UNEXPECTED
COMPANIONS

NICOLE STOUT

First Edition, 2021

ISBN: 9781838308117 (paperback)
ISBN: 9781838308100 (ebook)

Cover design/Interior design: Asya Blue

Published by Ceridwen Publishing
www.nicolestout.co.uk

For Emily

Dear Bosc

Here's to the power of woman's line strength!

Love

Nicole

AMY MELLO FAMILY TREE

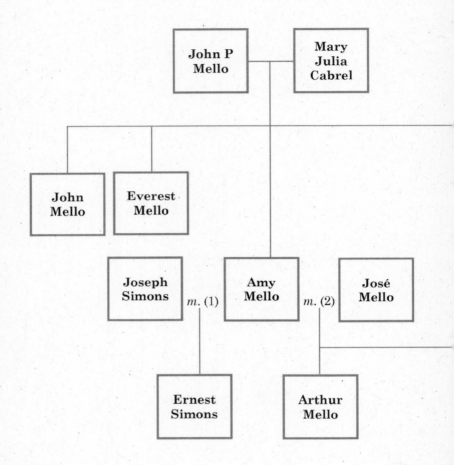

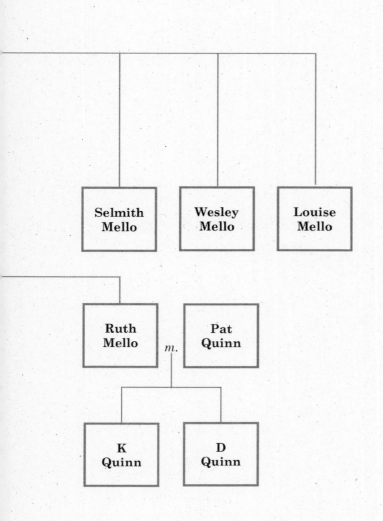

CHARLOTTE SOPHIA, A.K.A. 'LOTTY', BURNE FAMILY TREE

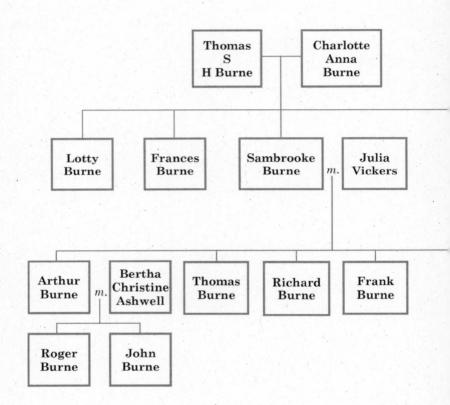

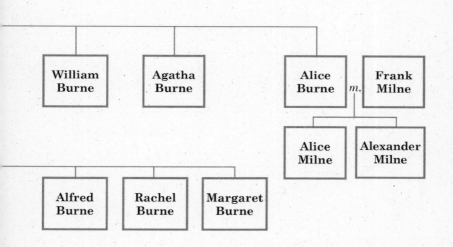

WINIFRED DAVIES FAMILY TREE

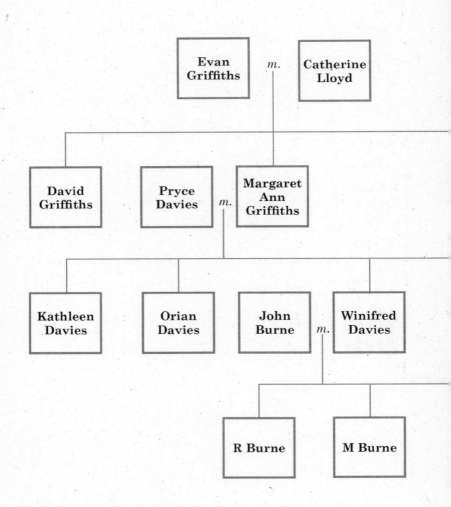

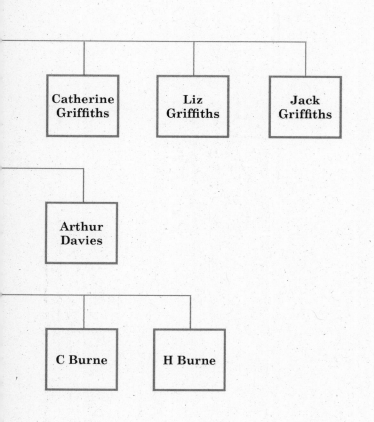

ELLIE

Ellie pushed open the heavy door and glanced around. *All clear.* She could see the gate at the far end of the courtyard and headed for it. The distance seemed endless but suddenly she was through the gate and hidden by the hedgerow. She stopped and caught her breath. If she went back now, no one would ever know, but she knew she couldn't. She checked her watch: 3.02 and a smile flickered across her face. She pulled her coat and scarf out of her bag and hurriedly threw them on as she headed down the road towards the train station. An elderly woman walked towards her. She wore a floral-print dress that looked suited to warmer temperatures than those offered at the end of October. The woman stopped and stood, waiting to cross the road.

Ellie frowned. *Why doesn't she cross at the lights? God, I sound like my mother.*

Ellie hunched her shoulders and concentrated on the pave-ment, hoping the woman wouldn't say anything about her not being at school. She passed the old woman close enough to catch a scent of lilies and vanilla. In ten more seconds she would be past the big magnolia tree, around the corner, and then there would be no sign of her leaving.

'Stop. Don't go.'

Ellie looked around. The woman was looking at her with a stern expression that didn't hide the concern in her eyes.

'Did you say something?'

The woman opened her mouth but seemed to struggle for

words. Ellie glanced back at the magnolia. A breeze whipped the bare branches and Ellie fancied that they were waving at her. *Hurry up, hurry up ... If I miss the train I won't get there in time and if I stay here I'll get caught. But she looks like she needs help. How annoying.*

Ellie took a step closer to the woman.

'Eleanor Hardwick, where do you think you are going?' Ellie looked down the road and bit her lip. Her headmistress strode towards her.

'I heard that old lady call out and was going to see if she needed help,' Ellie said, hoping this distraction would mean that the truth would be overlooked.

Mrs Walker frowned, 'What old lady?'

Ellie pointed to the spot next to her and then looked to her left when she didn't get a reaction from her headmistress. Her hand stayed in the air, as though if she pointed long enough the elderly woman would reappear.

'She was there. Just a second ago.' Ellie looked up and down the road but the woman had vanished. 'She can't have gone far, she was walking slow enough a snail could've overtaken her. And then she called out. I was going to help her up. Where did she go!'

Mrs Walker continued to frown down at her, then sighed, 'Back to class, Miss Hardwick. Really, I could set my watch by you. Every Wednesday afternoon. I have a good mind to post a sentry at the front door.'

———

The bell rang, celebrating the end of a school day, and over the voice of the teacher boys and girls began to pack up. Ellie stuffed the sealed envelope into her bag without a glance and jammed the last of the books in after it. Slinging her bag over her shoulder, she headed down the stairs, past the main office and out into the courtyard, where parents were gathered to collect the younger students. Now that she was fourteen she had told her mum that she was too old to be picked up.

Her friends were standing by the gate and one of them glanced in her direction. Ellie waved at her, although she wasn't sure that she'd been seen. *Please wait.*

Having failed to escape History, the one bright spot was that she had been given her monthly allowance today and she now had enough to buy her friends the bright sweatbands that they had been talking about ever since they had seen their favourite tennis player wearing them.

A gaggle of girls from her year bustled past, and one looked at her before nestling back into the laughter and whispering that hummed within the group.

Despite the short distance, when Ellie reached the spot where her friends had been, they were gone. She looked around and tried to hide her embarrassment by focusing on kicking a pebble that had been foolish enough to lie in her path. It skidded off to the left and abruptly stopped in a pile of leaves.

'Typical. Can't even kick a pebble properly,' Ellie muttered.

The daylight, which yesterday had kept her company home, seemed to now be fading as if in reproach. She passed the large house that celebrated every festive celebration. At the moment it was dressed in ghostly shrouds, giant spiders and eerie lights. At Christmas, the lawn would host a Santa and sleigh and the whole house would be lit up day and night, a beacon for wanderers braving the cold.

Soon it would be dark at home time, and Ellie didn't relish walking the fifteen minutes home in wintry darkness. This thought soured her mood even more. Ever since the incident in History last month, Mrs Milvern had been on at her. Ellie was sure she was singling her out for difficult questions or keeping her behind for the slightest so-called crime. It was bad enough that she had moved her to the front of the class 'so she could have a better view of board', but now there was a letter addressed to her mum which Ellie was couriering back.

Why even bother with a letter? Is she too stupid to know how to use email?

This barbed thought made her feel better for a moment. But Ellie knew that making her deliver her own execution warrant was an easy way for Mrs Milvern to show her who was in charge.

It hadn't even been Ellie who had started the whole thing; but to say that wouldn't help. *Really, this is all Mum's fault. If she hadn't made us all move just to be closer to her work none of this would've happened. I would still be at my old school with my nice teachers and friends who were funny and got me. But no, we had to move. And telling me it was for me so Mum could spend more time with me and that it was a better school was just a big fat lie.*

They're super snobbish, too. They just like the fancy touch screens. Think it'll make me cleverer. Ellie tried to laugh at her joke but it felt bitter.

The wind picked up as she rounded a corner and a plastic bag wrapped itself around her legs, almost tripping her. She stamped at it. *It's all so annoying. Plus, if Mum really was interested in spending time with me then why is she always at the restaurant? Why isn't she here, defending me, saying something to Mrs Milvern?*

Ellie bit her lower lip and tried to think of something else. Like that date Mia had mentioned at the start of term. Maybe it wasn't too late to say yes. And then Mia might be pleased with her. And Ollie wasn't *so* bad a person, even if she didn't really like him *that* way. She mulled over this idea as she mounted the steps of the railway footbridge, the halfway point from home.

It might mean they'll like me again and I'll be included in more stuff. But at least they are friendlier with me now.

Mia's comment, 'Well done for not saying anything. Friends stick together, yeah?' had given her a momentary glow. *But they still didn't wait for me. Maybe they didn't realise I don't have to go straight home anymore.*

Ellie had reached the top of the footbridge now. *If a train passes underneath the bridge before I've crossed it then I'll go on the date. Let fate decide.*

As she crossed the bridge, Ellie heard a train coming and picked up her pace. Despite her efforts, a train rushed underneath, the clatter of the wheels echoing as it went through, loud and ominous. *That's that, then.* She walked on in gloomy contemplation and when she next looked around, she was surprised to realise she was heading towards the river. *Why not? I have a little time before it's super dark.*

Enthusiasm pushed through her as she got closer to her spot, and within minutes she was settled on the bank, her school bag a makeshift chair, sketchbook on lap, pencil in hand. She preferred coming to the riverside in the early morning when the pervading stillness hid the river's energy. 'Always moving, ever still,' she murmured, watching a heron fly low over the water. *A sign of rain.* The bird landed below where Ellie was sitting. They both remained motionless. And then the scratch of pencil against paper disturbed the silence.

'Strange looking bird, in't.'

Ellie dropped her pencil.

'Oh, sorry. Didn't mean to scare you.'

She looked up to see a woman nearby, in the Surrey uniform of wellies, jeans and dark jacket. A dog sniffed at the shrubs further ahead. The heron didn't move.

'They can stand still like that for ages,' Ellie said. 'Makes them really easy to draw.'

The woman chuckled. 'You're very good – excellent eye for detail.'

'Thanks.'

The woman walked on down the path; the river rippled along its way; the pencil moved across the page. The heron didn't move.

When she next looked around, the river had turned into a

thick line of ink and car headlights flickered across the bridge. *Time to go.* She headed for the bridge, gripping her bag closer as the path ahead became murky with a cold mist. A sweet fragrance floated on the air and she glanced around to see where it was coming from. Through the mist she saw three figures standing together under the bridge. Their features were hidden in the growing darkness and all she could see was their outline.

She slowed her pace, her stare locked on the shadowy forms. Out of the corner of her eye, the bridge's steps promised safe passage to the world above. The figures remained where they were. No echo of voices or footsteps reached her. They were still: three dark smudges against a white background.

Ellie fixed her sights on the stairs, now only a few steps away. *Please don't follow me.* She looked again. The trio had disappeared. Ellie suppressed a shudder and took the stairs two at a time, appearing at the top to a surge of noise and light.

As she headed home, Ellie heard her phone beep and rushed to grab it, hoping it was one of the girls letting her know where they had gone. She could still go and join them.

Instead it was a message from Aria. 'Wanna come over and work on the play?'

Ellie cringed. She had been enjoying going to Aria's and sitting in her kitchen, the table covered in dictionaries and print-outs. But since Mia and the others found her typing out some of the translation during a break they hadn't stopped teasing her about it. At the time, Ellie had denied the accusation that she was doing 'extra work to be teacher's pet', but this had only made them laugh harder. She had been too upset to think properly and just kept repeating her denial. She still didn't understand why she had got so upset about it. Was it so bad to try to be good at something that wasn't tennis?

A younger pupil had walked past at that moment. She had recognised Ellie and her face had lit up with relief.

'Hi. I need to go to Mrs Milvern's room. Do you know where

it is? I thought it was on this floor but can't find it.'

Ellie had rolled her eyes at the girl. 'You are super-stupid if you don't your way around the school by now.'

The other girls had hooted with laughter at this outburst, and Amelia had chuckled about how the little girl's lower lip had started trembling. The memory made Ellie feel sick. She ignored Aria's message, put the phone away and stopped. Someone behind her made a comment as they skirted around her, but she didn't hear their words. Pasted to the tree was a small poster advertising the start of a new play. What rooted her to the spot was that the play was the one they were working on. And it was not even a translation. She stared at the poster. It was really no more than a flyer, the paper yellowed as if to make it look old, the drawing of a small German town like something off a traditional chocolate box. And under the title in bold, Gothic writing, the proud information that it would be in German.

'Who would do a play that, like, no one knew of? And of all the unknown plays there are out there, how weird is it that it's this play — *our* play,' Ellie said, too surprised to care that she was talking out loud. 'And in German; not even translated.'

She ripped the flyer from the tree and shoved it into her bag next to her sketchbook and the letter.

Finally on her road, she pulled out her house keys, checked her phone again for any new messages and unlocked the door. She stood for a second in the hallway, savouring the stillness that greeted her. It was one of the benefits of always being the first home, although when her mum had stopped meeting her after school and walking home alone had first become a regular occurrence, it had seemed sad and lonely. But it had begun to be embarrassing having her mum rushing to the school gates, late and breathless. Much easier just to tell her that she was too old for such treatment.

She dropped her bag and stood for a minute looking at an old family photo on the hall table. She had passed it so often she had stopped noticing it but the woman on the back row now caught her attention. She was wearing a similar floral dress and had the same white, curled hair as the person she had seen today.

'Isn't it funny how old people look the same,' Ellie said, her voice loud against the emptiness.

Her phone beeped again and she quickly checked it. It was her mum. 'Are you home yet? Mum x'

'I know who you are, Mum. Why do you always insist on signing your name?'

But she knew better than to ignore this message.

'Yes'

'Can you drop by the restaurant? I need help carrying a few things.'

'Ok'

'Thx darling!'

Ellie rolled her eyes and headed upstairs to change out of her uniform.

In her well-worn hoodie and leggings, she moved all her essential items — wallet, phone, sketchbook and pencil set, book and strawberry lip salve — to her favourite rucksack, which had an image of the album cover *Girls* on it, and left the house.

Pulling the door shut, she remembered the letter. *If Mum read it at work then she wouldn't be able to yell at me until we got home and by then she might have cooled down a bit.*

Ellie darted back into the house to retrieve the letter.

———

The restaurant Ellie's mum co-owned was only five minutes from their house, and as far as Ellie was concerned it was a stretch to call it a 'restaurant'; it was more like a wine bar with food. Chunky tables with metal chairs circled a bar that had bar stools around it. Across the back of one wall were wine bottles suspended in brackets against a blackboard. The bottles all had their labels missing and the prospective drinker chose their glass from the descriptions written in chalk.

'We want people to not be led by their prejudices but by the style and characteristics of the wine,' Ellie's mum had enthused. Ellie had wished she hadn't asked.

The restaurant wasn't very large but a wide window at the front and cleverly placed mirrors and lighting made the place feel light and spacious. When it was warm, they drew back this window and placed tables and chairs outside on the veranda.

Now, the window displayed ghoulish faces sprayed on with white frost, and carved pumpkins grinned at approaching customers.

In the last couple of weeks Ellie had picked up the habit of coming to the restaurant after school. At first, she had done it as a protest against an unjust punishment, but she had started to enjoy sitting among the noise and flow of the wine bar. She would sit up high on a bar stool doing her homework, half watching people filter through. It was fun to be there and absorb the atmosphere without taking a direct part in it.

Astrid would often be working in the afternoon and she was Ellie's favourite of the wine bar's team (her mum hated calling the people who worked for her 'staff'). Her mum had once told Astrid that Ellie was translating a play from German into English. In an explosion of claps and laughter, Astrid had turned to Ellie and said, 'Wie lange lernst du schon Deutsch?'

Ellie was too embarrassed by her mum's need to show off to reply properly, and, speaking at her shoes, said, 'Ich spreche nicht gut.'

She could feel two sets of eyes bearing down on her: one with a hint of sympathetic amusement and the other with a familiar impatience. After the silence had worn on, her mum had made some comment about how she should try to speak German to Astrid, and Astrid had just smiled and gone back to work. But ever since then, Astrid had taken to sneaking samples of the latest cheeses or meats to Ellie as she studied, leaving this mini food-board next to Ellie's elbow with a wink, as if they were conspirators.

Ellie pushed open the door and was relieved to see that it was indeed Astrid working today. She waited quietly for her to finish taking a customer's order. It was just after five p.m. and the place was filling up as people drifted towards home.

'Hi Astrid. Mum about?'

'Hello Ellie. Yes, upstairs I think.'

She took the stairs two at a time and felt light-hearted on reaching the top without breaking rhythm.

'Mum?'

The office was empty.

'Weird.'

The quiet was overwhelming. She couldn't remember the last time she had been up here, and after the bustle of the bar the silence seemed to fold around her like a blanket. Ellie stood in the middle of the room twisting a strand of her hair as she thought about what to do.

'I'll just wait, I guess,' she said to the room, and settled herself into her mum's office chair.

The chair faced out into the room, surveying the domain. The grey metal desk, like a narrow river on a cloudy day, lay between her and the space beyond. To one side was a bookshelf displaying volumes of wine and food knowledge, and to the other side was a small round table with comfortable chairs. On the wall behind the chairs hung a picture of Mount Fuji, its domed peak emerging from a collar of cloud.

The room was peaceful, a low hum from the closed laptop the only noise. Ellie reached into her bag and pulled out her book, *Wide Sargasso Sea*. It wasn't a school set reading book, which made it more enjoyable even if it had been her mum's idea.

'Don't just read the syllabus. Read around it,' she had said, plonking the book in front of Ellie as she wrote her notes for *Jane Eyre*. 'They don't seem to want you to read many female authors in this curriculum of theirs, so do it yourself. And this is an excellent example. Read about a voice suppressed, a different perspective that is not well understood and therefore feared. It's as relevant today as it was two hundred years ago.'

Her mum always went over the top when it came to female roles in society. Ellie had taken it politely without much thought of reading it. A few days later, though, she had found the book under a pile of clothes and a voice whispered to her to read it. She had started and had become so absorbed she had been late meeting Mia and Rosie and they had left without her. Only later did she appreciate how lucky she was to have been five minutes late.

But she struggled to lose herself in Antoinette's world of palm trees and spices. Thoughts swirled around her and the words blurred into a single line that she read over and over.

Where is Mum?

She thought she heard a noise and looked up. A book had dropped to the floor. She picked it up and was surprised to see it was a novel.

F. Scott Fitzgerald.

'What are you doing here?' Ellie said to the book. 'Will have to tell Dad that all Mum does is read books when she's at work.'

She replaced it and ran her fingers over the other glossy spines, with pictures of grapes and glasses brimming with deep-red wine.

The wine-tasting room. That must be where she is.

She left the office only to pause as she remembered that her rucksack was still in there. In the pause, a flicker of movement at the end of corridor distracted her and she moved forward without the rucksack.

'Mum?' she said, her voice not as certain as she would have liked. 'Is someone there?' She took a few steps, then some more as a hazy light at the end of the corridor urged her on.

The tasting room's door was bordered with light, and voices drifted towards her. The smoky, sweet scent of wood greeted

Ellie as she approached. Beyond the door, she could hear the crackle of wood in a fire and felt a momentary rush of pines, gentle water, darkness and starlight, as if back in Canada roasting marshmallows on open flames.

When did they put a fireplace in the tasting room?

She reached to push open the door and noticed that she was carrying the letter from school.

How did ...? When did ...? God, I'm going mad.

The door was ajar and she could hear the ring of familiar voices. Without knocking, she took the final steps needed to cross the threshold, only to be brought to an abrupt halt.

The three women stood together at the far end of the room, guarding the fireplace. One stood with her back to the door and the others, as if her bookends, stood either side of the mantelpiece. One of them had her hand on the marble, her fingers bent as if she had been tapping the cold stone. The conversation ended with Ellie's appearance and the woman moved her hand off the mantelpiece to pat her hair into place.

An elegant dining table, shrouded in a white tablecloth and surrounded by delicate wooden chairs, glittered with candles, cut glass and silverware. More candles sparkled from brackets on the wall and their flickering gold reflected back at Ellie through the large gilded mirror above the mantelpiece.

Ellie wondered if all wine-tasting sessions looked like something out of *The Great Gatsby*.

The women's manners were strange: they seemed awkward in their surroundings and all were visibly relieved to be saved further small talk by her interruption. Stumbling out an apology for disturbing them nevertheless, Ellie was retreating towards the corridor when a voice stopped her.

'Our guest of honour has arrived!'

Ellie turned and looked at the woman who had stepped forward as she had spoken. She seemed to be in her sixties although Ellie never could tell with older people. Her grey hair was pulled back and pinned in place and her skin was incredibly fair, as if she never went outside. Fine pearls hugged her neck, joining together to display a large silver and diamond pendant. She was a very large woman and the dress she was wearing seemed to emphasis this with its square-cut top framed in lace, fitted to the waist and then blooming out all the way to the floor. It was dark blue, with sequins patterned across it.

Ellie had never seen anyone wearing anything like it. *Why wear this to a local wine bar? Maybe it's a Halloween party.*

The lady bustled forward and for a moment it looked as though she might get wedged between the chairs and the sideboard where glasses and a bottle of wine had been set out.

'What odd attire young ladies wear these days. Trousers! And so fitted as well. Leaves very little for modesty.'

Ellie's retort was on her lips but the woman carried on before she had the chance to speak.

'Where is the maître d'hôtel?' she asked no one in particular. 'Really, this is very unsatisfactory. I am surprised this establishment has managed to remain operating given such a low level of service. Well, I am not above pouring out sherry when called upon. *Malarum rerum, omnium,* do you not agree?' she said, fixing her gaze on Ellie. Her eyes were slightly almond-shaped and as she took Ellie in they narrowed a little as if processing every detail of her. Ellie was reminded of a cat; watchful and waiting.

'Uh, sure,' Ellie replied with no idea what the woman had just said.

Then, with a small smile, the woman thrust the glass towards her. Ellie took a step back at the movement and a sweet scent of body odour followed her.

'Lotty, Eleanor isn't even fifteen yet. Perhaps some water would be better?'

'What nonsense, Winifred. We drank sherry before dinner when we were younger than she is. And if we were a little poorly, we would be given brandy. I remember my brother,

Willy, riding home and it was pouring with rain and he was quite wet through and had brandy and water for tea. He couldn't have been more than ten years old at the time.'

Ellie had frozen midway through accepting the glass. *They know my name. They know my age. Who are they?*

As Ellie jumped from theory to conspiracy, the lady opposite her carried on with a story about a sister who was allowed sips of the market woman's beer when she was only eight or nine.

'She came at eleven on Saturdays on her way to the market to get our butter to sell. The market woman was quite old-style, with a round bonnet over a neatly frilled cap ...'

Bonnet? Frilled cap? Who talks like that?

'Nevertheless ...' the other woman said.

She looked the youngest of the three and Ellie assumed she must be at university.

But what random clothes, like something out of those World War Two dramas Mum watches.

'How about we compromise and give her a *small* glass?'

The interruption came from the third lady, who until then hadn't said a word. She had moved from the fireplace and now stood away from the other two, hovering near one of the table settings as if waiting to claim this seat for herself. Everything about her was neat and precise except her dark hair, wisps of which had escaped despite the clear effort to keep it in curled control. The woman now patted at it again as the others glanced at her in response to her suggestion.

Ellie kept her eyes on her. *She looks familiar. Is she a friend of my mum's?*

'This *is* a small glass, Mrs Mello. It is sherry after all,' Lotty said, still holding out the glass.

'I've never had sherry,' Ellie said. She let go of her hair mid twirl.

'An excellent time to start, then.'

It seemed easier to accept it, and as the unfamiliar rich notes of the drink hit her nose, her mind went back to that evening when five minutes might have changed so many things. She hadn't found out what had happened until the next day. Her phone battery had died and, in her rush to get to Mia's, she hadn't noticed until it was too late.

She was almost tearful when Mia's mum told her they had left, and breathless by the time she got to the cinema. They weren't anywhere in the foyer and the man wouldn't sell her a ticket without ID so she had loitered around, checked the toilets, double checked the ticket area, hung around outside and in the end walked home, alone and dejected. Later that evening, her phone sprang back to life and so did the messages.

'Where are you?'

Then:

'We've gone without you'

And then later:

'We didn't get in the dumb guy selling tickets didn't believe we were 18!!! What a tool.'

After that, there was silence. She texted back explaining what had happened but they didn't reply. No one did. The group chat seemed so silent. Too silent.

Ellie felt awkward holding the letter in one hand and the glass in the other but she didn't put either down. She looked at the golden drink in its cut crystal glass and wondered if it would have been worth it if she had been there with them when they headed from the cinema to the riverbank, bottle hidden under Rosie's jacket. After all, better to be in trouble together than to be ghosted alone.

AMY AND ELLIE

Amy grimaced at being called Mrs Mello; it sounded so formal, so boring. It had been a long time since she had seen herself as a 'Mrs' and to hear it now in the stuffy tone of this Lotty Burne, with all her airs and patronising ways, made her skin itch with irritation. She picked up her glass and took a large glug of the sherry.

'Mmmm, not bad,' she said.

Lotty raised an eyebrow but didn't say anything. Instead, she turned the bottle towards Winifred, who shook her head.

'No, thank you. I will save myself for a glass of wine with the meal.'

'You don't drink?' said Amy, 'I've always enjoyed a glass, especially on special occasions such as this. Even in the middle of Prohibition you could get alcohol; some said it was actually easier.'

Memories of going to her neighbours for 'tea' flitted through Amy's mind. It hadn't always been very good quality and was usually a homemade attempt, either made too strong or having an aftertaste of soap. Or both. Even now, gin made her grimace a little. *But I've never been a spirits person, much prefer wine.*

As if her mind was rolling along without her permission, a new memory surfaced, of her father-in-law when he had produced two bottles of red wine at her wedding to Joe. Manuel had kept them hidden at the start of Prohibition and then, three years later, opened them with child-like excitement, waving away any protest by saying, "A celebration always needs something to mark it." Later that year, Joe's parents decided to return to the Azores, and as they had waved them off Amy had joked to Joe that they were only going back to pick up more wine.

'Why don't you just have one glass, Winifred?' she continued, but Winifred politely declined.

Amy sighed. *This is going to be a long meal.*

Amy passed her glass to Lotty for a refill and smiled conspiratorially at Ellie. She absorbed the details of this young relative. Ellie had the appearance of a fawn with spindly limbs that were waiting to grow into a body on the crest of adulthood. She was surprised at how much this girl looked like her granddaughters at the same age. No hint of Portuguese in her, but the bone structure of her face ... *It's like mine; oval shaped.*

Amy nodded her head in approval and drank some more sherry.

Emboldened by this woman with wispy hair and an air of defiance, Ellie had a sip. She started to cough as the alcohol hit the back of her throat.

'Tastes like old floors,' Ellie said.

'I am not in the habit of tasting floors,' Lotty said, 'so I am sure I would not know.'

Amy smiled, clearly amused, and Ellie took a second sip. This time she found there was a sweetness to it that helped dull the sharpness, and almost succeeded in enjoying it.

'I prefer my sherries a little drier than this,' Lotty said, her gaze never leaving Ellie's face, 'but it is not too sweet. My dear Aunt Mary once turned down an invitation to our cousin Peel's house because, amongst other things, she served her sherry sweet to a degree.' Lotty chuckled.

'How lucky to be able to choose friends and relations over such things,' Amy said. Ellie stared, open-mouthed, waiting for some reaction but none came.

'Winifred, if you won't have any sherry, how about I get you some water?' Amy asked. Without waiting for a reply, she leaned across the table to where a water jug was waiting. 'Your accent is quite unusual,' Lotty said. 'Where are you from?'

'Bermuda,' Amy replied.

Ellie jolted at the word. *Does she know I have family in Bermuda? Who is she?*

'Ah that is why I could not place you. I am quite good with accents; however, I could not decide on yours. How satisfying to have a little mystery resolved.'

Ellie realised she was staring at Amy and forced herself to look elsewhere. *It's the accent that's familiar, that's all. But she does sound exactly like my nan.* Something flitted through her mind, a vague memory, but it was gone before it established itself.

'I wonder if you knew my nephew? Arthur Burne? He was stationed in Bermuda during the Great War.'

Ellie looked from one to the other. *The Great War? Like World War One? Why would she know someone who was alive then?*

'No, I don't know the name,' Amy said.

'I cannot recall their address, Pageant Parish, perhaps,' Lotty continued.

'Paget,' Amy said.

'Yes, that is correct. Paget. And yet you did not know him? Perhaps his wife, Christine?'

'No.'

'Really? You were living there then, were you not? And Bermuda is small, is it not?'

Amy didn't think these questions warranted a reply.

'Where did you reside in Bermuda?'

'In different parts of the island.'

'But during the War?'

There was a pause.

'Paget.'

'Ah!' Lotty paused. 'Well, perhaps you socialised in different circles,' She did not hide her glance of assessment and Amy's lips receded into a thin line. Winifred stepped in before she could reply.

'Well, perhaps we should include our guest in our ramblings,' she said, smiling swiftly across the other three.

'Yeah, great idea,' Amy said, forcing herself to smile. 'After all, you must be wondering why we are here, Ellie, and how we know you. We can't give you all those answers now, but ...' she said hurriedly sensing Lotty about to interrupt, 'I suppose a good place to start would be introductions. My name is Amy Mello and I am your, let's see, I am your grandmother's grandmother, so that makes me your ...'

'Great-great-grandmother,' Winifred said.

'Yeah, your great-great-grandmother. On your dad's side.'

'You can't be. I mean, she's dead. At least ... she must be. NO! She is definitely dead.'

'Oh yeah, kiddo. Dead as a doornail! Died *years* ago. And much older than how I appear today. With one less leg as well!'

Ellie had to admit that she did look a little like her nan. There was even something of her Aunt Di about this woman. *The voice? The face? Both?* Ellie couldn't quite place it but the similarity was definitely there. Before she could process this information further, the door opened and a waiter, dressed in white shirt and black trousers, appeared carrying a silver tray with a selection of small dishes. He placed the tray on the sideboard near Ellie and left as silently as he had arrived. Ellie frowned after the stranger. Her mother was always complaining about the lack of reliable staff so perhaps he was new. *Where is Mum? Why hasn't she turned up to say hello to these people?*

'This is most unorthodox,' Lotty said. 'Are we not going to sit to eat the hors d'oeuvres?'

She reached for one of the small trays and popped its contents into her mouth. Amy stayed near her chair and watched the food disappear from the tray. *Why doesn't she pass the tray around?*

'I would expect hors d'oeuvres to be taken,' Lotty said, 'in a drawing room if not at the table. Certainly not standing as if one is waiting for a train.'

Ellie eyed the food suspiciously: small pancakes glistened with, what looked to Ellie, a pile of dark goo.

'What are these?' she said.

'Hors d'oeuvres,' Lotty said. 'Small, often salty, appetizers to warn the digestive organs to prepare for a meal.'

'Like canapés,' Amy said.

Lotty's brow furrowed, 'Canopies? I do not mean to contradict you, Mrs Mello; however, here in the United Kingdom we do not tend to eat the tops of trees.'

'She means canapés,' Winifred said, moving alongside Lotty and picking up the tray.

'Eleanor, would you like to try one?'

'What actually are they?'

'Blinis with caviar.'

Ellie moved the sherry glass to share her hand with the letter, and reached towards the silver tray, then paused. 'Caviar, like fish eggs?'

'Yes, dear.'

She pulled her hand back, nose scrunched. 'No thanks.'

At that moment, another waiter entered the room and announced that dinner would be served shortly. Amy sighed as she watched Winifred set the tray back down.

'Oh good,' Lotty said. 'I was mildly concerned that we would eat our entire meal on our feet.'

'Eleanor, why don't you sit down?' Winifred said, 'Your place is just in front of you.'

Ellie looked at the table and saw her name, written in a swirl of handwriting on a silver name holder. *Eleanor Hardwick.* She didn't move. The other women quietly sat down and waited. The darkness outside seemed deeper now and the only light came from the candles encircling the room and the ones in the candelabra on the table. Amy picked up the napkin barely noticing the mitre shape she had destroyed. She smoothed out the napkin across her lap and thought how strange it was to still be dictated by such habits. *But why not? I really like this dress. It would be a shame to ruin it.*

'You lose the light so early at this time of year,' Winifred said.

'And no moon tonight,' Lotty said. 'Although some would say it is unlucky to look at the moon through glass. When I was a girl, my school fellows used to rush with averted faces past a certain passage window through which the moon often peeped.'

'You didn't have a governess?' Amy said.

'To begin with, Mamma sent us to Grandmamma Goodlad, her mamma,' Lotty said. 'She was an excellent tutor and we also had a governess. After a while, with Papa still poorly, a more permanent arrangement had to be found so it was decided to send us to school and I was there for one year. We were unhappy, did not see Mamma for over a year and missed home dreadfully.'

Trays with bowls of soup arrived but Ellie still didn't sit down. A silence stretched across the room as the soup was served and the waiter gave Winifred and Lotty their napkins. Ellie's voice cut through it as the waiter passed her.

'Can you tell my mum that I'm here?'

He seemed panicked by her question. Ellie frowned as she waited.

'Your mother? I ... I don't know ... I mean ... I'm new here.'

He backed out of the room leaving the door open, and disappeared. Ellie felt an urge to follow him. She was close enough that it would have taken two steps to be out of the room. Nothing was stopping her. She looked at the women who sat quietly, waiting, watching.

ELLIE AND WINIFRED

There were few moments in Ellie's life when she hadn't had the security of her parents' presence. As a single child, she had always taken it for granted that they were there, ready to drop what they were doing to entertain or help her. She was even consulted on holiday ideas, although Disney World never seemed to make it to the short-list. Each time she was asked for her thoughts on where might be fun to visit, if she dared to suggest such a destination, her dad would reply that there were so many interesting places which *didn't* involve artificially engineered entertainment and paying fifteen pounds for a sandwich.

The last time they had gone to an amusement park was five years ago. Her parents had relented after she had deployed a strategy of constant begging, wearing them down through pure stubbornness and persistence.

It had started so promisingly: good weather, an early arrival for those first few, queue-free thrills. Ellie had been surprised by how much her mum seemed to enjoy it. While her dad hesitated, looking suspiciously at the tracks, her mum virtually pulled her to each new ride. They had laughed over strategies for where to sit to get the best experience or which line looked the quickest.

'Dad, did you see us?' Ellie had shouted coming off a particularly steep roller coaster. 'Mum and me took our hands off the bars and held them up in the air all the way down. It was so fun!'

'I saw. I was right behind you.'

Ellie had laughed and run on to look at the big map posted opposite the ride's exit. The park had filled up and people buzzed around her. She lost herself inspecting the map and working out which rides she could go on and where to go next. And when she turned around, her parents were gone. Ellie pushed her way through groups of smiling faces, yelled into the noise and ran up and down paths until the panic wore into despair. She finally remembered about the main fountain. It had been the first thing her mum had said when they had gone through the turnstiles: "If anyone gets lost, we will meet back here." Alone and anxious, she walked to the fountain and was almost surprised to see the same panic and anxiety she felt mapped out on her parents' faces as they scanned the crowd.

That feeling of aloneness sank into her now amongst these strange women and their intense casualness. And this time there was no fountain to head to.

'What a strange young man,' Lotty said. 'However, given our experience so far I am not at all surprised.'

'Never mind, darling,' Winifred said, smiling across the table at her. 'I'm sure your mother will come and find you when the time is right. Now, why don't you sit down and tell me how my granddaughter is? Does she still ride?'

'What?' Ellie blinked at her.

'Ride. Your mother used to ride horses. Show-jumping, as I recall. I remember her room when she was a little girl being full of rosettes.'

'Oh, yeah. Umm, no. No, not anymore.'

Ellie scuffed her foot at the wooden floor. *It figures that they would pick up on Mum's enthusiasm for sport.*

Despite a family filled with successful sports people, Ellie struggled to generate much enthusiasm for sports, preferring to lose herself in books. But that had all changed when she had become friends with Mia. Mia was popular and great at all sports. Ellie was sure her own tennis skills had improved a lot thanks to hanging out with Mia and the other girls.

'Well, what a pity. Of course, during your lifetime, Lotty, it was a common way to travel, wasn't it? Funny to think that a hundred years later horse riding would just be a hobby.'

'How can you *remember* what my mum's room was like? You aren't much older than me!' Ellie blurted out.

There was an odd silence.

'Ah, of course. I had forgotten what age I had chosen,' Winifred said, and glanced down at herself. She looked at the other women at the table. 'I thought that, given our subject, a younger version would be best. I was training to be a nurse when I was this age so it seemed appropriate.'

'What subject? Appropriate for what?' Ellie said, glancing at the faces around her.

'All in good time, darling,' Winifred said.

She gestured to the empty seat. Ellie wanted to resist but something overcame this urge and she obediently took her seat, sneaking the letter under her side plate as she sat down.

'What was I saying? Oh yes: nursing. That was how I met your great-grandfather,' Winifred said, her gentle smile never leaving her face. 'We were both training at Westminster Hospital. Although until that point it had been quite a different path for me.'

Ellie looked closely at the woman sitting opposite her. She had short brown hair which naturally curled, but with a bit of imagination Ellie could replace the dark hair with white and it would have been a close match to her mum's granny. *Weird to have seen a woman that looked like my great-grandmother earlier and now to have this person claiming to be her.* Ellie liked to think that coincidences had a meaning but these coincidences seemed too eerie to bode well.

She glanced at the door. It hadn't been shut properly but she couldn't see the corridor beyond and something about that made her nervous. *Where is my mum? If she doesn't arrive soon I am going to need to do something ...* Her mum was always encouraging her to solve problems or questions using her own initiative. 'What do you think the solution is?' was a favourite line of hers and it always irritated Ellie. Ellie's standard response was, 'I don't know, that's why I'm asking.'

She glanced around the room, taking in the table setting with its queue of cutlery, the white roses ballooning out of a small vase, bottles bubbling with water, crystal-cut glassware, and the women in their clothing from various eras, and an idea began to bubble inside her. She wasn't an expert on her family history but she must know enough about the ancestors they were pretending to be, to trip these people up. *After all, this must be some weird joke, what else could it be?*

Ellie sat a little straighter and tasted the soup.

'What is this?' Ellie asked, wrinkling her nose.

'Beetroot and horseradish,' Amy said.

'It's tastes really ... peppery.' Ellie moved her bowl to hide the spot where a drop of pink liquid had created a marbled pattern on the white tablecloth.

Amy reached for the silver salt cellar and smiled at Ellie. 'I would prefer it with a little more salt.' She sprinkled a spoonful over the soup and then threw some over her shoulder. She took a sip of the soup and murmured with pleasure.

Ellie looked suspiciously from the soup to the women around her. *This has got to be a joke. All of it. Who would choose beetroot soup, for God's sake? No one, that's who. It's a joke. The women, the soup ...* Her stomach clenched as she wondered who had set this up. *Mia? They can't be that mad at me, can they?*

Amy turned to Winifred. 'Why did you choose nursing, then?'

'I always wanted to be a nurse and be of help to others. Perhaps because of ... What I mean is, I was very good at science and maths and nursing seemed a good option for those subjects.' Winifred took a careful sip of the soup.

'How lucky you were to have had those opportunities,' Amy said, tearing off a chunk of bread and dunking it into the soup.

'I had a very supportive family and was fortunate to find

25

a position in a care home near my cousins in Kent so I could start my training,' Winifred replied, hearing the involuntary briskness in her voice.

'Hang on. That's not right,' Ellie blurted out. 'Your family's not from Kent. You're all from Wales.' She felt triumphant in her realisation and pleased with herself for remembering these details. Winifred's cheeks burned and Ellie assumed this was because her lie had been detected so easily.

'You are from Wales?' Lotty said. 'You do not have a Welsh accent.'

'I lost it,' Winifred said, her left hand pressed against her cheek, 'when I moved to Kent. It was sometimes difficult to be understood otherwise.' She continued to smile but there was a trace of sadness about it.

The small mantelpiece clock chimed and the sound took Winifred back to 1938 and footsteps echoing across another wooden floor in time with the rustling of paper bags. On the other side of the counter stood a girl, her forehead creased in concentration as Winifred tried to communicate what she wanted. In the end, Winifred had left with only half the things she had needed, head down in embarrassment as she passed a queue of curious people. She told her cousin she had forgotten the apples and carrots. But this was not an experience she wanted to share at this dinner.

'What did your family do in Wales?' Lotty asked.

'They were farmers.'

'Really? How much land did you own?'

'We didn't own the land,' Winifred said.

'Oh, I see.' Lotty concentrated on sipping her soup.

Amy turned slightly in her chair, 'What a coincidence! My family were farmers as well. Not one of the *very* well-off farming families. My dad was a farmer for one of the larger farms and worked hard. What type of farming did you do?'

Avoiding eye contact, Winifred ran her finger over the edge of the water glass. 'Sheep, mainly. But also beef cattle.'

Ellie shrugged. *That doesn't prove anything. Sheep farming in Wales, anyone could come up with that.*

'Where in Wales did your family reside?' asked Lotty, applying a thick layer of butter to her bread. 'I travelled to Wales quite often. Mamma would take us to Llandudno quite regularly to take the sea air.'

A shrill whine came from the water glass and Winifred abruptly removed her finger from it. She smiled and quietly said, 'Llandudno is a very nice part of Wales. I am sure the sea air must have been invigorating.'

'It was very pleasant, although for us Buxton-on-Trent was much closer if you needed a health tonic of that sort, not that it helped dear Frances.' Lotty sighed and adjusted the napkin on her lap.

'So, I think I should go,' Ellie said, putting her napkin on the table. 'I'm sure my mum is looking for me.'

She pushed back the chair and smiled, 'It's been nice to meet you,' she said, sounding just like she did when her parents introduced her to some friend or work colleague.

'Now look ...' Amy said, her chair clattering as it fell away in her haste to stand. Winifred squeezed Amy's arm.

'This must all seem quite strange to you,' Winifred said. 'One minute you are sketching herons, and the next you're attending a silver-service dining experience with three strange women.'

Ellie felt her mouth open but couldn't manage to shut it. 'How did you ... were you ... who *are* you?'

Lotty turned in her seat to look at Ellie. 'The answer depends on whether or not you believe in souls.'

'Souls?'

'No need to pretend ignorance. Belief in souls as a separate entity having an existence independently of the body is found even in races very low on the scale of cultural development. Obviously, it lies at the root of belief in ghosts, revenants or *gjengangere* ...' With an air of practised ease, Lotty used the correct pronunciation for gjengangere. Despite Ellie's confusion, she supressed a giggle at the sudden use of a different accent.

'... So it naturally leads to the conclusion that if you believe in souls, you can believe in ghosts. In order to answer your question as to *why* we are here, you first have to decide if the latter option is viable to you.' Lotty paused as if allowing the others to digest her words.

'So if I believe in ghosts then you are real?' Ellie said. 'That doesn't make sense. I can believe in fairies and elves but that doesn't mean they exist.'

Lotty took barely a second to reply. 'How do you know they do not? Besides the Gods and their foes, the Giants, the northern mythology recognised other races of beings more familiar to man. The mischievous, sullen Dark Elves, and the bright and airy Light Elves.'

'We went to Iceland when I was little and they had houses for elves,' Ellie said with a rush of enthusiasm.

If Lotty heard her she didn't acknowledge the comment but continued with her train of thought. 'In modern days, the study of the Bible by the poor has had much to do with extinguishing certain phases of folk-lore. Fairies and goblins are never named in it, therefore people's faith in them began to die; and the stories formerly told of them are now attributed to ghosts and witches. Beings of whom, on the other hand, some mention may be found in Holy Writ.'

Amy let out a sigh and took another sip of sherry. Ellie's eyes left Lotty's face and settled on Amy. *She really does look like my nan. It's super-weird.* Somewhere she had seen a photo of her nan's nana and now she tried hard to bring it back in memory. The hair, wispy and dark, the jut of the chin and the pale pink dress suddenly rushed at her as she saw the face and dress in the framed picture in the living room in Bermuda. Ellie sat down again, a lump forming in her throat as she looked again at these women.

'... Where stories of these classes of beings exist,' Lotty was saying, 'the effect of Christianity has been to give them a more unpleasant character. As the stupid, brutal giant is transformed into the arch-fiend, so the friendly household spirits become troublesome uncanny inmates.'

'His house, so they say, was haunted by a jolly ghost,' Winifred said in an attempt to halt the monologue.

Unable to resist, Lotty continued the quotation: '... that shook the curtains, whined in lobbies, tapt at doors and rummaged like a rat.'

Winifred started to say something but Lotty got there first.

'As it happens,' Lotty said, 'ordinary sleep as well as fainting-fits, stupor and unconsciousness are often explained by saying that a man's soul has left him in those moments. There was an account of a Welsh reaper whose soul was seen running about while his body lay asleep in the harvest field.'

Amy relaxed her posture and a deep laugh broke from her.

'I can assure you it was not considered a laughing matter.'

Ellie looked at Amy and Winifred, who were both now smiling in amusement. Lotty glanced at the women, a frown upsetting her pale, smooth forehead.

'The story was not uncommon among people more backward than the Welsh. There are soul-traps brought back from countries which may be seen in the British Museum.'

Amy laughed even more and looked at Winifred.

'Isn't that good to know, Winifred? That there are nations "more backwards" than yours,' Amy said. Winifred kept her smile but carefully put her spoon over her bowl.

Lotty stopped. 'I did not mean to say ... I meant rather that.... Wales is a delightful country. As I mentioned, my family took trips to North Wales often. My ... my sisters climbed Snowdon. I have many very pleasant memories of Wales. It is rich in folklore and I was merely referring to the fact that you can find ballads and beliefs in uncivilised as well as civilised countries. It was really not intended as an insult ...'

Lotty squeezed her hands together, the unconscious movement partly hidden in her lap.

'Please, Lotty, it is fine. I know you did not mean anything by it.' Winifred turned to Ellie. 'To answer your question ... differently, we are here with your best interests at heart,' she said. 'We can see you are having some ... difficulties at school and we simply want to give you some ... guidance.' Winifred's nose scrunched slightly at the word.

Ellie shrugged and looked at the purple pool in her bowl.

'Only you can make the right choices for yourself but we feel we can offer some ... assistance,' Winifred said.

Out of the corner of her eye, Winifred saw Amy take a sip of her sherry. She seemed to have stopped listening to the conversation.

'Never minded nurses really,' Amy said. 'They always seemed nice cheerful types. But doctors. Always talking down to you as if you didn't know anything just because you didn't have a fancy certificate.'

Winifred opened her mouth to say something, but stopped. *Best not go down that route.*

'My education was not quite on the same level as any of yours. Besides, most of what I needed to know couldn't be taught in a school.'

Winifred kept her smile in place but her hand adjusted her necklace as she watched Amy. *Where is this going?*

Amy waved a finger in Ellie's direction, 'Now look, my life wasn't full of privileges to squander away. I had to work and save. None of this skipping school for the fun of it, that's for sure.'

Ellie looked up from her soup and stared at her. Winifred looked at Amy but Amy kept her gaze on Ellie, whose arms had wrapped themselves around her chest.

Winifred cleared her throat. *We need a softer approach. If only Amy would look at me.*

'We were there long enough to learn how to count, read and write, but my parents needed us to work. When I left school, I helped my mae around the house. It wasn't big or a fancy place but she still needed the help. I was the third of seven children. She was a strict woman, my mae. Traditional. Old-style Portuguese. Everyone was afraid of her.' Amy chuckled and helped herself to another slice of bread.

'But she taught me a lot. Even before I left school I had chores and responsibilities. She had me helping in the kitchen, I learnt how to cook and not waste anything. Every morning I had to light the kitchen range and help get the younger children dressed. No time to feel sorry for myself ...' She fixed her gaze on Ellie, her finger stabbing the air towards her. Ellie wriggled in her seat and became fascinated by the swirls she could create with the soup spoon.

'If you do not wish to eat the soup, please put down the spoon,' Lotty said.

Ellie dropped the spoon into the bowl and a splash of pink liquid spread across the white tablecloth. Lotty clicked her tongue and Amy shook her head.

'It's not my fault. I don't like soup,' Ellie said.

'You do not like soup? What an odd dislike,' Lotty said.

Ellie shrugged. Winifred took a sip of her soup to hide her irritation.

'You should've tried my sopa de couves,' Amy said. 'Potato and kale soup. My nana brought the recipe with her from the Azores.'

'Sounds like watery salad,' muttered Ellie.

Amy narrowed her eyes a little as she looked at Ellie.

'I changed it a bit: more potato, less kale, and with some meat added, too,' Amy said. 'Everybody wanted seconds. My first husband used to love it. Would always ask me to make it for him.'

Her finger slashed at the air around her as she continued.

'Now, *there* was a man who knew the value of things. And

had ambitions. He didn't want to be stuck on a farm for the rest of his life, breaking his back pulling onions from the ground in the heat. We got on a boat, me, Joseph and Ernest, he was three at the time, and set off for America.'

Amy brushed some breadcrumbs onto the floor.

'We weren't alone, my older brothers and their families came with us. Farms were struggling thanks to the War. All of us wanted a better life. We hadn't all had the opportunity to educate ourselves well but that didn't matter, some things can't be learnt: like setting yourself high standards and working to them ...'

Ellie squirmed, unsure why, but sure this was a criticism aimed at her.

'... Joseph swore he would never step foot on a farm again!' Amy went on. ' And God bless him, he never did.'

Winifred shifted in her seat and rubbed her arms. *Is it cooler in here all of a sudden?* She checked the fire. Only a small glow of pale red winked from the embers and charred logs.

Winifred stood up and tried to rekindle the fire. The others watched her efforts and once she sat back down, Amy asked her about her farm in Wales. *Of all the topics to choose.*

'It sounds as if many things were very similar for us,' Winifred said after a pause. 'We also never wasted anything. The good vegetables would be sent off to the market to be sold and we would keep the small or disfigured ones. My aunt would spend hours peeling those tiny potatoes. My mother's family was very good to us. Mam had to run the farm all by herself with four children to raise, so her brothers and sisters would do what they could to help.'

Darling Uncle Jack. Winifred's face softened, remembering all those summers when Uncle Jack, Aunt Mary and her cousins would arrive. The children, taller versions of their previous-summer selves, were fresh-faced and clean, noisy and excited at the prospect of the freedom of being at the farm.

They would all pretend that they had walked the six miles from the station like locals, although everyone knew they had sat in the gambo, getting off the cart only when the house came into view. It must have felt so crowded with all those extra people sleeping in the tiny rooms upstairs but her mam never seemed to mind. With the memory of her childhood to drive her, Winifred had ensured her own children had their own rooms, all four of them. She would shake her head in bemusement at their excitement at sharing a room when the occasion arose. In *her* childhood, a shared room had been normal. Not even that: a shared *bed* had been normal.

Winifred lingered on this memory, a time in her life she had tried not to reflect on, but now as she searched for the right words for this girl sitting opposite her, she remembered those summer harvest days. Her Uncle Jack would spend any spare time tinkering with machinery, grumbling that no one looked after it, and the boys would chase about the fields, hiding and climbing over the hay bales, pausing occasionally to help gather straw. They would throw it in high arcs, much of it missing the gambo.

'My aunts were very invested in the harvest, at Loynton and also, later, at Shackerley,' Lotty said. 'Always making note of the weather, the weight of the bales and the price that year. They oversaw the whole process. What was your role at harvest time?'

Winifred looked at Ellie, who clearly wanted to leave but wasn't sure how to, and an idea bubbled.

'My sisters, cousin Mair and I were in charge of preparing the meals. Bread and cheese for lunch, which would be sent out with the labourers in the morning as there was no time or money during haymaking for them to stop for a proper lunch. Then there would be suppers to make for hungry stomachs, an endless series of pies and stews.' Winifred smiled at Ellie. 'I can still make a hot crust pastry without needing scales, thanks to

all those summers. It was hard work but rewarding in its way.'
Winifred watched Ellie, who was still only partly listening. *We must impress on her the importance of hard work and people you can trust.*

'It also helped that it was a close community. People would always drop by our farm. You needed your neighbours as the nearest big town was six miles away and people didn't have cars in those days.'

'If the town was so far away and your mum was so busy, how did you get to school?' Ellie asked, her eyes suddenly alert. *I know this for sure. Let's see if she says the right thing.*

Last year, Ellie's mum had suggested a road trip to Wales. Ellie would have preferred Europe, or even to stay home with her friends, but was told that wasn't an option. On the trip, she had been shown where her great-granny had gone to primary school – a small stone building now converted into a house – and recalled it being only a five-minute drive from the farm, not miles away in a town. She smirked at her own cleverness.

'Well, the primary school was in the village, which was two miles away, and we all walked. Always, whatever the weather. There was the gambo that carried bags and crates, but only Townies used that for rides. Locals walked.'

Ellie nodded in confirmation. *Okay, that's right. But anybody could guess that.*

'My parents decided to move into my great-uncle's farm because it was a better walk for us children to the primary school,' Winifred said. 'The land was not as good as the farm they had been at, but they were concerned that walking across wet fields instead of along lanes would make us ill. That walk had already given my older sister, Kathleen, several bad bouts of flu so it seemed a sensible move.

'As things turned out, it might have been better to have risked the walk, as the farm was very hard to run when it was just my mother. Kathleen had to go into service and Orian, my other older sister, left school to help on the farm. In the end it was only me who went to secondary school.'

Ellie stopped breathing for a second. She couldn't remember all her great-granny's siblings' names but she did know that only Winifred had gone to secondary school.

'I had to walk to the village and get the bus from there into Builth. In the winter, the snow was so thick that there were times when we had to get out of the bus and help push it up hills. I remember so clearly the first time that happened. We all got out of the bus even though the snow came up to our calves and it was bitterly cold. The driver herded us around to the back and picked out the strongest ones to help him push. One of the older girls was sent to act as driver and steer the bus.'

'She could drive?' Ellie said.

'Not exactly ...' Winifred took a sip of water. 'But she was the tallest of those not picked to push the bus and could see over the steering wheel. The boys and the driver slipped about, pushing the bus, with us younger children shouting out encouragement from the sidelines. I even joined in, pushing from the side. Despite slipping in the snow and the bus's side being so cold it numbed my fingers, it all felt like a big game.'

Ellie realised that she had heard this story before, too. Her mother pulled out a shorter version of it whenever she thought Ellie needed reminding of how lucky she was not to suffer the hardships others faced. Ellie wondered what her mum would say if she told her that the kids had found pushing the bus in the snow an adventure.

'During the winter, even with time on the bus, we would arrive at school wet through and have to try to warm up by a little cast iron stove. We'd hang our coats around it and even take off our shoes if the snow had been particularly slushy.'

'That doesn't sound as fun as pushing a bus up a hill,' Ellie said.

Winifred looked at her, sensing that she was making progress. 'No, it was not. However, I wanted to live a better life than my mother had had, and education was the answer. Our water came from a stream and we had to collect it from behind the house; we bartered for things we needed; there was no electricity; and the only fire was in the kitchen.'

Winifred looked at Ellie but didn't see her. She saw her mam, chopping vegetables while a pot bubbled on the fireplace. One afternoon when she was about five, Winifred had sat at the kitchen table, surrounded by the smells of smoke and onions, and asked for butter to put on her bread, the standard snack when she got home from primary school.

'We don't have enough butter right now for it to be used so freely,' her mam had said.

Winifred had sulked and picked at the crust.

'It's so unfair. Sarah says she has bread and butter every day.'

'Well, that's lucky for Sarah. Always someone worse off than you, mind.'

Like Gladys and David, the tailor's children. Their coats were lined with newspaper and when they got to school they would stand close to the small stove warming red hands. For them, what they got at that little primary school was the only hot meal they would have that day.

'Quite simply, Eleanor, a good education is a luxury and I wasn't about to let it go to waste. Mam would never pay for anything with money if she could help it. We didn't have it, see. She would barter with eggs and vegetables. That was how we used to get ice creams in the summer.' She shook her head. 'No, it was not for me. I wanted to leave as soon as I could.'

Winifred looked at the women. Amy was leaning slightly forward, taking quick sips of her soup as she listened; Lotty sat upright and still, her head tilted slightly as she absorbed the story.

'I was proposed to once when I was still at school,' Winifred said, keen to make her point to Ellie as clear as possible. 'I was sixteen and a Baptist minister wanted to marry me. But marrying a local boy and being tied to their fate was not for me.

Poor Kathleen had no choice and I didn't want that. I wanted to travel. I wanted to see the world. That ambition kept me going on many a cold winter morning.'

'What happened to Kathleen?' Amy asked

'Oh, she married young. We didn't care for him.' Winifred looked directly at Ellie as she continued, 'Funnily enough, all those miles of walking came in quite useful when I was training for nursing. I was finally accepted to Westminster Hospital as a trainee in 1941 and the following year I was posted to Basingstoke. One of the drawbacks was the distance we had to walk to get on duty and to meals. It was about half an hour's walk from the units to the nurses' home. You couldn't be late either. Matron was very strict about such things.'

She took a sip of water before adding, 'All hospitals were like that back then. There was very strict decorum and discipline was rigidly enforced. There were also very exacting hygiene rules: beds had to be straightened properly and you always had to be dressed appropriately; the matron wouldn't accept anything less.'

Ellie leaned forward and pushed her soup to one side. Winifred watched her great-granddaughter adjust her position, resting one arm on the table as she listened. Winifred's face brightened in response.

'The Christmas of 1942 saw us doing rehearsal after rehearsal every night for the pantomime. I was quite sick of it. You should have seen me as Prince Charming.' She chuckled at the memory and shook her head. 'Or rather you shouldn't have. My costume consisted of shorts and a Russian blouse. I am afraid Matron would not have approved. In the midst of it all the old girl paid us a visit one day. We marched along the corridor like a lot of schoolchildren to be shaken by the hand. She asked us each in turn how long we had spent on the ward and began telling us what wonderful work we were doing. Through all this I was hiding one arm which had no cuff!'

Winifred chuckled again. 'Oh dear, listen to me rambling

on like this.'

She felt flushed by talking so much about herself. In the brief silence that followed, Winifred looked around and assessed the list she had created for the evening.

The table: It looks nice, the roses an elegant touch, although a little more colour would have been nice. All this white reminds me of funerals.

Lighting: Lotty was right to insist on candles. Softer than electric lights, although I think those candle lamps might have been better. The fire: Glad I rekindled it, as it is lovely and warm in here now. I hope it doesn't go out so suddenly again.

The food: Ellie needs to eat something. In hindsight, perhaps caviar and beetroot soup were a bit too unusual. I'm not sure I would have managed to get any of my children to eat them. Hopefully the next courses will be more to her taste. She seems to be warming to us, though. It was touch and go there for a moment; Amy is quite direct. Yes, this is going well. Would have preferred to have maintained our previous tactics a while longer, but never mind. No point dwelling on that.

ELLIE AND LOTTY

'I have often observed that nursing a person requires particular skills,' Lotty said. 'My dear Mamma fell ill when I was nineteen years of age and the responsibility of looking after her and our younger siblings fell to Frances and me. Mamma was never the same again and had to be pushed about in a chair; whenever I pushed her, she found great fault with my making her go so slowly. She would also get so tired if guests were visiting. My father's sisters used to visit from Loynton and –'

'Now, that's the second time you've mentioned this "Loin-tin". Where is it?' Amy said.

'Loynton? It is the family seat.'

Amy looked at her blankly and Lotty's eyes narrowed with impatience. *What did I say that was so confusing?* She sighed, squeezed her hands together and said, 'Loynton is a hamlet in Staffordshire and the estate had been in the family since 1649, the year Charles the First was executed.'

'So you could say your family had a better year that year?' Amy said.

Lotty paused to digest the comment. *Is she attempting to be amusing?*

'Loynton Hall, on the other hand,' she continued, 'was built circa 1671. The Hall and estate were Sambrooke, my brother's, inheritance and when he came of age the Aunts moved to Shackerley in Albrighton. Loynton was quite delightful, with well-proportioned rooms, extensive kitchen gardens and a farm that we would often visit and help feed the lambs, although I always thought the cows quite smelly.'

Lotty took final sip of her soup and then carefully put her spoon down.

'However, I am getting ahead of myself. I was referring to Mamma and the Aunts' visits. They would stay for hours, talking their loudest. Poor Mamma would have such a headache. On those occasions she would go to bed early and often stay in bed all of the next morning. Frances was much better at looking after her than I. Mamma used to say I washed her as if I did not like to touch her, and nor did I!'

Lotty laughed and checked the other faces to ensure they had understood the joke. Amy opened her mouth to say something, so Lotty raised her voice as she said.

'Frances was often the one we would send to look after family if they were in need of help. She was so patient and thoughtful, even though when she was in charge of Sambrooke when he was recovering from scarlatina, Mamma was quite convinced she was not doing as much as she ought.'

'What's scarlatina?' Ellie said.

'Scarlet fever,' Winifred said.

Lotty sipped her sherry. *Why is Winifred talking as if she is hurrying to somewhere?*

'... very common in small children.' Winifred went on. 'Nasty rash and fever, and very infectious. Before antibiotics it was dangerous enough to make whole communities panic if there was an outbreak.'

'I've never heard it called "scarlatina",' Ellie said.

Lotty shot a look at her. 'It is the scientific name. New Latin, to be precise, originating from the medieval Latin "scarlata".'

Ellie shrugged. 'I don't know Latin.'

Lotty put down her sherry glass and stared at Ellie. 'You do not know Latin? It is not compulsory learning? Not even for the boys? The basis of legal, medical and religious doctrine? You should tell your mother to find a tutor who can teach you.

It is an important and very interesting language.'
She could see that Ellie didn't look convinced.
'I'm not great at languages. Besides, most people speak
English when you go abroad, so it's not really a problem.' Ellie
wasn't sure she really meant that but she knew it would annoy
Lotty.
Lotty didn't say anything; her face darkened and she took
a long sip of water. A tree branch tapped against the window
and the candles flickered. The fire suddenly flared and a spark
dashed across the floor towards Lotty and Ellie. Lotty watched
the spark fizzle out. *Beware of a quarrel.*
She changed her position to look more directly at Ellie. 'I
always found it extremely beneficial to speak the language of
the natives. In the summer of 1873, I went on a Swiss tour
with my aunt and uncle Whitelegge and was quite thrilled to
be able to practise my German, I can assure you. Speaking
the tongue of the natives often enables you to gather so much
additional information and knowledge. It shows a courtesy
and culture that would be otherwise lacking.'
Ellie didn't say anything and watched the candles flicker
and dance as they tried to stay alight.
'During our visit,' Lotty said, 'we were travelling up a particularly steep, stony path when my uncle's horse began to flounder.
Seeing that the horse was evidently in difficulties I contrived to
open a conversation with my man. I had tried English, French
and German on him previously with no success and could only
assume that he had no language. However, through my German and his slender French, we made out that it was unsafe to
continue to ride. My uncle was told that he was *très lourd* and
would have to descend.
She chuckled. Her uncle had taken the comment in good
humour and walking hadn't ruined his mood.
'If I had been unable to communicate with my man it might
have led to a serious accident or misunderstanding. And the
next day when we reached the Reichenbach he began to shout

the points of the prospects in stentorian tones, much to our astonishment.'

She smiled again as she remembered their collective surprise. The man's face was not visible to her memory; she could only recall his dark hair, weather-worn skin and plain brown clothes. But etched in her mind was the sound of small stones skittering under the horses' hooves and seeing birds soar soundlessly in the sky; too high to identify, just black marks on nature's blue and white canvas.

Lotty looked at Ellie, who watched her from behind a shield of crossed limbs. 'It was most useful to know languages oneself and not rely on others. I was obliged to do my learning around other household commitments, especially after Mamma was taken ill. Just as Winifred and Amy, I am sure, had chores they were expected to do, so did I: preparing and packing for the boys to ensure they were ready for school, for example; it would not do if they did not have enough shirts or their socks were not darned. And then there were food orders: Mamma would often require me to send the order to the butcher's or, if she was away, arrange for the carriage to meet her off the train.'

Ellie saw Amy shake her head, and her mouth moved, although Ellie couldn't hear what she said. Lotty didn't appear to notice, and carried on talking.

'If I had had the opportunity to learn languages in a classroom setting with no other responsibilities …'

Her gaze drilled into Ellie's forehead but Ellie steadily refused to make eye contact.

'They had schools for children in my time,' she added. 'Indeed, it was during my lifetime that attending school became compulsory, although children of the upper classes were not required to attend the national system.'

Ellie's foot kicked repeatedly against her chair leg. Lotty stopped talking and looked at the foot, then at the folds of her dress which were dangerously close to this moving extremity. The foot jerked to a stop and Lotty continued.

'Public schools were different, of course; however, these were mostly for boys and the ones for girls tended to provide a curriculum designed only for future domestic duties. Mamma, though, was firm in her view that we girls should be well educated.'

'When I was a child, she had to look after my papa and younger sisters, so Frances and I spent much of our time with family, especially Grandmamma Goodlad, who also assisted in our education.'

For a moment, Lotty found herself in front of her grandmamma, standing on the patio, clasping her hands to hide the ink stains that hadn't come off with the scrubbing she had given them.

Her grandmamma sat in her chair, a light blanket over her lap despite the heat, her eyes shut and her head gently nodding. Frances stood next to Lotty reciting the verbs they had learnt that day. Thinking her grandmamma had fallen asleep, Frances stopped.

'Continue, child,' Grandmamma said immediately, without opening her eyes. 'Remember your pronunciation. To get on well with a language, you must use the correct accent.' She waved her hand. 'Start again ...'

'Later, there were governesses who lived with us in Edgmond,' Lotty said aloud, now back in the room and keen to continue her story. 'Our younger sisters did not benefit from our grandmamma's tutoring, which I am sure was why they had such ... different interests to myself.'

Lotty sat a little straighter, her eyes locking onto Ellie once more, as she came to her main point.

'However, Latin was not a subject any of our governesses knew, so I taught myself. As a girl I knew all the scientific names for the local flora and fauna, and as a young lady, with the assistance of Uncle Richard, I became fluent in the language. Uncle Richard provided old deeds and legal books and I would translate them.'

Her steely gaze left Ellie's face and she gave the room a look of proud satisfaction. Her stare fell on Winifred.

'I even tutored my nephews for their Latin exams many years later and they passed first time. Unlike their father!' she chortled, revealing a missing tooth.

'Sambrooke had to re-take his Latin exams at Oxford, but I did not think he would appreciate my assistance so did not offer it. Besides ... I am sure there were other reasons why he failed the first time.'

Lotty pushed back a wave of feeling.

'Frances was —'

'Eleanor. Tell me, what subjects do you enjoy?' Amy said.

Lotty sucked in air through her teeth.

Ellie fidgeted in her chair. 'I don't think I have a favourite subject,' she said, biting her lower lip. 'I guess I'm not bad at maths and science.'

Winifred beamed at her. 'Those are very good subjects. I always enjoyed maths as well.'

Ellie glanced at Lotty, who still looked irritated by Amy's interruption.

'My favourite subject, though, is art and design,' Ellie said, and her lips twitched.

'Sketching!' Lotty said, 'I used to enjoy tracing church epitaphs, but it is hardly a replacement for learning the foundations of a language.'

Lotty's mouth drew a pale line across her face. *As if I went out to dinner to talk of sketching.* A candle sputtered and went out.

'My interests lay in other areas: dates and the history of places. I asked my Aunt Rachel once how old Norbury church was. After a pause, she replied, "Medieval". I know now that it is nothing of the kind.'

The memory made Lotty feel a little better. Ellie re-filled her water glass, wondering how much longer her mum would be. Her stomach rumbled and she considered attempting another spoonful of the now cold pinkish-purple soup. When she was little, her mum would read to her as they ate their meals. If Ellie wasn't eating the food, her mum would prompt her: 'Have a mouthful and then I will turn the page.' Eyeing the soup now, she thought the silver lining in her mum not being there was that no one was trying to force 'one more spoonful' down her.

'You seem quite pensive, Eleanor,' Lotty said, and Ellie realised that she was being scrutinised. She shook her head. Lotty continued her story.

'Of course, we were fortunate to have Mamma, as she encouraged our education. One year, a journal we subscribed to called *The Monthly Packet* announced that next year's Christmas number would comprise stories on one subject, a proverb: "What the snow conceals the sun reveals."

'We thought it would be great fun to do a Christmas number of our own and each write a tale on the proverb. It was rather amusing to see the different ways that authorship took us. Alice, who was only fourteen at the time, was the most fluent; she kept a little book in her pocket and whenever she had a few spare minutes she took it out, smiling to herself.'

A chair creaked and Lotty stopped talking. She sat in silence as Amy leaned across the table with a lit candle to relight the one that had gone out. A surge of orange light appeared and Lotty continued, suppressing a tut of annoyance.

'Although I was tolerably fluent, I could not always get into the mood for writing and did it more by fits and starts than the others. When I was in the mood I wrote easily and lived in my tale. I would stay up at night because my hero and heroine would talk so. Frances used to tease me saying that I would have got on very fast if only I did not polish and rewrite every sentence.'

'It sounds like a fun story —' Amy began, but got no further.

'Not to be left out, Mamma volunteered to write one,' Lotty said. 'She laughed unceasingly for three or four days, then gave Miss Berry, our governess, a few sheets of paper to copy it out fairly, and it was done.'

Lotty shook her head at the memory, took a sip of water and glanced at her audience.

'It was only out of the sternest sense of duty that Agatha and Frances wrote at all. Agatha could not think of anything to say and Frances complained that she could not express the ideas that floated in her head. She was always too modest, my dear sister Frances. Her powers of learning were always very surprising. Once she had learnt something, she never forgot it. And her imagination was vivid; the village children loved to listen to her stories. However, I digress. Once we had completed our stories we arranged for our Burne aunts to visit from Loynton and judge our efforts. They were an excellent audience, interested but not too critical. We gathered together in the drawing room and Alice went first and it was very elaborate, the best for her age; very unequal but showing great cleverness and amusing to the last degree. Agatha's was a sad story about a girl's jealousy and wounded pride; Frances declared it her favourite as it was so simply done.'

Ellie twisted her hair over her finger, let it go and twisted it again, all the time her mind dancing with ideas for an elaborate escape.

'Mine was the greatest possible contrast to Agatha's grey-toned story,' Lotty said, unaware of Ellie's lack of interest. 'A bright, sparkling tale of how a grave, shy, sweet girl, living a secluded life, fell in love and married a lively captain in a garrison town where life was completely different in all respects. Part of the amusement in my tale was that the characters were modelled from life. They all had such a laugh deciding who the characters represented, and they all guessed correctly that the heroine was my dearest Frances.'

Lotty was silent as she remembered them all sitting together in the drawing room, a fire warming the room against the ever-present dampness, and the large windows warning them that the afternoon light was fading. The bitter sweetness of marmalade still coated her mouth and around her the sound of teacups greeting saucers was barely noticeable against Alice's and Agatha's voices as they called out names and laughed at their own silly jokes.

Sitting closest to the fire were the aunts, who watched the younger generation but did not join in, being unfamiliar with the local villagers' names that were being thrown around. And, of course, there was Frances, sitting next to Lotty on the sofa, twirling a loose strand of hair while protesting at the characterisation.

'You have exaggerated once more, Lotty,' she had said. 'The heroine is too pretty and clever to be a true likeness.'

'She was the best of us, my dear sister,' Lotty said with an abruptness that made the words sound angry. 'Everyone loved her. She was very clever and talented but had such sympathy and concern for others, too, regardless of who they were.

'Her tale was a very good one. She declared she had not aimed high with it, but she was always self-effacing. The setting was Longmynd, Shropshire, and the main protagonists were the children of a poor farmer who had recently remarried. The only items she brings with her are her family spoons, which the children throw away. After various adventures and twists, the last one is found finally when the snow melts. I can see her now, standing in front of the drawing-room windows, as tall as myself despite being two years my junior, telling the story through her facial expressions as much as her words.

'We all agreed that hers should be sent off, and indeed it did win the competition ... In the end, however, it was not published. Not until many years later.'

'Why not?' Amy said.

'Why not what?' Lotty said.

'Why wasn't it published?'

'... The timing was not right.'

'What had it got wrong? Its Latin verbs?' Amy winked at Ellie.

Lotty gave Amy a look that shrivelled the warmth of the room.

'What was the tale called?' Winifred said, her voice quick and clear.

'"Margaret's Marriage",' Lotty said. 'It was a lovely little tale; I published it privately on her behalf.'

In the corner of her eye, Lotty saw Ellie start. Lotty studied the girl as she slowly said, 'A blue cover, because blue was her favourite colour.'

'Yes, that's right.' A shiver ran through Ellie. The only surviving copy of that tale was in her bedroom, contributing to the piles of books that had failed to make it to the bookshelf.

Lotty clapped her hands, 'I knew it! You've read it!'.

'Umm, no, I haven't. I've got it, though. My mum gave it to me for Christmas last year, she thought I would enjoy it.'

'And despite that, you have not read it?' Lotty pursued. 'It would do you good to have a little more curiosity.'

Winifred said her name and Amy started to say something about the colour blue but Lotty ignored them. 'My Burne aunts would often complain that we were being raised "to be seen *and* heard". And indeed Mamma's favourite axiom was "How are children to learn if they don't ask?" Ah, dear Mamma. She was always so good and answered all our questions even if it meant writing several letters to us.'

Lotty turned her head towards Ellie, 'If she had given a book to one of *us* to read, I can assure you, we would have read it.'

Ellie crossed her arms. *It's not fair. I haven't got round to it, that's all.*

'She expected us to constantly aspire to improve ourselves. When we were visiting Grandmamma Goodlad (I must have been ten years of age), she wrote quite concerned that the last letter she had had from me was in such very small writing. She feared that if I got into the way of writing so very small at that age, I would quite spoil my hand so she provided the last letter I had written where my handwriting had been of

a pattern that she liked. She requested that I show it to our
governess and ask her to assist me in achieving this preferred
style of writing. What would she have said if I had not? If I had
said 'I have not found the time for it, Mamma?'

Lotty's sharp eyes bored into Ellie, who sat stubbornly staring at the tablecloth, biting the corner of her lip.

'I'm sure Eleanor's mother doesn't mind *when* Eleanor reads
the story,' Winifred said 'Would anyone like some —-'

'It is not a question of "mind" but of curiosity that concerns
me. To be content with a life devoid of collecting knowledge?'
Lotty tutted. 'It was thanks to Mamma's encouragement, and
my own natural curiosity, that I pursued a vocation so fulfilling. One that challenged the present, explored the past and
made us question what we thought we knew.'

As she talked, she pinched her thumb and index finger
together as if her hand was yearning for a pen.

'This would not have occurred if I had not had curiosity; if
I had merely put aside the notebook my mamma had given
me and refused to take note of what was occurring around
me. Instead, from childhood, I followed the trail of antiquities curious to learn the traditions of the lower cultures,' said
Lotty. 'Later, I travelled across Shropshire speaking to the poor
regarding their beliefs and making note of them.'

Lotty leaned forward, her eyes locked on Ellie.

'It was not easy. It takes more than simply jotting down
a note or a phrase to be a true collector. I had to learn from
mistakes and be humble in asking for guidance. The main
secret of success when interviewing less-cultured people is
to adopt a sympathetic attitude. Encourage them to talk and
listen rather than ask questions. As Plato said, the wise speak
when they have something to say.'

Amy made a noise that sounded like a half laugh, half
sneeze. Lotty fell silent. *This will not be the success she wants
it to be.* Ellie tried to ignore the tree branch that scratched
against the window. She glanced around the room noticing for

the first time a painting of two crows, one perched on a branch, the other in mid-flight. She looked at the opposite wall, where the mirror hung. The crows were reflected in the mirror going the opposite way. *Has that picture always been there?* The wings of the flying crows fluttered in the mirror; Ellie snapped her head to the picture and back to the mirror. *I imagined it.* She tapped the edge of the letter against the tablecloth to distract herself from the shudder that swept over her.

Amy broke the silence. 'What's in that envelope? You've been guarding it ever since you arrived.'

Eight pairs of eyes studied the envelope with Ellie's mother's name clearly stamped across it. Ellie dropped it as if it had caught fire.

'Nothing important,' she said

'Stick to the sciences because acting really isn't your strong suit,' Amy said. 'Come on, what's in the envelope?'

'None of your business!' Ellie cried. 'I don't have to share everything with you people, just because you seem to think some weird intervention is needed. I don't even KNOW you!'

She pushed back her chair and rushed towards the door, prepared to put an end to this strange meal.

'There's no need to get all defensive,' Amy said. 'You can't leave yet, sit down.'

Ellie focused on the door. The sherry had affected her more than she'd realised, as the door seemed further away than before. A gust of wind shot down the chimney. The curtains billowed, their bustling ends reaching like hands towards Ellie. The door slammed. Ellie grabbed at the handle and missed. The letter floated away and fluttered to the floor, propelled by the cold draft that pushed at the door. Her throat tightened and she scooped up the letter. The three women still sat where she had left them. Two frowned and watched Ellie with a strict intensity. The other was pale, her eyes closed; her lips moved but no sound came out.

AMY AND ELLIE

It's probably no surprise that she's stubborn and strong-willed. I was the same. And if Lotty's anything to go by, there are single-minded genes on the other side of the family as well. What's in that letter? Why is she so anxious about it? Wonder how her mum will react to the news if it's bad. Probably not as badly as Eleanor fears. That's the thing about being a kid, you never fully understand your parents until you're much older. Although she's not really a kid, is she? Fourteen. I was working on the farm and in the house by that age. And Gloria travelled across the ocean by herself at twelve. Gloria ... Funny to think of her. She was another one though: independent, doing things her way. Just like me. Not that my mae approved of my independent spirit but then she didn't understand.

'This isn't the right time to be going to America,' her mother had said. 'You should stay.'

Amy remembered it so clearly: April 1918. Standing in that small cottage she and Joseph had on Joseph's dad's farm. Joseph had found an excuse to leave when her mother arrived; this wasn't the first argument they had had over their plans. And now all that interrupted their discussion was the noise of Ernest clashing toy soldiers on the stone flags of the kitchen.

'Please, Mae. We've been over this. There are better opportunities in America. You and Dad, of all people, should understand why we want to do this.'

'*We* had no choice. This was where there were opportunities.' Her mother's finger stabbed in the direction of the floor and then moved in a crescent to take in the whole room. 'And there are still opportunities here. You don't have to leave your family like we did. You can make a life here. With your family. That's why we left our home and families. So our children wouldn't have to.'

'Most of Joseph's family are in the States and he has lined up work in New Bedford. Better paid and not as back-breaking as farming.'

'Nothing wrong with farming!'

'I never said that, and you know it.'

'But why don't you wait? It isn't safe.'

'We're not gonna get torpedoed, Mae. We'll be in the middle of the Atlantic.'

'That's not what I meant.'

Amy looked at her mother. Despite Amy being the taller of the two, her mum could still make her feel like such a little girl.

'Bet you're not telling Everest or John they can't go?'

'It's different.'

'No, it's not.'

'You will be almost seven months —'

'Now look, I will be fine. There are doctors in America, good doctors, and we'll be in a city, with lots of access to anything we need.'

'There's everything you need here in Bermuda.'

Amy had her retort ready but her mum picked up some clothes and began folding them, so she said nothing. Joseph returned a few hours later, bringing the earthy smell of the farm with him. Amy had always found it strange to look at this tall, thin man with his sweet, childlike face framed with sticking-out ears and see him digging up vegetables or harnessing ploughs to the work-horse. But that was one of the reasons they had left. Because it suited him even less than it suited her.

He sat down, pulled off his boots, and tucked into the pastries Amy's mum had left.

'Now look, those are for the journey.' She waved a wooden

spoon at him but he just grinned and took another bite.

'My last day on a farm. Hopefully. Worth celebrating, I think.' He eyed the bags waiting at the door.

'How do you think we are going to get all that all the way to New Bedford? Why don't you leave some? John's Maria can make some dresses for you if you need any.'

'It's all essential — for Ernest. Remember, it could still be cold when we arrive and he's not used to it. And I won't be relying on Maria, or anybody for that matter, so it all comes.'

He had finished the pastry; he brushed his hands free of crumbs and kissed her on the cheek.

'Whatever you and the baby need,' he said, letting his hand fall to her protruding stomach.

———

Of course there had been doctors, not that they had helped us in the end.

Perhaps that was why I hadn't gone back. Unable to face my mother and give her back the little clothes she had so lovingly knitted.

But I had had Ernest to think about. And what would there have been for me in Bermuda? A single mother expected to live with her parents and work on the farm. Besides, I couldn't leave America. And it had been the right decision. Because Arthur and Ruth had come along. What gentle creatures they were.

Amy watched a waiter silently appear behind Ellie.

They had needed so much protection. Ernest, on the other hand ... All those nights waiting up, wondering where he was, if he was safe. He had been such a sweet child, not that he wasn't sweet when he was older. Always kind but he developed a devil-may-care attitude to life that was worrying.

But he had been so good when James was born that July. Wouldn't run around shouting and banging toys like other peo-

ple's children did. No, he adored his little brother and would do anything for him, even silence.

Ernest would sit rocking James' cradle, with childish seriousness, while Amy trundled about in the kitchen, usually with a pot bubbling with the scent of tomatoes and garlic. The smell was made more intense by the stuffiness of the house. Even with the windows open as much as they could be, all that seemed to happen was that more hot air came in.

Not like the heat of Bermuda, which was humid but had the relief of the Atlantic breezes. This heat was the pitiless heat of urbanisation, of factory fumes, dust and buildings. That first summer Amy was constantly forcing Ernest outside.

'It's too hot to be holed-up like this in the house,' she said.

'But James is inside. I want to stay with him.'

'James is a baby. Different rules. He needs to be in away from the dust and the sun.'

And then August had turned to September and no matter how hard the sun beat down, Amy didn't notice. To her, all was dark. If the leaves had turned black and caught fire, she wouldn't have cared. The shock and misery were overwhelming. Now it was Ernest cajoling *her* outside. They had gone for a walk through the small park by their house and her sweet little boy had picked a flower for her 'because she was sad'. She didn't know then how much darker that month would get.

The waiter cleared away the soup bowls and two more waiters appeared, one holding plates of fish in a cream sauce and the other carrying a bottle of white wine.

Amy watched the waiter finish laying the plates. The plates had the same pattern as the soup bowls and it reminded her of Bermuda and the family meals at Vicinity House. Except this pattern was blue and white. Amy shuddered. The waiter placed Ellie's plate down last. 'Can we be of service?' he asked her, for she stood in his way. She clutched the letter to her chest and stared at him.

'No, that is all, thank you.' Lotty stood up and signalled for the waiter to leave.

She looked at Ellie with an eyebrow slightly raised.

'Please take your seat, Eleanor. *Nolens volens*, we have not finished our conversation.' Lotty smiled at the other women. 'Or our dinner.'

Nicely done.

Amy frowned and moved thoughts of the past to the back of her mind, where they had always lived. Ellie still hadn't moved, but the warm smell of baked fish and allure of the cheese sauce tempted her back. She sat down and shuffled her chair in, feeling a little sheepish about her outburst.

'What did you say?' she said to Lotty. 'What's nolens boless?'

Lotty exhaled. '*Nolens volens*. It is Latin and translates as 'whether you like it or not'. What do they teach you nowadays?'

Ellie, feeling better as she ate, took a second mouthful of the fish.

'I told you: art.'

Winifred chuckled. Ellie smiled back, pleased with the reaction, and nudged the parsley garnish to the side.

'Parsley is an uncanny herb,' Lotty said.

Ellie looked at her, surprised to see that her action had been so closely watched.

'It is extremely difficult to grow it from seed,' Lotty said. 'Perhaps that is why some say that 'where parsley grows in the garden, the missus is master'.

Ellie shrugged. 'It's just parsley. We don't grow it these days. It comes from the supermarket.'

Winifred choked on a laugh. Ellie looked at her and Winifred carefully layered her fork with fish and sauce. *What did I say that was so funny?*

'Now, why don't you tell us about that letter?' Amy asked. She saw Winifred pause, her forkful of fish hovering mid-air.

'Perhaps now is not the right time,' Winifred murmured.

'It's okay, I'm going to have to tell my mum anyway before she opens the letter.' Ellie sighed and looked at the letter.

'A few weeks ago, I locked someone in a cupboard. I mean, she wanted to be locked in the cupboard. At least, that's what she said. But then a teacher came and caught us and when she was let out she said I had forced her into the cupboard. Which wasn't true!'

She stared at her plate. In front of her, files lay scattered on the floor and Rosie was squeezing herself onto the lower shelf.

'Come on. Help me shut it, Ellie. This will be such a joke! Think of the look on Mrs Milvern's face!'

The look on the teacher's face had been bemused irritation at finding the room in such disorder. And then Rosie had started knocking on the inside of the cupboard door. She emerged, eyes wide, with a tale of being forced inside. Mrs Milvern's bemused irritation had turned to a fury so complete that only Ellie saw Rosie's smirk.

Ellie felt as perplexed now as she did then about that event. The result had been the public humiliation of being moved to a different table, away from her friends. Rosie had always been really nice to her, so she was sure it had been a mistake. After all, it had been Rosie who had pulled her from the dark void of unpopularity back on that warm day in March, in Month Three of her sentence. New to the area, with Aria the only friendly face, it had been a miserable existence. And then Rosie had bounded over, her dark hair flicking wildly as if trying to free itself from the confines of a ponytail.

'Are you doing anything now?' she had said.

'No, not really,' Ellie said, wondering if she had sounded casual enough.

'Great! We need a fourth for tennis and I saw you were dressed for the gym, so ...' She had smiled broadly.

Ellie had looked down at her clothes: she had changed out of her uniform but was heading to the river to sketch, not planning to go to the gym.

'Oh ... well, I don't have a racket.'

'No problem. I always bring a spare. S'you're in? Great, come on. We've only got the court till 4.30. Oh, and do you have any cash on you? I forgot my wallet and we owe Mia money for the court. She never allows IOUs.'

Ellie's tennis skills were acceptable but nothing impressive, and that was demonstrated on the court that day. But the next day, Rosie came up to her and, linking arms, escorted her to their History class. And from then on she was included in that group of girls. Perhaps always slightly on the edge, never a fully-fledged member, but Ellie decided not to mind. She preferred being on the edge of a group to sitting by herself.

———

'*You Locked Someone In A Cupboard …*' Amy repeated. And then she burst out laughing, a deep, throaty laugh.

'I am sure I do not see what is so amusing,' Lotty said.

'No, I'm sure you wouldn't,' Amy said. 'However, some kids get into much worse trouble. Oh dear, Eleanor. Why didn't you just tell the teacher that she had asked you to do it?'

'I guess it does sound kinda funny,' Ellie said. 'It was really annoying at the time, but Rosie is so nice, the teacher would never believe she was lying.'

'She can't be that nice if she got you in trouble.'

'I'm sure she was just scared of getting told off, y'know?'

Amy looked at Ellie. 'No, I don't know.'

'Well, we agreed afterwards that there had been no point in both of us getting into trouble. Mia said that Rosie's parents had told her she had only one chance left after … after something else that had happened. And Rosie apologised to me later.'

'I had a strict mother, but I would never have let a friend take the blame, that's not what *friends* do,' Amy said.

Winifred touched her arm. Amy pretended not to notice.

'And what was this "something else that happened", kiddo?' She didn't wait for a reply. 'Now look, when I was growing up,

I had a very close friend called Mary. After my sister, Selmith, Mary was the next closest person to me. The three of us were inseparable and would be in and out of each other's houses whenever we could escape chores. I had no interest in farming. Neither did Selmith.'

The smell of onions straight from the ground, watching her brother troop slowly down the road to pick bananas at a neighbouring farm and voices urging the plough horse across fields drifted through Amy's mind.

'We both wanted to get off the island and have adventures. America seemed so glamourous. We had lived there for a little bit and I longed to go back. Childhood illusions of a life filled with games and candy, I suppose. And Bermuda had banned all motor vehicles when I was ten years old, so the thought of cars and omnibuses became much more exciting and dangerous.

'My day-dreaming drove my mae mad. Had very firm views on a woman's role and how a girl should behave.'

Amy laughed, 'I certainly didn't fit the mould. Her life was all about the house and the farm. Had eleven children in all. All those pregnancies and then only seven survived.'

A baby's pitiful cries filled Amy's ears.

'It is heartbreaking to lose a child, but Mae never showed it. Concentrated on the living, I guess.'

She took a sip of wine and swallowed the lump that had formed in her chest. *Not now. Everyone is watching you.*

'Of course, their memories lived on. My youngest sister was called Lydia because the baby who had died before my sister was born had been a little girl called Lydia. So they kept her memory in the name. A sad number of our relatives are named after dead siblings.'

She shook her head to free herself from the young faces that were beginning to form in her vision.

'Anyway, I had no interest in staying on a farm. I thought I would do things differently.'

She took a deep breath, 'It was only later that I understood her concerns and could empathise with her. But I think everyone grows up to feel that.'

Ellie scoffed.

'Now look. We all thought our parents didn't know what they were talking about.' Amy pointed her finger at Ellie, 'You're not the first to think that they don't understand you.'

Ellie shrugged and concentrated on the patterns she was making with the leftover sauce.

'I've gone off the subject; I was talking about the value of real friends. When I was too young to work at one of the big houses or on the farm, my mae had me doing chores at home. One of my jobs was to weed the path and vegetable patch. There was no shelter, my knees would get encrusted with little pebbles, my hands were always dirty and it was very boring and very hot. I would do it so slowly that Mary would often finish her chores and come and keep me company. On one of these days, I talked her into going down to the beach. My mother was dead against us girls playing about like that but I didn't care. We would strip down to our petticoats, clamber over rocks, hunt for shells and splash about in the surf anyway.'

Amy grinned and leaned forward as she said, 'We thought this was a great game so we snuck over the fields to the main road. We hid in the shrubs checking that the coast was clear and then made a dash for it to the beach. It felt like a real adventure. And, oh, we had such fun. Came back with sea salt in our hair and sand between our toes. We were so pleased with ourselves.'

She interrupted her story to take on a mouthful of fish. When she had finished she said, 'I thought I was so clever! But Everest soon turned up to warn me that Mae knew that I had abandoned my chores. I denied it, of course, right down to stamping my foot and putting my hands on my hips like I'd seen my mae do when she was cross. But Everest reached out and pulled some seaweed from my hair.'

Amy patted her head, 'Even back then my hair let me down. My mae was furious and then Mary turned up carrying a basket of treats her mae had made. She was going to take the blame for the idea but I refused to let her in. It would have been so easy, as my mae had a soft spot for Mary, and for pastries! I was given extra chores for a month, but rather that than let a friend take the blame.'

She looked seriously across the table and jabbed her finger in Ellie's direction. 'Friends look after one another.'

Ellie looked down at the table and adjusted her fork and knife.

'Well, I don't want any trouble. I haven't explained very well ... They're nice, really. And they're my friends ...'

'*Antes só do que mal acompanhado*,' Amy said: 'Better to be alone than in bad company.'

'But they do help me out. I'm not very good at sports and stuff,' Ellie said, 'and they always play with me. Once Mia said it was because she liked to win, but she was joking. They are really popular at school. It's nice to be part of that.'

'That may be so, darling,' Winifred said. 'But believe me, popularity has a very thin veneer.'

'I agree,' Amy said. 'If I have learnt anything, kiddo, it is that the best kinds of friends are those who admire you for who you are. Not what you can do for them.'

WINIFRED AND ELLIE

'A simple misunderstanding. I am sure it will blow over,' Winifred said. 'However, it is very easy to think you are doing something nice, like protecting someone, when really you are making things worse.'

Winifred took a sip of water.

'It's more complicated than that,' Ellie said.

Winifred looked at her for a minute and a moment from her childhood came to her. Without thinking, she began, 'I was not a naughty child. I did what I was told and was always on time for things. Neighbours said they could set their watch by Winnie Troedrhiw. However, even under the guise of doing good, I had my share of misunderstandings. Darling mother, she was never angry, though. Always laughing, despite —'

'How do you pronounce your family name? Lotty interjected.

'Davies.'

'Did you not just call yourself Troydrew?'

'Oh yes, that was the name of our farm. You often called people after their farms rather than by their surname.'

'How interesting,' Lotty said. 'Please, do continue.'

Winifred held on to her smile, absent-mindedly adjusting her necklace. *Remember, she's not doing it on purpose. It's just how she is. I'm simply a bit on edge because of earlier.* It had been a strange energy: the candle going out like that, the wind blowing through the room. *And was it my imagination or did it have a hold over Eleanor? She snapped so quickly. What had been the purpose of it? And where had it come from?*

She glanced at the other women. *It would have been easier to suppress if I had had more help.* Winifred sighed. *That is probably being unfair. After all, it was Lotty who got her back to the table.* She adjusted her necklace again and returned her attention to Ellie.

'One day I really tested Mam's patience. I thought I would be useful. I was probably about six years old and although I already helped with my baby brother, the housework and finding kindling for the bread oven, it was the farmhand and sometimes my older sisters who did the share of the major farm work. So there I was, six years old and desiring to be helpful. I thought I could assist by giving the chicks a bath. I got a pail and filled it with water from the stream then carried it around to where the hen coop was. I put three of the chicks into this pail of water expecting them to splash about like I had seen the ducklings do. Instead they promptly sank. It took me a moment to realise they couldn't swim and by then it was too late for them, the poor dears.'

'You mean they drowned?' Ellie asked.

'Yes, sadly. My mother was so good about it. I was incredibly upset and couldn't stop crying and darling Mother just gave me a big hug and never spoke of it again. My sisters were less forgiving and gave me a very hard time.'

'Mum has shown me where you lived,' Ellie said. 'She says it's converted now but once was both a farmhouse and a cow-shed. Is that true?'

Winifred's hand reached for her necklace and her fingers twirled one of the beads. The pictures Ellie had seen of the Burne residences flashed through her mind and she twisted a piece of her hair in her fingers. It was Winifred who came to her rescue. She smiled at her great granddaughter.

'Yes. That is right. One part was a cowshed and we had the other half of the building. Call it semi-detached.'

Ellie smiled even though they both knew it was a weak attempt at a joke.

'The kitchen was the main living area. There was a big fire in there, which made it the warmest room in the house. It had pots and pans hung across the lintel and a bread oven to one side.'

Winifred could almost smell the warm bread and creamy rice pudding promising hungry stomachs a little luxury.

'My mother was an excellent cook and made delicious stews, pies and puddings. Her cooking was why labourers were always willing to help with the harvest. Her Welsh cakes and pasties were the best in the area. So good that the farm hands would overlook the fact that she never allowed beer.'

Winifred slipped further into reverie as the warmth of the room and the glow from the fire evoked her childhood parlour. All that was missing was the clanging of pots and voices laughing and talking over one another.

'We were a close family; working all together does that, I suppose. At harvest time we would be out at all hours picking vegetables and tying the wheat into sheaves. And during sheep shearing we would be involved, too, holding the sheep down while our neighbour shaved the sheep clean of their wool.

'I surprised my children once when I wrung the neck of chicken without a second thought.' Winifred's eyes glittered. 'We were living in Dartford and, if they thought about it at all, they probably just associated me with meals, the church and care. Then there we were in Wales visiting my mother and brother, and Mam says, 'we're having chicken tonight as a special treat.' So I offer to get the chicken.' She nodded at Ellie. 'Your granny, my oldest daughter, came with me, although I have no idea what she was expecting. Probably a fridge somewhere that we had been keeping secret from her! Along with running water and lights.'

Next to her, she heard Amy chuckle in empathy.

'Your granny, Eleanor, watched dumbfounded as I caught the chicken and wrung its neck. I'd grown up doing it of course, so it was quite normal to me. But my suburban children were not accustomed to that lifestyle ... thank goodness.'

She paused and took another sip of water. Ellie was too distracted in studying this woman opposite her to say anything. Winifred wore a cream wool dress with a matching belt. It had a simple, classic look to it and appeared to be new. A large beaded necklace was the only accessory. It was hard to imagine this person sloshing about on a farm killing chickens.

'We once had a labourer who stayed with us for a couple of seasons,' Winifred said. 'He was quite superstitious and would never allow us to throw stones in a stream, especially when they were getting the hay in, for fear of rain.'

Lotty clapped her hands together. 'I have heard of such a superstition but never had a first-hand account of it.'

Lotty's hand went for the fold in her dress where her notebook once lived, but Winifred carried on talking and was relieved to see Lotty give up the search.

'Another labourer, Rhys, loved carrots so much we used to joke he was eating the donkey's breakfast!'

'We once had a farm hand who would eat onions raw,' Amy said. 'He used to tell us it was to scare off evil spirits. But I always thought the only thing it did was scare *people* away!'

A low laugh echoed amongst the diners.

'You mean, he would just bite into it? Like an apple?' Ellie asked, scrunching her nose up.

'Yes, exactly! He peeled it first, of course.'

Ellie didn't think this improved the idea. Winifred piled flakes of fish and cream onto her fork, noticing that the other plates were already scraped clean.

'We've gone off topic once more, but what I was trying to say was that things do have a way of working themselves out,' she said.

Ellie's cheeks flushed as she realised Winifred was referring to the letter. But she also felt a lot better. Ellie took in the faces around her. *They'd been super-nice about it. And haven't quizzed me or demanded that I explain it over and over.*

'And don't forget, Eleanor, that a good night's sleep will often help,' Winifred said.

'Absolutely,' Amy said. 'And if that doesn't help I always found a good old session with my favourite soap opera made everything better!'

Ellie's giggle echoed around the room.

ELLIE AND LOTTY

'Did you celebrate harvest time?' Lotty asked.

Amy's brow knitted and her mouth curled a little. 'I don't remember any.'

'I merely ask as in Shropshire they had a variety of traditions that took place when the harvest had been brought in. Farmers and labourers all over the county performed a ceremony at the end of the reaping called Cutting the Neck, and another at the end of the harvest called Crying the Mare. I wondered if there might have been similar in Bermuda.'

'Never heard of any. Eleanor, do you have —'

'I was always very interested in customs and traditions,' Lotty added. 'Even as a small child I would carry a notebook with me so I could write down what I observed.'

'Yeah, you've mentioned it,' Amy said, tapping her index fingers against each other.

Lotty turned her head towards Ellie while her body remained in corseted stillness, giving the movement an owl-like quality.

'It was my papa who inadvertently sparked this interest of mine. He was taking us to visit Grandmamma Goodlad and our Goodlad aunts. They lived in Ilfracombe, Devon, so we would take the ferry part of the way there. I do believe he always loved visiting Devon and, of course, Grandmamma Goodlad and my aunts were so fond of him that they quite spoilt him.

'It was a pleasant day, with a blue sky and a breeze that encouraged the ferry's flag to flutter and dance, like the daffodils of Wordsworth, and there was Papa, away from his troubles, enjoying the boat journey so much that he started whistling. Then a sailor told him to stop: 'We've enough wind as it is without whistling for more,' he said. This made an impression on me so I got a notebook and set it down, and as time went by I added various curious customs.'

'What sort of customs?' Ellie asked, surprised that she was interested in the answer.

Lotty nodded, pleased at the question. 'Any sort I came across. They varied depending on the time of year and where you were in the country, or even county. Take this time of year, for instance: the poor children in Edgmond used to come around singing on "Souling Day".'

She started to sing in a melodious though loud voice:

'Soul, soul, for an apple or two,

if you have no apples, pears will do.

One for Peter, two for Paul and three for him that made us all.

Up with the kettle and down with the pan

Give us a good big'un and we'll be gone.'

Ellie held her breath, willing her mouth to stop twitching. Amy caught her eye and the giggles bubbled inside Ellie, her eyes sparkling with the effort to remain still. Lotty glanced around the room and paused on Ellie, who refused to look at her.

'There were also songs referring to "soul cakes", and in 1863 there were few old North Salopians who could not remember when soul cakes used to be made at the farmhouses to be given away on Souling Day. However, when I was a child, the village children expected apples, pennies, or "any good thing to make us merry", as they would say.' Here Lotty's voice took on a Shropshire accent, mimicking the children's voices.

'One of our maid servants said that she heard that people used to go away shouting "A good house!" if they got anything, but if they were sent away empty-handed they cried "A bad house!".'

Lotty paused, her mind flickering back to that time. One of her governesses, Miss Mitchell, had taken her to visit an old woman in the village who had agreed to talk to Lotty about her childhood. They had walked down the hill, Lotty clutching her little bag containing her notebook, pen and inkpot.

'Now remember, Charlotte,' Miss Mitchell had said, 'you have to first establish friendly relations with old inhabitants like Mrs Dowly. When once you have, they do like to talk about the old times.'

Miss Mitchell had been correct and it had been one of the best lessons she had taught Lotty. Mrs Dowly had invited them into her cottage and they had sat around her table sipping tea from mis-matched, chipped cups and listening to her stories. It was Mrs Dowly who had told her that her children used to get slices of bread and mead, bread and cheese or other 'broken victuals' on Souling Day.

'Never heard of Souling Day. Is that the same as Halloween?' Ellie asked, her giggles now under control.

'Well, in Shropshire, All Saints' Day is known as Souling Day,' Lotty said.

Ellie's face contorted into bemusement and Lotty wrinkled her brow.

'You surely know when All Saints' Day is?' she said.

The crease in Lotty's brow deepened. *How little this girl knows. To think at her age I could speak four languages, identify birds by their song and had a better grasp of English history than my school-taught brothers.*

'It was a common practise of heathen peoples to hold a yearly feast in honour of the dead,' Lotty said. 'Thus the Fathers of the Church did but consecrate an already familiar custom when they instituted the Christian festivals of All Saints' and All Souls' Days. In the first half of the 8th century Pope Gregory II instituted the observance of All Saints' Day on the first of November but it stood alone for a hundred years until the Abbot of Clugny began to offer mass on the day after

All Saints' for the souls of the departed.

'As beautifully as the ancient Feast of the Dead had been consecrated to Christian purposes, popular non-religious customs still clung around it. Hallowe'en, or the Eve of All Saints, hinged on the idea that this was the time the spirits of the dead were abroad.

'The day's feast consisted of food and drink set out for the use of the dead but presently consumed by the living. Traces of this feast survived in North Shropshire when poor children would go out "souling" on All Saints' Day, reciting a ditty peculiar to the day and looking for a dole of cake.'

'Oh,' was all that Ellie could think to say. She stared at the rows of cutlery, unsure where else to look.

'I think what Lotty is trying to say is that All Saints' Day is the first of November,' Amy said. Lotty looked across the table at her, her mouth moving into a thin line.

'A little additional knowledge has never harmed a person,' Lotty said. She turned her icy stare away from Amy and smiled at Winifred.

'Dates are particularly interesting, I have always thought. It is a curious detail that both of Roger and John's grandfathers died on the same date, 19th October. Of course, not in the same year, and before either of the boys were born. Nevertheless, an apt time to pass away given the heightened level of superstition there is at this time of year.'

Lotty took a sip of wine and looked at the fire, which had reduced itself to glowing embers.

'Understandable, given it is the beginning of the dark days of winter when the falling leaves and dying year seem in themselves to suggest thoughts of death and memories of the past.'

Ellie caught a brief flicker of emotion across Amy's face. Ellie couldn't decide if it was anger or sadness she had seen, or a mixture of both. Amy stood up and placed a log on the fire.

'I mentioned earlier that the eldest of my brother's sons, Arthur, and his wife, Christine, spent time in Bermuda,' Lotty said, watching Amy. The log seemed to stifle what little heat was left and Amy prodded at it. Amy knelt down to blow into the embers.

'Posted there during the Great War. I do not believe he saw any fighting, unless a fierce game of tennis counts.' Lotty laughed at her joke.

'Did you have family serving in the War? I believe Bermuda did send men across.'

'No,' Amy said. 'Most of my family were too old or too young. When we moved to America, Joseph, Everest and John had to register for the draft but by then it was June 1918 and they weren't called up.'

'Arthur was fortunate to be posted to Bermuda,' Lotty said. 'He was in no danger and their oldest son, Roger, was even born out there.'

Lotty noted that Winifred had sat up straighter, and knew she had touched on something. *I will not pursue it just yet.*

'Not that he would have objected to being sent to fight elsewhere, of course,' Lotty said. 'Nevertheless, a relief to Sambrook and Julia, especially as all the other boys were in danger, one in Singapore and two in France. All came back safely having served their nation well. Alf was mentioned in dispatches four times. Julia was very proud of him. He was always so cheerful and loved history. Very smart boy.'

A twist in her stomach stopped her. 'Of course, not all my nephews were as fortunate as the Burne boys. Dear Alexander was killed at Ypres not a month past his twenty-first birthday. He was the youngest of that generation and quite an adventurous boy. Opposite to his sister. And his mother, for that matter.'

Ellie watched Amy sit back on her heels and wait for a spark from the fire. The room already felt cool.

'My sister, Alice, was very proud of him. She had had him when she was quite old—thirty seven years of age. But she would wait for Frank. I never did understand why; however, he was decent enough, I imagine. Limited prospects, though, in my view ... and Mamma's. Nine years they were engaged and even then they married despite Mamma's reservations.

'When he proposed to her, she came to me in the drawing room where I was writing and said "I'm engaged". And I replied, "Engaged in what?" Alice was most put out by this response.'

Lotty chuckled and sipped her wine. A ribbon of flame shot out from under the log and Amy returned to the table. Ellie watched as the flames, once so hesitant, now enthusiastically devoured the latest offering.

'And then to lose her boy like that,' Lotty went on. 'She was never the same after he died. I believe the intention was to follow his father into law, however it was not to be. When the War came Alexander signed up immediately. He was only eighteen, and within four months he had received the campaign medal.'

Lotty did not try to hide her pride, her smile spreading as she savoured the memory.

'A fellow officer described Alexander as the most gallant officer ever to have served in the Army. "They were staunch to the end against odds uncounted; they fell with their faces to the foe".'

Lotty felt the presence of those lines as she spoke them, and then let out a sigh as the days after Alice had received the news came to her mind. It had reminded her of Mamma all those years earlier. Suddenly older, quieter, and their light gone, even in laughter.

'So much promise, stolen at such a young age,' she said. She could feel her lower lip tremble. She took a deep breath and regained control. 'Of course, it is best not to dwell on such matters,' she said in an attempt to finish the conversation.

'It was a waste of a generation, in my view,' Amy said. 'All that death and horror. And you think, Okay, for what?'

The room went still. Lotty stared at Amy and then turned to Winifred.

'Did Roger also going into law?' she asked. ' I assume as

the heir to Loynton it would have been expected of him.' The room's stillness cracked.

'Yes, he trained as a lawyer.'

'And when did he take over Loynton? Arthur, of course, had to run it from afar while his mother lived on at the house.' She leaned forward still looking at Winifred. 'Which I always thought was a foolish arrangement. My brother was rather more brawn than brain.'

'Yes, Julia had life-long tenancy and lived another twenty seven years — she died in 1942. At the time there was another war, and then later ... things were different.'

Winifred adjusted her necklace. Lotty watched her. *She's avoiding the question.*

'In what way were they different?' Lotty said.

Winifred hesitated. Lotty repeated the question. Winifred met her stare and said, 'Roger had died, and with him Loynton. Not that it was as simple as that.'

WINIFRED AND ELLIE

'Grief, see, does strange things to people,' Winifred said. 'Love's tragic twin. We could avoid grief if only we would not love, but none of us would be without those we love. "I am half sick of shadows, said the Lady of Shalott".'

The poem brought back memories of walking with John through the bruised streets of London. *So much of that life could be linked through our poems.*

But it was an earlier memory of the war that won her attention as she searched for ways to make their stories relevant for their young charge. Here it was, an experience that had made her work harder, romanticise less and be forever grateful.

Winifred's mind left the room and found its way to a steam train where her younger self sat in a third-class carriage, clutching her small suitcase. Beside her, Eileen flicked through a magazine oblivious to the crumbs from her sandwich that flecked her dark green skirt. The train chugged slowly out of Swanley and made its way towards the south coast. The weather was mild, the storm which had been forecast hadn't arrived, and the view through the window was nothing but green hills and sparkling blue skies.

'Is it wrong to feel excited?' Winifred said, watching Eileen fold up the magazine.

'About what?'

'This ... whatever "this" is. It's as if we have volunteered for a mission or something.' She put on a low voice, trying to sound male. 'Information on a need-to-know-basis.'

Eileen laughed. 'Not sure I would make a good spy. Would probably leave some secret message in a cafe!'

Winifred giggled. 'Come on, though. You must have some thoughts on what we might be needed for.'

Eileen stared out the window and then, with a big smile, offered, 'Maybe we are needed to keep a German spy fed and watered so he can be interrogated.'

Other passengers in the carriage looked over at them and Winifred hissed, 'Keep your voice down.'

Eileen took in the stares that gradually faded along with their interest.

'The uniform would make a good disguise, though,' Eileen said, patting her bag. 'No one would suspect a woman dressed in a Red Cross uniform.'

'No one would suspect a woman.'

'Also true. I do hope it isn't dull, Winnie. If I am just going to be washing up teacups and plates I will think I could have been doing that in Swanley.'

'Eileen! What a thing to say. We must do our bit, no matter how mundane.'

'That is why I volunteered: doing my bit.'

'Looking for cute boys, more like.'

Eileen faked shock. 'What a thing to say.'

Winifred smiled. 'Well, glad you're here whatever your motives. Washing up cups would be dull without you but still better than cleaning out bedpans.'

Eileen let out a loud groan and eyes swivelled towards them again.

———

Winifred moved the fish around on her plate, no longer interested in eating it. *If only Eleanor could find friends like Eileen. That is what she needs right now, friends who'll bring out the best in her, not play on her worries. Friends who go on mystery trips, no questions asked. Not that either of us were ready for what met us.*

The wavy lines of sauce she was creating with her fork seemed to turn into waves of seawater splashing against the docks, and before she realised it, her mind was back in Dover, and May 1940.

At first there were only a few ships but as the days went on more and more destroyers arrived at Dover. Hundreds of men trooped down gangplanks, some walking in silence, some helping others. An army without boots, clothes or weapons. All filthy. All tired. But they were still an army, and Winifred felt pride in them as she watched them gratefully accept a coffee and sandwich.

All had stories: stories of standing for hours chest-deep in water, waiting with no shelter on a beach, sand in everything, bombs so regular the men could tell the time by them. The worst cases were carried out on stretchers and lined up or propped against sandbags. Young faces disfigured by burns. Limbs held in place by makeshift splints. Many wouldn't receive proper care until they reached a hospital. Those who could walk were sent to wait for trains. Many fell asleep where they were standing, their relief expressed by succumbing to exhaustion.

For days there was a constant swirl of action: handing out hot drinks and food, smiling and comforting, as the moment required. Any illusion she had had of the glamour of war was lost at the seaside that May. Before the bombs fell like confetti over London, before the summer skies were decorated with vapour trails, she had seen the effects of war.

Was it Divine Providence or luck that had saved so many? That there was a second chance she liked to think was because God's will had prevailed. And yet, *were* those men saved? After all, she knew only too well that some scars cannot be seen or healed.

Winifred's thoughts finally brought her firmly back to the dinner table. It surprised her that only a few seconds had passed since Roger's fate had been forced out of her. As she had sat remembering that train journey and those busy days, three pairs of eyes had waited for more. The steel-blue eyes of Lotty barely blinked as Winifred picked up the story's thread once more.

'Roger was always very military minded. Like Alexander before him, I suppose,' Winifred said with a nod to Lotty.

A look swept over Lotty's face and Winifred stalled, distracted by a strange niggle that the look had given her. But by the next blink of Lotty's eye the look was hidden and Winifred carried on.

'Roger had joined the Territorial Army after leaving school so when the war began, he was automatically moved to the Regular Army.'

Winifred pushed her unwanted plate to one side.

'Army life suited him,' she continued. 'Right down to the uniform. My darling John always looked a bit uncomfortable in it, as if it was a little bit too big for him. He was constantly adjusting something or pushing at his glasses having imagined that they were slipping. Roger, on the other hand, wore it with a natural assurance.'

Ellie noticed a little spider crawling around the rim of her water glass. She put a finger out and the spider crawled onto it. *Unlucky to kill a spider.* She watched it dangle from her finger for a second before it fell onto the table.

'... Roger's unit was based in Ramsgate when John and I married, so he was able to come to our wedding even with only four weeks' notice. We married from John's aunt's house because it was down the road from where John was taking his hygiene course ahead of being sent to India. Quite romantic,' she gave a short laugh. 'I did manage to get a hat, as they were not rationed. And for all the rushed decisions and practical compromises, having Roger as his best man was truly special for John. They were very close, those two. Always sharing jokes and laughing.'

Winifred watched Ellie cajole the spider onto her knife. A knot twisted in her stomach. *We need to change the topic.*

'This was all a long time ago. I always felt it was best left there. Now —' Winifred said.

'Dear Winifred, I must insist upon knowing what you know. What did you mean that Loynton, the seat of our family since the Civil War, died with Roger?'

Winifred took a deep breath. 'We married in February 1944. In June, Roger's unit was sent to France. About five weeks after he arrived, he was hit by a shell. Poor Roger died almost immediately, on 3rd August 1944, six months after he had stood with us as our best man, so full of life.'

The flickering glint from the bronze statue of two hares standing on the sideboard behind Lotty and Ellie caught her eye. The dulled metal seemed so enduring, like a memorial of memories of all who had had contact with it.

'Once the war was over,' Winifred said, 'I took a nursing role in Nuneaton just to be closer to Arthur and Christine but I couldn't fill the void that had opened with his death. The loss was too great for all of us. John rarely talked about him and Arthur and Christine's grief turned them in on themselves.'

'So I presume John inherited Loynton?' Lotty asked.

Winifred looked at Lotty. 'No. They sold it.'

Lotty let out a noise and her eyes blinked. A second later she was still.

'Did not even tell John about the sale until it was completed,' Winifred said. 'Arthur and Christine never lived there, you see. They rented it out after Julia died and the intention had always been for Roger to take over the running of it. They could not see past that and so, for them, all meaning for keeping Loynton Hall died with Roger.'

'Fame, jealous-wing'd, shall bear along the bounty, he has shown,' Lotty murmured.

Winifred wondered what Lotty meant but was too distracted by the immediate topic to give it more than a passing thought.

'I always thought John was warming to the idea of taking up residence there and becoming a country doctor. Obviously he had never thought of inheriting Loynton as a boy, but with things as they were and a family of his own to pass it down to, I think he would have seriously considered it. But it was not to be. I am sure we were far more suited to Dartford anyway.'

Lotty raised her head as if Winifred had said something insulting to her.

'It must have been for the best,' Lotty said eventually. 'But how like Arthur and Christine not to communicate over something so important. I learnt of their marriage through a tenant from one of the farms and so looked in the Stafford papers and found the announcement. At the time, I remarked to a family friend that I had heard nothing from Sambrooke or Julia about it. He replied that Arthur had never told his parents; they had read it in the Stafford papers, too!' She shook her head at the memory. 'It must be hereditary, as I first heard of his father and mother's marriage from a neighbour!'

Ellie placed the knife on the floor and watched the spider crawl away. The knot in Winifred's stomach tightened.

———

Ellie watched the spider scurry to the safety of the table leg. In the shadows of the table, she couldn't see where it had crawled to or whether it was still there. For a second, she couldn't understand why these shadows seemed so unfamiliar. *It's the candles. The light doesn't reach here. But why use all these candles when there are lights?* Ellie glanced around. *There's no light switch. Weird.* She looked around again, more quickly this time. *Hang on, when did they take the plates? Is this another course? What is it? Lamb? I can smell mint. How long was I watching that spider?*

'This is incredibly dull. I am sure being with friends would be much more amusing,' Lotty said.

Ellie's head snapped around. Lotty appeared to be listening to Amy. Ellie looked at the women on the other side. Neither gave the appearance of having heard Lotty. *Did I imagine that she said something?*

AMY AND ELLIE

She really can talk. Look at her, tapping her fingers even with her hands clasped like that, so desperate to interrupt. Wonder what Lotty is short for. Charlotte? Leticia? I'd ask her but she would probably give me a lecture on the meaning of names.

Amy inspected the two round portions of lamb in front of her. She could see it had been pan-fried and the browned meat shone against the crisped fat. She cut into the circular display with relish.

'Now, this is very nice,' she said chewing on the morsel. 'I prefer a good side of beef, course, but this is nice. Perfectly cooked, y'know.'

Her mention of beef reminded her of Bermuda and her wonderful kitchen, equipped to manage catering for the large family gatherings that took place at Vicinity House. It had been her dream to have a kitchen like that. Especially after the small ones she had put up with in Massachusetts. She took a sip of the wine, now a red. *Tastes like cherries. Not sure about it.* She took another sip.

'Now look, Winifred, I also found I changed my accent when I moved to the USA.'

Ellie sensed that Winifred had virtually jumped in her seat at the change of subject, and wondered how Amy couldn't tell that this was an uncomfortable topic for Winifred.

'Well, it was not a conscious decision.'

'No? You think it just happened?' Amy said.

Winifred paused, weighing her words, and Ellie took the

moment to eat a morsel of the lamb. 'More a survival technique,' Winifred said finally.

'Oh yeah? How come?'

Again the pause. Winifred looked at Ellie as if considering something. Ellie realised she was holding her breath.

'I was seventeen, straight out of school with no experience of the world beyond those hills. Going to a grocer's was a novel experience in itself. And as it turned out, a girl from the Welsh hills was as novel an experience for those from the North Downs.'

Winifred adjusted her necklace.

'What do you mean?' Amy said.

Ellie smiled at her plate, and for a moment was back in Bermuda, sitting on a kitchen stool being grilled on school, friends and what her new home was like.

'It's okay, I guess,' she'd said.

'What do you mean?' Nan said.

Ellie shrugged. 'The school's fine, that's all.'

'What about friends? Have you made many friends?'

Ellie had savoured the word 'many'. That Easter trip to Bermuda was just after Rosie had pulled her along for tennis and the friendship with all of those girls was still new and uncertain.

'Uh, yeah. A few.'

Her nan sighed in exasperation. 'Do you ever use full sentences, Ellie, huh? Y'know, give people some colour, some details?'

'Yes.'

But she met her nan's eye and they started laughing.

Ellie realised Winifred was still looking at her and that her smile had been caught. The smile faded but she relaxed as Winifred's smile grew. Winifred answered Amy but she did so while keeping eye contact with Ellie.

'On my first trip to the grocer's, I had to repeat myself several times. In the end I left with only half of what I had wanted.

I could hear them giggling and mimicking my accent.

'It wasn't done to be cruel,' she added hastily. 'They just were not familiar with a Welsh accent. There is no doubt that it was easier to be understood with a more ... neutral inflection.'

'Oh, I agree. I think you have to change when you move somewhere new,' Amy nodded her head. 'Adapt, y'know? When I went home to Bermuda, everyone said I sounded like a Bostonian! What you've got to realise is that's the thing with America: it doesn't accept you, you accept it.' Her fork waved in the air.

'And it's better that way. Helps you make it Home. But it wasn't easy. For a long time I couldn't understand what they said. You should have heard how they said my name! Amy. Not a hard name to say but you would see people trying to work out what I had said and then coming up with something totally different. Annie was the one most people landed on. And you'd think: okay ... I started answering to it after a while!'

Amy cut into the lamb and, with a sweep, moved the morsel from the plate to her fork to her mouth. She gave a satisfied grunt as the buttery hints of the meat, mixed with the taste of mint, melted on her tongue.

'And Simons—that was my first husband's surname—oh, that got them,' she added as she swallowed the mouthful. '*Soin-monds*, that's how they said it!' She shook her head, sighing at the memory.

'And my second husband, José, he went by Joe. José was too foreign, even in a place like Cambridge, Massachusetts. He said it was much easier to Americanise it than to spend twenty minutes trying to help someone say José properly!'

Amy took a sip of wine and glanced around for the bottle.

'It constantly happens,' Lotty said, 'and perhaps especially among the English, that uncouth-sounding foreign names are changed to ones that more nearly resemble the vulgar tongue. Our blacksmith, upon shoeing Papa's Irish horse Usquebaugh, entered the name again and again as Huskeyball. Now, imagine: if we speculated on the meaning of such a name as Hus-keyball, we would have a very good idea of the way legends are almost invariably formed.'

Lotty smiled intensely at the others.

'Mmmm. Anyway, I used to joke that I only married Joe because his name was the same as my maiden name and easy to pronounce,' Amy said, and spied the wine bottle on the side table near Lotty. *Won't ask Lotty for it. Will wait for a waiter.*

'So you were not Mello when you married Mr Mello?' Lotty said.

'No. Like I said, I was Simons first.'

'I am not sure it would work,' Lotty said.

Amy tapped impatiently at the base of her wine glass, oblivious to the flat thump, thump noise it created. *What is she talking about? Quick, think of something to —*

'A woman who has married without changing her name is able to cure whooping-cough, according to folklore. Do you know how to bake bread?'

'Of course I do.'

'I knew one woman living in Edgmond in 1884 who, having married her cousin of the same name, during an epidemic of whooping-cough, had so many requests for her bread as to be quite a tax on her good nature. In savage cultures, if I may be allowed the expression, marriage with one of the same tribal name was forbidden, even if no blood relationship existed between the pair.'

Amy exhaled. Lotty frowned.

'Winifred. How long were you married for?' Amy said.

'Fifty-five years.'

'That's impressive,' said Amy. 'And to think I had married twice by the time I was twenty-four.'

She stopped herself saying "and a widow twice over by the time I was thirty". *Not worth picking up that thread. How to bring this back to Eleanor ...*

'Now look, Eleanor,' Amy said. 'Doing what is best for you

isn't always the easy thing to do. After Joe died, I decided that I wasn't going down that route again. I was clearly unlucky with marriage! I had three children, the youngest barely out of diapers, and had moved too often, so I stayed in America and carved out a life as best I could.' Her finger moved in small arcs with each word.

'The easy option would have been to go back to Bermuda,' she said. 'But I had already moved poor Ernest about so much: Bermuda, Cambridge, New Bedford, back to Cambridge, and then,' she counted out on her fingers, 'three different homes once we got back to Cambridge. So I couldn't move him again.'

'What did your husband die of?' Lotty said.

Amy stopped, her hand frozen in mid movement. *What does it matter what they died of?*

'Which one?'

'Ernest's father.'

The sound of rasping, shuddered breathing rushed at her and framed other sensations. The impersonal, hurried footsteps of doctors, the clinking of bottles, the soft caress of a handkerchief. And afterwards, a little boy asking for his daddy ... Her chest clenched. She looked down at her plate and the blue and white colours stared back at her.

'Pneumonia.' She continued to stare at her plate. A vision of Joseph's lifeless face, once so beautiful and warm, snapped across her memory. The pale skin, sapped of colour; and his lips, faded blue, as if slightly bruised.

'We'd only been in New Bedford a few months. And then I packed up Ernest and moved him to Cambridge to be near Everest and Charlotte. They had children as well and Everest even sorted out boarding for me. It just made sense and I knew I could make it work; but it was hard for Ernest. I've always wondered if that is —'

'And your second husband? What did he die of?' Lotty said.

Amy got up and walked over to the sideboard. *Oh no. I can't talk about this.* She picked up the bottle of wine and returned to her seat. Carefully, she poured the contents into her glass. There was a satisfying glug as the liquid hit the bottom of the glass. Ellie's eyes widened in surprise as her glass was filled, and Amy suppressed a smirk as she heard Winifred's tongue click.

'A car accident,' she said.

'Oh, were there many cars in Cambridge?' Lotty said.

Amy slowly put the wine bottle on the table, catching a drip with her finger as she did. *What is with the interrogation?*

'Yes, of course there were. Lots of cars, trams, wagons; it was a very busy city. Full of businesses and action. You had to be careful and pay attention when crossing any road. There were always stories of kids ... I mean people ... being hit by vehicles.' *Stop talking. Change the subject.*

'Anyway, what I was saying, kiddo,' she tapped her index finger to her lips, 'is that doing what is right takes guts. I could have left, gone back to Bermuda, many times, but I stayed because that was the right thing to do. *Aquele que não sabe nadar*: He who can't swim sinks; and that was very true of those first years in Cambridge. You had to be prepared to knock on doors, ask for help, make connections.'

In the end her neighbours had become her family. Everyone was from somewhere else. Intense friendships were made in days; help and support then given for years. That was what Joe had been at first: just another part of a network of support. He worked as a meat trimmer in a butcher's near her apartment and would save her cuts of meat or give a 'friends' discount when he could. Amy had a brief vision of a butcher's apron, hands casually being wiped on the front of it while their owner offered a calm, quiet smile.

But it wasn't a life for everyone. Everest and Charlotte had left pining for fresh sea breezes and the calls of kiskadees. Then, later, Joe's family had gone back to the Azores. But Amy had liked the detached attitude of the city. The noise, the movement, the cauldron of languages and flavours.

'In that environment you find out who your friends are fast.' She waved her finger at Ellie. 'Who is standing by you. Who can you rely on for help. Friends who aren't prepared to do that aren't worth it.'

Amy frowned as Lotty started to search in her dress. *What is she doing now?*

'I am sure I requested a notebook. A notebook with detachable leaves. It is indispensable.'

'Why do you need a notebook?' Ellie said.

'I must note down that saying,' Lotty turned her storm-blue eyes on Amy. 'Is it Bermudian or Portuguese? Both, perhaps? What a nuisance not to have a notebook. Proverbs always remind me of my dear friend Miss Jackson. She gathered a mass of homely wit and wisdom. Miss Jackson was closer in age to my mamma, being only four years her junior; however, she and I had a friendship that spanned the age gap.'

The rustle of fabric died away as the search ended and Lotty placed her hands back in her lap.

'It was Miss Jackson who laid the foundation for what became *Shropshire Folklore: A Sheaf of Gleanings*. When illness made her fear she would not be able to complete the task of writing the book, she placed her notes into my hands and begged me to carry on the work for her. So whilst she did not write it, without her it would never have come to fruition. So I fully agree with Mrs Mello: good friends are rare and worthy of treasuring.'

Across the table from Lotty, Amy smiled. Ellie hadn't been listening so much as watching this exchange. *How strange they are. One minute they are snapping at each other and the next they are sharing anecdotes.* She reached for her phone. *Where's my bag? Oh yeah, it's in Mum's office. Frig. I wonder what Mia and the others are doing now. Did they go to the green like they normally do? Maybe I should have headed there. They probably just assumed I would catch them up. But why didn't they text?*

Amy watched Ellie glance at her watch. *She looks bored.*

Amy leaned into Winifred and cupped her hand to her mouth. 'We aren't getting through to her.' Winifred cocked her head towards Amy but her eyes darted towards Ellie. Amy could feel Lotty's frown. *She really doesn't like to be left out but we need to do something else.*

Ellie glanced at her watch again. A minute had gone by. *How can I get out of here? They might still be at the green if I leave soon. I need my phone. Why did I leave it like that? What if someone steals my bag? Why is Amy looking at me so seriously? It's super-spooky how still she sits. Has her face paled or is it just the light?*

ELLIE

'That's a pretty watch,' Amy said.

Ellie looked at it again. It had been a present from her parents for her birthday. She had wanted one that received messages and you could call from, but her dad had said no. Apparently it would be too distracting for school.

'Besides, you can't have a better one than me,' he had said. He didn't wear a watch except for running, so Ellie assumed it was some sort of Dad joke.

'Yeah, I guess,' Ellie said absently.

'What do you guess?' Lotty said, the crease of a frown running like a watermark across her forehead.

'What?' Ellie said, still trying to bring herself back to the conversation.

'You said "I guess". You guess what?'

'Nothing. I mean, I don't guess anything. It's just a phrase.'

'Indeed? How curious. Mmmm, I have always marvelled at wristwatches,' Lotty said. 'Such strange little contraptions. As if you are carrying a miniature clock on your wrist. My sister, Agatha, adored hers. She said that with it she need never be late, as if being on a time was an impossibility until then. I wonder, though, if mankind's need to control time has rather resulted in time controlling man?'

She looked expectantly at Ellie. Ellie fiddled with the watch strap unsure if she was up for a philosophical debate.

'Well, I never worried about time. I would arrive when I was ready,' Amy said. 'Except for work. You have to be on time for work, but otherwise, ten minutes here, ten minutes there doesn't matter in the scheme of things. That's why I've never had a watch. Loved other jewellery, of course, and not cheap trinkets — good-quality stuff.' She pointed a finger at Ellie. 'Spend money on good-quality jewellery and furniture and you will never regret it.'

A rack of glittery hair clips and bracelets distracted Ellie. The image was so clear it felt as if it was right in front of her. She half wanted to reach out just to check that she wasn't back in that shop instead of sitting at this dining table. *Why had it popped into my head? Cheap trinkets. I've heard those words before.* Ellie twirled her hair as pieces of memory gathered together.

'When we got on the boat to Canada, I left anything valuable behind. We could only take what we could carry,' Amy said.

Ellie's fragments of memory splintered with the interruption.

'It wasn't the time for sentiment. We had to make sure we had enough warm clothing for us and the kids. Ernest was three by then, and Everest and Charlotte had little Sally, barely two years old, and baby Olive. Sally and Ernest had great fun on that journey. Took over our whole deck and played together with other kids for hours. I didn't enjoy it as much; couldn't stomach any of the food. But it wasn't a long journey and the sickness had left me before we got to Canada.'

'I thought you moved to America,' Winifred said.

'We did. But we went round from Halifax. It was the quickest route.'

'Quicker than simply getting a boat directly to an East Coast port?' Lotty asked, and Ellie could see the surprise and scepticism written across her face.

'Yeah.'

'Surely not, it must have been many more days of travel. Remind me where you were destined?'

'Massachusetts.'

'So Boston would have been the best port, surely?' Lotty said.

'Yeah, well, this route was better for getting a visa into the country.'

Ellie thought Amy looked a little irritated by the fact-checking. *And, to be fair, did it really matter why she went through Halifax?* Ellie sighed and rubbed her finger across the glass face of the watch.

'Anyway, the boat journey was cold! I had to wear many layers and Ernest was dressed in the only woollen sweater and coat I had for him. New England winters teach you what cold really is. The first part of our journey was simple and we got over the border no trouble. But in Vermont it was slower, y'know. We were told to get off the train because it was needed for the war effort. There wasn't another train going towards Cambridge until the next day.'

Ellie put her knife and fork together and raised the wineglass to her mouth. A smell similar to fruit seemed to waft from the dark red liquid, but on sipping it a tangy, almost peppery flavour made Ellie put it down abruptly. She tuned back into Amy's story

'...There we were in some town in Vermont, bags in hand, no place to stay, no one expecting us. Charlotte, Naomi and me waited with the kids at the station and Everest, John and Joseph went to look for lodgings. They came back very pleased with themselves and we headed into town.'

Amy took a sip of water and then carried on talking.

'The kids loved it, their little eyes like plates looking at the cars and large buildings surrounding the high street. But they also had those elegant houses with porches at the front and white shutters, and it was to one of these that we went. Painted blue. I like bold colours. Not cold, lifeless colours like blue and white ...' She shuddered. 'They are like the shades of death. But the house had a cute wooden sign, hanging just above us, welcoming us in with those beautiful cursive letters, the old-fashioned writing they used to do.'

She was looking straight at Ellie as she said this. Ellie could see the sign, a swirling flow of letters. But on the sign she saw, it didn't say "B and B"; it said "Gingers and Pickles".

———

Ellie had stood looking up at that curling writing, engraved on a wooden board that swung slightly as a breeze toyed with it. *Ginger and Pickles.* As she had stood there, building up to the moment, her mind refused to let her concentrate. *It's a funny name for a corner store. Didn't Ginger and Pickles in the story go bust? Somewhere we have the book, so I should know. Come on, focus.* She glanced back. They stood in a cluster out of sight of the shop front, trying to look like they had a purpose.

In theory, it was going to be easy. How many times had they said so? No cameras. And the woman behind the till was always reading a book or on the phone. Ellie was wearing an oversized jacket with deep pockets that was too warm for May but perfect for her mission. Her heart sounded too loud. She was sure it could be heard thudding away as if trying to expose her.

The bell went. The door clicked behind her. The woman looked up from her phone. Ellie looked back at her, trying to maintain eye contact because that was what she had been told to do. Rosie's warning: 'Don't look shifty. Just act your usual mousy self.' But that was hard to do with a heart beating your guilt onto your face. Ellie managed a shaky smile but the woman seemed to look at her for longer than usual. *She knows. She knows.* A crackly voice said something. *Smile. Act normal.* The woman behind the counter went back to her conversation.

Ellie walked to the back of the store where the hairbands and clips glittered. *Don't forget nail varnish as well. Has it gone quiet?* Ellie glanced to her side. *No, she's still talking.*

As Ellie moved her head back to her prize, a shadow shifted in the far corner of the shop. She peered at it, trying to make out what she had seen against the fluorescent, artificial light. *Is someone else here? They will see ...*

The thought that she would have an excuse to leave steadied her. But after a better look Ellie realised that there was no one there and that her imagination was just teasing her. She rubbed her hand on her jeans. *Now or never.*

'Now, why would you take such a risk just for some cheap trinkets?'

Ellie cried out and spun around. *Nan?* The woman looked up from the phone and asked if she was okay. Ellie nodded. Her mouth moved but no sound came out.

ELLIE AND LOTTY

Ellie had run out of the shop unable to hide her shock. Her hands were still shaking and the girls just laughed at her, called her a coward. But no one else was coerced into doing it; it was just her, it was always just her. Mia had been annoyed. Not that anyone wanted the hair clips. They just liked the drama of it. She had let them all down but there had been nothing else she could have done.

That voice. How could it have been my imagination? It had been so real. That evening she had rung her nan 'just to say hi'. She was in Bermuda. She hadn't been in a corner shop in Richmond. *Of course she hadn't.*

The girls had been cooler with her after that. She hadn't been invited to Rosie's house or when they went to the cinema. A few weeks later, her mum offered to take her and a friend to Murray Hill to watch Wimbledon.

'Why?' Ellie said, not bothering to hide her suspicion.

'Well, just for fun, really. You've become so interested in tennis, I thought you might like it. You could bring a friend if you like ... Aria, maybe?'

'Aria doesn't play tennis.'

'Oh, right.'

'But maybe Mia or Rosie could come?'

'Sure, darling. That would be fun.'

Ellie merely nodded but inside she glowed with excitement. She had seen Murray Hill on TV and it had always seemed so much fun, sitting in the sun, picnics laid out and everyone with big smiles as the cameras panned over them. Maybe they could even get on TV. She hoped that this offer would be an olive branch, but when she suggested it to Mia, she had shrugged and said that she had tickets for Court Two and didn't need to 'sit on Beggars' Hill'. Ellie had told her mum that she couldn't go after all; she had too much school work.

'What do you like about maths and science?' Amy said.

Ellie glanced around and then back at Amy

'Me? Oh, ummm. Dunno.'

'You said that those were the subjects you were good at. What do you like about them?'

Ellie shrugged.

'Well, what else do you enjoy?'

'At school?'

'Yes.'

'Not much.'

'No other subjects? History, English, music?'

Ellie said nothing. She was still locked in the emotions of her memory.

'What else do you like? Come on. You must have things you like doing?'

Ellie thought of Antoinette Cosway, of her vivid world of herbs and heat. The bright colours and sounds of the Caribbean. It sounded like Bermuda in some ways. She loved pretending to be part of a book: to be there, living in the character's world, a heroine of immense bravery and beauty. Ellie was a slow reader; she had been reading this book for over a month, although that wasn't her fault. She had had to read it around her allotted books from school. But it was a refuge, books like *Wide Sargasso Sea*. She could forget the drowning sadness that pressed at her chest at times. The feeling was almost a constant companion although she tried to pretend it wasn't there. *Why had she been late that day? And why hadn't she just taken the bracelets like she was meant to?*

Then it would all be different and they would like her more.
Amy's voice pushed into her thoughts.

'Which subject is it that you have to sit at the front for?'

Ellie saw Winifred's mouth disappear into a thin line. *She doesn't like this interrogation either.*

'History.'

'And that's the class you skipped today?'

Ellie wrapped her arms around her. 'It's only History.'

'Ah, the next course is here,' Winifred said.

Ellie thought her enthusiasm sounded forced. Aromas of roasted duck and spiced plums seeped across the room. Two other waiters with bowls of buttered potatoes, green beans and braised red cabbage followed the whole roast duck. Plates and glasses were cleared and new ones presented like a faultlessly choreographed ballet.

The conversation halted as they watched a waiter expertly carve the meat into thin slices. As Lotty took a large portion of all the food offered, she could see Amy sitting still except for her hands, which kept moving, steepled fingers tapping each other.

The waiter moved to Amy with the silver tray and serving spoon and fork and she helped herself to slices of duck and large spoonfuls of the potatoes, but took only a small sample of the beans and cabbage. Lotty smiled, amused by the impatience Amy was trying to hide as Winifred and Ellie each took a small selection of the dishes. As soon as the waiters had disappeared and etiquette allowed, Amy returned to her questions.

'What about outside school? What do you do?'

'Not much.'

'Nothing at all?'

'Mum takes me to a play sometimes. She likes supporting fringe theatre.' She hadn't meant to sneer quite like that. They had seen some pretty good stuff.

'Okay, plays ... Anything else?'

'The girls play tennis. I've started playing it more because of them. I'm getting quite good now. Not as good as my dad, but I can beat my mum or Aria.'

'Whose Aria?'

'A friend.'

'Tennis is a rather frivolous pastime, do you not think?' Lotty said, taking a sip of water. 'My sister, Alice, would spend whole summers going to tennis parties. She would get most upset if she was not asked to play. "I was not asked to play tennis once though I carried my racket all the time," she would say. Often I was unable to attend such gatherings due to other commitments. I was regularly needed for the Girls' Friendly Society, or was collecting stories. I did not have time for such frivolity.' Lotty cut the duck into smaller slices as she talked.

'However, on one visit to Loynton, when Sambrooke was living there and his children were still quite young, we elders played on the tennis ground. Alice called it "mild tennis" as Sambrooke, Julia and Ada were all inexperienced players. Even I was made to play despite preferring to make conversation than run around on a lawn. Alice complained afterwards that I had only hit three balls! "And what of it?" I replied. After all, I would rather excel at more useful skills than that of being able to hit a ball.'

The story had brought back happy memories of those times with her siblings. Eating gooseberries on summer afternoons, tea in the garden, putting on plays or charades when the weather was too cold to venture out.

Lotty looked around to see if the others had enjoyed her joke as well. Ellie was scraping food onto her fork and refusing to look up, Amy shook her head a little at her and Winifred mouthed something. Lotty's eyes narrowed. *What is she doing? What strange manners people have developed.* Winifred nodded in Ellie's direction and gave Lotty a look. *More and more puzzling.*

'However, it is good to have different interests, don't you think, Lotty?' Winifred said.

'Of course, I have many interests; history, geography, art,

literature —'

'Well, yes. But also to have more ... outdoor interests. Tennis is an enjoyable sport —'

'Did you play?' Lotty asked.

'No ... No, I never learnt. However, John would play with the children in Stafford, when we visited Arthur and Christine. They would draw lines on the grass and put up a net as there was not a permanent court. The children enjoyed it so much. Eleanor, does your granny still play?'

Ellie looked up. 'Yeah, she does.'

'Oh good,' Winifred said.

Ellie knew she was trying to make her feel better. 'We do a lot of walking as well. Mum and Dad like hiking so we do that some holidays,' she said.

Winifred smiled at her as if Ellie had just announced that she had won a Nobel Prize.

'I never thought of walking as a pastime,' Lotty said. 'We walked in order to reach our destination: the church, a call on friends, sometimes even to the train station.' *Why is Winifred looking at me in such a strange way?*

'We used to take the children hiking,' Winifred put in. 'I always believed it was a Burne interest. If we visited Stafford, we would always go on a hike to the top of the Wrekin.'

'Oh, I suppose it was, for some.' Lotty said. 'My dear sister Frances always enjoyed walking. One year, we walked Snowdon. Such a long way. I went by pony as it was quite steep in places. Frances strode ahead, eager to see the top. Of course when we arrived at the summit, it was covered in cloud and you could not see further than your hand. She was most disappointed.'

Frances's face danced in front of Lotty. She always remembered Frances laughing at a joke someone had made, or her face animated by a story she was telling.

'She was never disappointed for long, dear Frances. She fixed to go again the next day. It was a clear morning and nothing could dissuade her from venturing out. She was so keen to see the view from the summit. I declined as I was quite tired from the previous day's excursion —'

'Had it been *so* tiring, riding a pony?' Amy said.

Lotty's eyes widened in piqued astonishment. *Did you ever!* She turned her body in order to see Ellie and Winifred at a better angle. 'The pony was most helpful, yet it was still tiring. I struggled with a weak chest due to a childhood illness which would often seize me and I would be reduced to bed rest. So I was always cautious of over-exerting myself.'

Winifred smiled at her and Lotty softened. *She understands, at least.*

'I visited Scotland with my aunt and uncle Whitelegge in 1870. My uncle was also an enthusiastic walker. We visited the Wallace Monument, it was quite new, a high tower on the top of the hill two miles from Bridge of Allan. We had a steep walk up the hill and my uncle pulled me most of the way. I thought I would have got on better had I had my alpenstock; however, my uncle had expressed such a horror of travelling with it that I had offered to leave it behind in Glasgow. He made no answer, but when I came down the next morning he had already posted it.'

Even now, Lotty could still feel the surprise of that discovery and heard it in her voice as she told the story. Ellie smiled, her two front teeth biting into her bottom lip. Lotty glanced in Ellie's direction as she smiled.

'The people of Glasgow were very—'

She could feel them waiting but she couldn't speak. Frances used to smile exactly like that.

Lotty studied Ellie. *How had I failed to notice that she has the same almond-shaped eyes as Frances and me? The Burne eyes. And her hair colour: the same caramel-brown.* Ellie shifted under her gaze.

'I seem to have forgotten myself.'

'You were talking about Scotland.'

'Yes ... yes. Frances stayed at home to care for Mamma. It was not long since Mamma had suffered her heart displacement and she was in quite a bad way. Some days she did not come downstairs at all. Frances was so patient. She had to run the house by herself, which caused her no end of botherment and messages at times. She also had to pack up both boys for school. Even with her best efforts, Sambrooke did not have all his socks darned and went one pair short. She was naturally good with children, though: patient, and had a wonderful imagination. We described her as "our leader" in make-believe plays.'

Lotty had stopped seeing her audience. She saw only her sister putting the finishing touches to the stage they had erected in the drawing room. *That smile again.* Lotty stacked a small slice of duck with potatoes and vegetables onto her fork. She was grateful that the meat was nicely cooked and not chewy. Her tooth always struggled with overcooked meat or crunchy pieces. She had resorted to cutting the crusts off her bread towards the end, just to avoid the worry.

'Frances was always natural with children; she found adult parties and pretty little company talk so dull. Whilst I was in Scotland, she was invited to Loynton to make up the numbers for a shooting party and she wrote in concern that it would be her part to sit in the drawing room in the morning with some fancy needlework and talk "young lady". I do recall her finding it all quite dull.'

Lotty took another mouthful of food and watched Amy as she topped up her wineglass. Lotty nodded in acceptance as the bottle reached her glass.

'Thank you. Do you speak Portuguese, Mrs Mello? I only enquire as it is a language I am not as familiar with.'

'I spoke it with my family at home but not all the time. What you've got to remember is that we spoke English everywhere and were taught English at school. Even my kids didn't speak it often. Y'know what kids are like. They don't want to stick

UNEXPECTED COMPANIONS

out. English was what they were taught in the US and Bermuda, and that is what they preferred.'

'What a shame not to have passed on the knowledge of a mother tongue,' Lotty said. 'Frances and I did enjoy languages. She would often mix her sentences with French, Latin and German for a little amusement.'

'What fun you had,' Amy said.

'We thought so,' Lotty said. A frown wrinkled her forehead. 'I suppose it was not to everyone's taste. Our aunts, I know, found us challenging to converse with. Our interests were quite different. My Aunt Sophia was much perplexed when she learnt I was translating a play from German to English. "Whatever for?" she had asked. "Are there not plenty of English plays you could read?"'

Lotty chuckled. 'Yet it was a great success in other circles. I stayed with our friends the Vallings soon after I had translated the play and it had been published.'

Ellie picked up her water glass.

'Jim was very much taken with *The Burgomaster's Guest*,' Lotty said, 'and he and I managed to turn some of the incidents in it into the charade of witchcraft, which was very successful.'

Ellie's glass stayed suspended in the air. Her mouth remained open, still waiting for the promised water. Lotty didn't notice.

'I was Anna, with him for my Muses; and my sister Alice was the grandmother, much to the surprise of the company. His brothers took part as well: Hal was Klaus, in his father's uniform, and Teddy a splendid burgomaster. He threatened, "I'll marry you to Sparrow, Miss Burne, after all," whenever I disagreed with him afterwards.'

Lotty frowned at Ellie's gaping mouth. *What can the matter be now?*

'Sparrow?' Ellie said, her eyes still staring. '"He sticks to me like a burr and chatters like a magpie."'

Now Lotty stared.

100

'Yes.' Lotty's voice was so quiet only Ellie heard her.

'It is not a well-known play and was published in a very obscure magazine,' Lotty said recovering from the surprise. 'Many people did not come across it and remained in ignorance of its existence. Yet you know it?'

All eyes turned on Ellie. She slunk lower in her chair, willing her cheeks to cool down.

'Aria's dad found it for us. We ... we thought we would do a translation for a school project. Aria helps me with my languages 'cause she's really good at them.'

It had been Aria's idea and for a while they had searched for a good play to do, but nothing had seemed quite right. Then one day, sitting in Aria's sunny kitchen, scouring the internet, her dad had appeared and dropped a pile of publications on the table. The musty smell of forgotten pages puffed out as he shuffled through them.

'It is here somewhere,' he said. He had never lost his German accent and certain letters were reproduced with a Germanic inflection.

'Ah-ah! Here it is.'

And from time-stained pages, stapled together, with some corners creased over by a careless handler, came the play that Aria and Ellie had been looking for. Funny, with a variety of characters, but not too long, and written in German.

'It's probably going to be horrible,' Ellie said. 'I struggle with the *der, die, das* and stuff; but the play is funny so we thought we would give it a go.'

Ellie glanced at the faces around her. She expected Amy to say something about it being a waste of time and so braced herself for the mockery she knew would come just like at school when Mia had found out; she could almost hear Mia's laughter echo across the room.

'That sounds very challenging, Eleanor,' Amy said. 'Translating a whole play. That's really impressive.'

Ellie smiled and sat up a little bit straighter.

'Yes, very impressive,' Lotty agreed. 'When I undertook the translation from German I had my governess to assist me.'

'Well, Aria's dad is German.'

'Even so, Frances —'

'Eleanor.'

'Pardon?'

'You called me Frances.'

'Did I? How strange.'

'I'm Ellie to everyone. Only my teachers call me Eleanor.'

'I rarely used my full name either and was Lotty to family and close friends. Charlotte was used for formal occasions and by those within the Folklore Society.'

Lotty smiled on Ellie, who kept her eyes on the table but her cheeks glowed with newly found pride. In the reflection of the window, there was no sign of the waiting shadows; the candles burned bright and a warm glow glinted off the glasses and cutlery.

ELLIE

'My neighbour in Cambridge was German,' Amy said. 'She was a strange person in lots of ways; no care for her appearance. Would just pull out clothes from a pile on the chair in her kitchen, all scrumpled, and wouldn't iron them or anything. Just put them straight on as they were.'

Amy shook her head and her hand moved once more, drawing an imaginary line through the air. 'But she made the most incredible stews and potato rostis. The fragrance of onions and garlic would hit you way before you got to her house; I could never make them as good as her.

'After Everest and Charlotte left, she looked after Ernest till I got off shift. She was the kindest of people and we were very close. I felt sorry for her. She had made some bad choices. Married a terrible guy. I know I shouldn't say that but it's true. He ran off and left her one day, never came back. I always thought that was the best thing that could have happened to her. And she stayed on in Cambridge by herself, strong woman. There for twenty years but still had the strongest German accent.'

'Where in Germany was she from?' Lotty said.

'Oh, I can't remember. The south somewhere.'

'Stuttgart? Munich? Kempten?'

'No, no, no. It started with an L. Loo ... Laa ...'

'Lucerne?'

'Yes. Yes, that was it.'

'That is in Switzerland.'

'Yes. That's right. Switzerland.'

'So she was not German. She was Swiss.'

'Yes, exactly. Swiss.'

The good feeling from earlier was still warm in Ellie and she found this exchange funny. She didn't need to look at Lotty's face, though, to know it was etched with frustration.

'I always found the Swiss accent quite horrible. Very difficult to understand their German and certainly easy to distinguish against someone from Germany.'

Lotty picked up her fork and, still shaking her head, skewered food to it. Ellie smiled behind her napkin. Amy shrugged and Lotty continued.

'I visited Lucerne in July 1873 as part of the Swiss trip I was undertaking with my aunt and uncle Whitelegge. I remember Lucerne quite well as we had to get up at 4.45 to get there. Aunt Mary thought at first it would be too fatiguing, and Uncle William professed to be astounded and declared us mad creatures at the prospect of such a start. It turned out to be a great success as we got our journey over before the heat of the day and Uncle William declared, after, that he would have more faith in women henceforth.'

Lotty, having paused to eat her food, continued, 'Did your neighbour reside by the lake or further up? We got rooms *au troisieme* in a *pension* behind the cathedral, up the hill. There was a nice breeze from there. At tea, I was quite excited to discover my aunt's niece, Anastasia, sitting at the table opposite. We were there for ten days and spent a good amount of that with Anastasia and her aunts. They were three regular old maids...What was your crossing like when you emigrated to America?'

Ellie found it hard to keep pace with the change of direction, but Amy didn't seem to miss a beat.

'It was very rough at times. Many people were very ill. Although the food didn't agree with me, that wasn't because of seasickness. Let's just say not everyone has the stomach for a crossing like that. Naomi, John's wife, was sick for almost the whole journey.'

Ellie took a mouthful of duck and tried another sip of the wine. It tasted bitter and she put the glass down.

'... What I really remember was how cold it —'

'I enquired, as on our crossing to France not more than half a dozen gentlemen escaped being ill,' Lotty said. 'Directly we started, all the husbands wrapped up their wives and —'

'It was the wind. That made it so cold. I had been warned but —'

Lotty raised her voice. 'The wives were settled on benches in readiness to be ill. I really believe that made them worse. I followed my uncle to the gangplank after —'

Amy jerked her finger in the air, caught Winifred's eye and continued. 'Now look, after our first winter in Massachusetts I had a much better idea of what cold could be! But even when we arrived in Canada in May, it was cold and there was snow in places. In May!'

Lotty's knife and fork clattered on her plate, the fire spluttered. Ellie reached for her water glass even though she wasn't thirsty. *Why are they both being so weird.* As she reached across, her hand knocked against the wineglass. Glass and wine cascaded across the table. *Oh God.* Ellie could only stare as red wine splattered across the tablecloth and the remains of Lotty's food. She let out a breath and then saw the polka-dot pattern on Lotty's dress.

'Oh God! I'm sorry. I don't know what happened.'

'It appears you spilt red wine.'

'Yeah, but I ... mean ...'

'Never mind, darling,' Winifred said. 'It was a simple accident. No use crying over spilt milk.'

'What a shame. Do you think it will stain?' Amy said.

Lotty shot her a look. Amy took a sip of wine.

'Salt might get it out although there doesn't seem to be a lot here,' Winifred said. 'Or white wine works.'

Ellie spied a bottle of white wine on the sideboard behind her and Lotty. 'I'll get it,' she said.

'No need,' Lotty said. 'I will fetch it.'

The chair glided back, she stood to a rustle of applause and carried herself to the sideboard.

'But to go back to our original conversation, I believe we were discussing your friend and this play you are translating together. What a wonderful project,' Winifred said, straightening her napkin on her lap. 'How is your dress, Lotty?'

'It will be fine, I am sure.'

'Oh good,' Winifred said. 'Fortunately, most of it spilt on the table. Perhaps you could give Eleanor, sorry ... Ellie, some advice with regard to the play?'

Lotty stood in the dim light between the fire and the candlesticks on the sideboard. Her face was half shadowed and she looked at Ellie carefully as she thought of what to say. In the silence, Ellie glanced over at Lotty and goosebumps rose on her arms. Her breath caught in her throat.

It's her. It's definitely her. The woman on the bridge.

'I don't think it's a good idea,' she said, but she didn't see Lotty dab at her dress or Amy return her attention to her duck. Instead, Ellie saw a concrete wall and heard the impatient thud, thud of a tennis bag hitting a hard floor.

———

'I really don't think it's a good idea, Mia,' Ellie said, peering at the wall and assessing its height.

'You saying I'm lying?'

'No, 'course not. But it's been raining and it could be super-dangerous.'

Mia scoffed and Ellie's stomach clenched as she watched her friend roll her eyes. Ellie glanced again at the wall of the bridge. It was low enough to climb up onto it, and although she didn't want to doubt that a younger version of Mia had done so, Ellie wasn't convinced *she* wanted to do it.

'It's just like walking across a balance beam,' Rosie said.

'Well, you do it, then,' Ellie said. *Why did I say that? They'll get annoyed that I'm causing arguments.*

Rosie muttered something and went back to tapping her tennis bag on the footbridge.

'I haven't asked Rosie to do it, I've asked you,' Mia said.

Ellie looked again at the wall and pretended to not see Rosie's smirk.

'I'm starting to think you don't want to hang out with us,' Mia said, casually picking at her nail. 'I mean, you let us down with the cinema. We didn't get in and I reckon we would've if you'd been there. You look old. And then, because we weren't at the cinema, Sam's dad caught us drinking down by the river. Told our parents, too. I'm lucky that my parents are so cool but Rosie ...' Mia frowned in mock sadness. 'Rosie's parents were really mad. Said if she gets in trouble again they will stop her allowance.'

Ellie was tempted to say that Rosie never seemed to get an allowance, but she didn't feel brave enough. They'd been through this conversation so many times. There was no point explaining that she *had* gone to the cinema and also been turned away, and how her phone had been out of battery. They would just shrug and point out that there was no way of her proving that any of it was true. Aria had once asked her why she felt she had to prove anything to them.

'I don't. I mean, it's not like that,' Ellie said, knowing that the answer sounded weak.

'They just seem like total emos,' Aria said. 'But I guess I don't know them.' She had kept her face down, hidden from scrutiny so Ellie couldn't tell how much of what she said she really meant or if she just didn't want an argument. But Ellie told herself that that was it: Aria just didn't know them.

Ellie stood on the footbridge looking at the flickers of different emotions rippling over their faces.

'What if a train went underneath? I'm not sure it's that safe,' Sam said.

Thank you, thank you. Ellie tried to catch Sam's eye but she wouldn't look at her. She looked nervous. *She's not gonna push it.*

Mia sighed. 'Well, we can't wait here all day for Ellie to find some guts. I told you, it's not hard. Don't you trust me?'

'I'll do it,' a little voice piped up.

Ellie shut her eyes to ward off the sickening feeling that swept over her. *No, Beth. Please.* She turned around and looked at the younger girl, who had trailed after them from the tennis club. She was ten and followed them all with glazed admiration. Ellie took a deep breath.

'No, Beth. You won't. It's too dangerous, no matter what Mia says.' She was angry and knew she would regret these words later.

'So, you'll do it then?' Mia said. She was watching Ellie and her eyes in the diminishing September light seemed to have a cruel glint to them. *Would she let a ten-year-old do it if I refuse? Probably.* Ellie put her bag down and cautiously put a hand on the wall. A noise stopped her. At the far end of the footbridge, someone was watching them. The woman stood in gathering shadows but it was light enough for Ellie to see her face. Ellie couldn't tell if she disapproved or was just curious. The woman seemed to be weighing up the scene and processing the details before her.

'Come on, get on with it before someone sees us,' Mia said.

'I'm just waiting for that woman to leave,' Ellie said.

'What woman?'

'The one over there, in that long dress and shawl.'

'There's no one there.'

'Yes, there is.'

'Oh, let me do it. I have great balance.' Beth tried to push past Ellie.

'No, Beth don't. I'll do it.'

Ellie put her hands on the wall and pulled herself up. She shot a look of appeal at the woman in the hope that she would come and intervene, but she stayed where she was, watching. Slowly Ellie started to move across the wall. She felt light-headed. *Just like in gym. One foot and then the next. Look straight ahead. Don't look down.* Ellie was halfway across. Out of the corner of her eye she could see the woman. A frown of concentration ran across her brow but there was no other sign of movement from her.

A train rattled under the bridge. Ellie's foot slipped on some loose cement. She cried out, her free foot frantically trying to balance her. Then she fell, landing in a pile on the footbridge. From far away she heard the others' footsteps and shouts. She dragged herself to the wall and leaned against it. Her wrist throbbed and blood and dirt mingled on her legs and arms. *Help! Where are the others?* Ellie glanced around, hardly believing that they had run off. She looked for the woman but she too had disappeared.

ELLIE AND WINIFRED

She had been lucky. Just scratches and bruises. Nothing lasting to remind her of the incident. She told her mum that she had fallen down the stairs of the footbridge, which wasn't a complete lie, and pretended not to see the strange looks her mum gave her for a while afterwards. But she knew her parents had their own ideas about it all. That evening, when she had been banished to the kitchen to wash up, her parents sat in the sitting room in whispered combat.

'It's those girls ...'

'I know, but she found it so hard to settle in ...'

'That was almost a year ago now ... there must be other kids she could be friends with.'

Ellie had closed her ears to the conversation, willing away the wish for her mum to come in and hug her. The girls were all a bit distant with her after that. So she had been really glad when Rosie sought her out. Maybe that was why she did it. She hadn't wanted to mess around with the cupboard. It hadn't seemed a good idea. But she had to make up for the bridge and it was Rosie who she owed so much to. But the look on her mum's face that day, as she had waited for Ellie at the school gate, had sent a chill through her. If her mum had been angry it would have been bearable, but she didn't seem mad, just sad.

'Come on,' she had said. 'We're going home.'

If she was furious she didn't show it, and when she spoke she sounded dejected. 'I'm going to meet you from school for a little while. I think you need to start focusing more on your studies than on ... extra-curricular entertainment.'

That was the only thing she said the whole way home. True to her word, her mum started meeting her from school again, and the girls would melt away under the gaze of this adult disapproval. On the second day of her home-time escort, a voice had stopped them as they had started out of the school gate.

'Ellie! Mrs Hardwick! Wait for me.'

Aria rushed past other groups of people, her bag waving at her side as she struggled to get it to stay in place.

'Aria, please call me Natalie.'

'Sorry, Mrs Hardwick—-I mean Natalie. Ellie said you were walking home together and I thought I would join you. I hate walking back by myself.'

Ellie's mum had looked at Ellie, who took a firm interest in what her friend was saying. Aria then started to walk home with Ellie and her mum each afternoon, the conscious buffer between them. She wasn't embarrassed to spend the mile trek with a parent, and talked easily about her day and teachers.

But the woman on the bridge never left Ellie. The imperious stare, the slight frown. *How could I not have seen it before? To be fair, she had been wearing a simpler dress and was younger and thinner.*

'There is no need to sit there gawking, Ellie,' Lotty said. 'It might seem a lot to ask; however, I can assure you that attention to detail and slow, methodical work is the only sure approach to success.'

What? Oh, the play. Ellie shut her mouth and moved her features into a smile.

'It doesn't sound a lot to ask for. Umm ... thank you, Lotty.'

Lotty watched her a moment longer and then moved back to the table.

'Frances used to twirl her hair in the same way. Quite unconsciously. If a strand was loose she would twist it as she thought. She also had the habit when she was tired or bored.

She once wrote about a dinner she had to attend at Loynton where the evening was dullish and that she sat under the arch and nearly went to sleep. It left me with an image of her prising hair loose and twirling it as she watched the guests sing and talk around her.'

Lotty smiled.

'You were close to your sister, weren't you?' Winifred said.

'Yes, I was. I am indebted to her, as well as Georgina Jackson and Mamma, for steering me along the folklore path. She was more than a sister. She was my dearest friend and confidant. She was ... irreplaceable.'

'I was close to my sisters,' Winifred said, hoping this subject would be a safe one. 'Especially Orian. She ended up marrying one of the local boys. We all thought him very handsome. They managed to buy their own farm near my parents, the first of our family to own their own farm. She never left Wales, only ever wanted to be a farmer.'

'That is the true definition of a fulfilling life,' Lotty said. 'Doing something you are passionate about.'

Winifred watched the pale, soft hands opposite her glitter in red and gold as they casually manoeuvred the silver fork from the plate to the mouth.

'Of course, being passionate about something might not satisfy hungry stomachs,' Winifred said.

Her father's face flickered in front of her. Winifred rarely thought of him. He was surrounded by too many hard memories. It had been easier to simply pretend it had never happened.

She turned her attention back to Ellie. *She hasn't said anything for a while. She looks sad. Oh dear, we do not seem to be doing a very good job of this. Too many voices.*

'Is Aria a good friend?' Winifred said.

Ellie shrugged. 'Yeah, I guess. She's fun and really clever. And she doesn't care what other people think.'

'I had a very close pal when we were nursing in London,'

Winifred said. 'Eileen. We used to have such fun. She was quite outgoing; the opposite to me, in that sense. Once she was caught by the night watchman after curfew and when he asked her name she gave the name of a Russian actress, Olga Chekhova. The man did not find this amusing but we called her Olga from then on.'

Ellie managed a smile.

'I found, Ellie, that having just one or two close friends will stand you in good stead over time; unlike a great pile of uninterested acquaintances.'

Ellie mumbled something, although even she wasn't sure what she had said.

'I agree,' Amy said. She tapped her finger to her lips. 'Now look, it sounds like you have a great little friend in Aria. You should keep her.'

'She's not a pet.' Ellie pushed her plate away.

Amy pointed her finger at Ellie. 'What you need to remember is that you can't take those sorts of friendships for granted. When I moved me and the kids back to Bermuda, I found a house close to my friend Mary precisely because we were close. Ernest even married one of her girls.'

She tapped her finger to her lips and then stabbed the air with it. 'I mean, I knew I wasn't going to live in that small cottage forever; I had a bigger goal. And I knew I could make it happen.'

Ellie nodded although she wasn't sure what Amy was getting at. *Why is she still watching me? What does she want me to say to that?* Ellie darted her eyes across the other women, hoping to avoid the intense look waiting at the far side of the table.

'How did you and John meet?' Amy asked.

Winifred sat for a second before realising the question was for her. *How does she jump from one conversation to another like that?* But seeing Ellie lean forward, Winifred relaxed.

'We were both training at Westminster Hospital. I was in

my first year of training as a nurse and he was a second-year medical student. It was April 1942 and I had been posted to an evacuated maternity unit in Ripley. We worked together treating a baby and later that day he walked around to the nurses' unit to ask me out.'

Winifred stopped but continued talking as she realised that Amy was waiting for more details.

'I was in the bath when he called and one of the other nurses came in with the message. I told her that I could not go on a date as I had nothing to wear, and she offered to lend me a dress, blue with a velvet bodice. Quite decadent really. So I agreed to the date.'

'Wow. Just think, you might never have married him if your friend hadn't lent you a dress.' Ellie said.

Winifred cut her duck slice in two and skewered a piece with the beans. 'If ifs and ands were pots and pans, there'd be no need for tinkers,' she said and smiled at Ellie. 'Soon after we met, we were transferred to different hospitals. I went to Park Prewett, a Service hospital in Basingstoke.'

Multicoloured tiles, criss-cross shadows ... Winifred pushed the thought away.

'I was not going to write to him, but Eileen persuaded me. So I did. You see how big a word those two letters *i* and *f* make? You could even go further back, as without the war I would not have been able to train at Westminster Hospital. They refused my initial application, you know. They said I was too young, although I always thought that was nonsense, but it was why I was working at Parkwood Convalescent Home in Kent when I initially came to England. And then...'

She stopped to eat the amalgam of duck and beans, hoping the pause would encourage someone else to talk. But she was wrong.

'And then...' Amy prompted.

'And then, when John and I married, I was one of the first married women to be allowed to continue to work. That was the reality in those days: social concerns took second place to the needs of wartime. The war taught us that "if" was a pointless word to focus too much attention on. You just had to get on with things. If something was going to happen, it was going to happen.'

The noise of glass crunching under foot, the sight of a building crumpled in on itself, and the smell of burning wood surrounded Winifred. She sealed off her senses to the memory and took another forkful of her food. *This duck is delicious, almost as good as the ones Mam reared.*

'What was it like to live in England during the war?' Amy asked.

Winifred sliced a potato, the knife slipping easily through it. She watched the pale middle turn pink as it mingled with the red cabbage. *How strange to start talking about this now.*

'For the first months of the war, it didn't even seem like there *was* a war. You could drift along almost oblivious to the troops gathering at ports and railway stations, and the activity on the Continent seemed another world away. It felt so ... aimless and, in truth, fairly safe. That was why I volunteered for extra duties, just to do something and feel useful. I suppose I have always found hard work a relief; however, for the most part it was fire watching, and even that seemed pointless, especially in the early months of 1940. We used to joke that there were more dangers from the gardener than from the German bombs!'

Winifred took a sip of water.

'But then things started to change and you had to work out how to get by. A lesson for any time of life,' Winifred said, glancing at Ellie. 'How to manage change. Some might draw or read. A group of us coped by reciting poems or comic verses whilst walking. It's what kept us going whether in uniform or not.'

'Do you remember any of them?' Lotty said.

'Oh, some were quite silly really,' In her mind she sifted

through the collection of poems and riddles, before choosing one:

'"What did the Doodle-bug say to its fellow traveller? I'm going down now so Doodle-oo!" The Doodle-bug was a type of bomb.' She smiled but it seemed that the joke was lost on the group. 'Perhaps you had to be there to appreciate it ...'

Lotty was still looking at her expectantly so she chose another from her mind's anthology.

'We also entertained ourselves with modifications.'

She could hear John's version of 'The Walrus and the Carpenter' floating in the air.

'"They wept like anything to see such quantities of
sand.
If this were only cleared away they said, it would be
grand.
'If seven stukas with seven bombs bombed it for half
a year,
Do you suppose, the walrus said, that they would get
it clear?'
'I doubt it said the carpenter and drank a bitter
beer."'

'Lewis Carroll,' Ellie and Lotty said. They laughed in unison. Winifred smiled. *Lotty looks more at ease than I've seen her all evening.*

'Yes. You see, there was more than enough real war to be getting on with, so comic and curious poems were in. The radio broadcasted music and comedy, though not many of us had access to a radio.'

'Do you have any other such ditties?' Lotty said.

'Oh, plenty. We would make up alternatives while walking or sometimes just recite poetry ... a favourite was "The Lady of Shalott" ... nothing to do with onions.'

The joke had been one of John's and his eyes would twinkle

in lexical amusement every time he made it. The joke softened Winifred's memory-armour, but she realised that the humour hadn't hit home beyond a small smile from Lotty.

'It was a coping strategy,' she said by way of explanation. 'You had to learn how to remove yourself from the emotions of others. No choice, really. You see, so many men came back scarred from their experiences, not just physically but emotionally as well. And they would attach some importance to you and your presence as they adjusted to their new reality. As a nurse I was looking after servicemen and used to receive letters and small gifts from some of them. 'Some were funny — once, an RAF pilot sent a poem to four of us who had been looking after him. He called it "The Ballad of the Night Nurse".

'The verse he wrote about me went something like:

"Davies is my name, Always working, happy to, spirit never fails,
tea preparing, toenails paring, emptying the pails,
changing sheets, washing feet, tucking in their tails.
Jolly little nursling I, may the patients never die!"
'It was very funny and clever.'

When no one spoke, Winifred continued, 'Of course, there were others who found it harder to recover and weren't able to ... express themselves so eloquently. I received one poem from a patient and, well ... let's just say it contained some quite graphic, and indeed aggressive, language. I was no shrinking violet; as a nurse *and* having grown up on a farm I had seen enough of the world not to be shocked easily, but still ...'

It had reminded her so much of what had happened to Kathleen that she had barely been able to read it.

'It ... well, it did not make pleasant reading. I gave it to John without a word and we never spoke of it again. I do not even know what he did with the poem.'

Darling John. He was so good like that. Nothing fazed him.

A favourite memory of hers from that time had been the first time she had taken him to Wales. He had accepted this different way of life without a murmur of complaint. Her father had met them at Garth and without a word put their bags on the cart and drove off.

'How do we get to your farm?' John had said.

'We walk.'

She didn't tell him it was six miles. She just set off, walking across farmland and over hills. The weather had been warm and dry and she hadn't even bothered to change out of her city shoes.

And then there had been their visit to the big house where Kathleen was working as a maid. He had headed down the drive towards the front door.

'*This* way,' Winifred said, and led him around the side of the house to the servants' door.

'I've never been in through the tradesman's entrance,' he said, and walked into the servants' quarters as naturally as if he had been doing it all his life. Winifred adjusted her necklace.

'I like your necklace,' Amy said.

Winifred touched it again.

'My mother-in-law gave it to me, she thought it would suit me. She always did have an eye for jewellery. I wore it with this dress for a photographic session soon after we were married. It was July and John was leaving for India. I wanted him to take a photograph of me with him.

'We didn't know how long he would be away, you see. It was 1944 and no one knew how long the war would last. I'd saved up my ration coupons to be able to buy the material, but even so it wasn't easy to find something.'

She ran a hand over the material and smiled. 'I was determined, though. We had only been married a couple of months, I wasn't even twenty-four.' *Why am I brooding on such sentimental nonsense? Love in wartime should be confined to books.*

Winifred looked at Ellie, who sat with her arms on the table, her plate pushed to one side. *At least she is interested.* Winifred leaned back in her chair. *Perhaps being a bit off-topic isn't the end of the world.*

AMY AND ELLIE

A man entered the room. Tall, olive-skinned, his dark hair cut in a sharp line across his forehead. He looked directly at Amy and smiled. Her question stuttered to a halt. *Joe.*

'Amy, is everything all right?'

Winifred's concerned face came into focus. Amy looked back at the man, who was collecting plates. It wasn't Joe. *Of course it isn't.*

'I'd like to be a doctor. Or if not, then write books. But I don't think my grades are good enough.'

'Well, they won't be if you don't value yourself.'

Ellie's head snapped up. Amy said with a sigh, 'Now look, if you don't believe you can do it, you won't. If you only aim for B's don't expect to get A's.'

Her hand shook as she adjusted her napkin. *Joe.* The waiter picked up her plate and his arm brushed against hers. *Is it my imagination or does he have the same smell? Don't be ridiculous.*

'Joseph and I believed we could make a better life for us in America. I was seven months pregnant when we set out. My mae was against the whole thing, but we were determined. As I said, we sailed to Canada and travelled down to Massachusetts. Just doing that wasn't easy.'

She looked around the room.

'What with the war and trains being delayed or taken over for war supplies it took a lot longer than it should've. But we eventually got to Cambridge. And then New Bedford. My brothers and Joseph had to register for the draft. It was an uncertain time for us, especially with a new baby on the way. But exciting, too. And I knew we could make it work.' *It didn't work out how I had expected but that couldn't be helped. It still worked out ... in some ways.*

'We had a lovely house in New Bedford. Near a park and close to Joseph's brother. I liked it from the minute Joseph told me he had found it. There were steps going up to the front door, two bedrooms upstairs and a room and kitchen downstairs.'

Amy glanced around the table, including everyone in the story. 'That first summer in America was hot. I'm used to heat, of course, but this was different. This was dirty and suffocating.' Her face scrunched up at the thought.

'New Bedford is on the sea and we were less than a mile from the harbour but you may as well have been 100 miles for all the sea breeze you got. Too many buildings.'

She hadn't even gone down to the harbour until that November. It had been too far to go when heavily pregnant, and then James has been too little to take out for so long in that heat.

'Besides, the stairs were difficult with the pram so I didn't really go out that much those first weeks with the new baby. Of course, it wasn't much cooler indoors. The rooms were small and the windows didn't open properly ...'

Amy sensed that Winifred was watching her but she refused to look at her. *I don't need to see her pity.*

'Mind you,' she said pointing across the table, 'the houses in Cambridge weren't much better. And in the middle of winter you would wish for the heat of the summer. Garbage covered in snow and frozen to the ground, the roads thick with black sludge. Walking anywhere was a bitterly cold obstacle course.'

'Why did you move to Cambridge?' Lotty asked.

Winifred shifted in her seat. Amy watched the waiter leave the room.

'My baby died ...'

Amy watched the wax drip down the candle on the wall

behind Lotty. It collected on the candle-holder like a clump of earth. The small comfort had been that she had been there, holding his tiny, struggling body. And hoping. Hoping her touch, her murmurs, would make him stronger. *But what chance did a two-month-old baby have?*

'And then Joseph followed him a matter of weeks later.'

Left to fend for herself, in a strange, impersonal place, surrounded by the futile promise of instruments and medicine. James' illness had come on so quickly and taken him so fast that the reality of it hadn't even properly taken hold when Joseph fell ill three weeks later. At the end of August 1918 Amy had had a happy young family, and by the start of October she had buried her son and her husband. Her world had seemed blank. *And now I'm seeing the ghost of my second husband.*

'I thought about staying where we were,' Amy said, tapping her fingers against each other. 'I knew I didn't want to go back to Bermuda. No money, relying on my parents and in-laws. Not for me. I knew what it would be like: each day folding in on the day before like a piece of paper getting smaller and smaller. And I knew Cambridge. We had lived there for a while when I was a kid. And Everest and Charlotte were there.'

Ernest had become very needy in the months after Joseph's death. She had tried to make his fourth birthday that following February a fun experience. Children from the neighbourhood over for a birthday supper; a cake and a toy train she had saved every spare penny for. But no amount of frosted icing was going to replace Joseph. Ernest had needed his dad and she had needed a better-paying job.

Amy watched the wax drip faster, and the candle wavered as the melted wax pooled around its wick. *Everything has to fight to survive.* That cold November day in 1918 sifted through her mind. Standing at the door to the harbour office, trying to ignore the smell of fish. The man had sat in his chair, feet up on the table, smoking a cigarette, looking her up and down.

'Can you read?'

'Yes.'

'Type?'

'Yes.' *No, but I will learn.*

'You'll need to be here early.'

'That's fine.' *Ernest is up early anyway.*

She had trudged the mile back to Joseph's brother's house too cold to be pleased about the job. Thoughts had bounced about, a constant stream of questions and statements. This feeling was new to her; she had never doubted or worried before. She had also never relied on anyone but herself or her own family. Now, she was the poor relation-in-law to be pitied. She didn't like it. And it had been hard to be grateful when the house was so crammed with children and furniture. And Mary expecting another in about a month.

She had pushed her hands deeper into her coat and buried her face in the collar. How she hoped Mary would have a girl. And how she hated living next to a cemetery. More to fear in that twilight than desperate men.

––––––––

Amy assessed Ellie as she cut the green beans and potatoes into bite-size pieces. *Perhaps this cupboard incident will be the thing that helps her see what little value these girls are to her.*

She pointed her finger at Ellie. 'Kiddo, what you've got to realise is that sometimes you need things to go wrong in order to see the strength you have to make things right. For me, it was that crowded house, the promise of someone else's new baby and that cemetery that gave me the strength to find a proper place for me and Ernest. I didn't wait around for something to fall into my lap, I went out and made it happen. Got a job with barely any education and no experience, simply because I had to make it right. The pay was a joke but it was enough to get me going.'

She stopped hearing the words that had, indirectly, fated her to find her way to Cambridge. '*Many girls would do it for less,*' the breathing cloud of smoke had said. It was one of the rare times Amy hadn't made a retort. She'd kept quiet. Every day she arrived on time, did her work and kept quiet. Every long, slow, boring day until she quit.

A smile now flickered across her face as she remembered the day she had resigned, fed up with the leers, the early mornings and the mind-numbing boredom. She had accepted a job at one of the textile mills. Better pay and she wouldn't smell of fish. It felt like a step in the right direction. But she hadn't known what to expect. What she saw was a large room with hundreds of women bent over machines. The noise had hurt her.

'You get used to it,' the woman in charge of new recruits said. 'The bell for a break goes at 10.00 and the lunch bell at 1.00. Don't leave your station at any other time.'

It was the air that decided it for her. Hot, humid, dense air, worse than the worst days of the humid season in Bermuda. The feeling of dust filling her lungs and clogging them; of not being able to breathe. She stood there and stared around her, then back at her 'station'. A cough started to tickle her throat and she gasped for air. *No. I won't do it. I can do better than this.*

She had walked out, ignoring the shouts from the floor manager. Not caring that she would lose a day's wage. The next week, Ernest and she were on a train, watching New Bedford disappear. Two small bags and a toy train to keep them company.

Amy sat up a little in her chair and tilted her chin as she looked around the room. 'In 1919, being a single mum or a woman needing a job was not unusual. If the war hadn't taken or ruined your man, the Spanish flu had ...' She paused, caught out by the bitterness in her voice. She patted her hair before continuing.

'But it still wasn't easy. Men were coming back from Europe

and people didn't think that women should be taking the men's jobs. There were very set ideas of what type of roles a woman should do. And you'd think: okay ...'

Amy rolled her eyes. Ellie smiled, her eyes never leaving Amy's face. *She is a total mix of Nan and Auntie D. Wonder if they even know about Joseph and that they wouldn't've been born if he hadn't died. I've definitely never heard any of these stories before. They probably don't know either.*

'As that year proved, I was lucky to be in Massachusetts,' Amy said. 'Cities like Cambridge were booming. The big rubber factory there needed workers and paid a lot better than anywhere else. I was a fast learner and talked my way into an apprentice job. Never looked back.'

And then Joe had walked into her world; or at least his wife had. Amy took a sip of wine and stared into the fire. The flames flickered and crinkled like rustic-coloured leaves, tripping over the log. The image echoed of other orange leaves, caught between tram tracks, a busy road and a woman with her hair piled in rolls on her head struggling to get a pram onto the pavement.

It was October 1919, just over a year since Joseph had died. Amy manoeuvred herself and Ernest between the cars and horses to the other side to help the new mother, and together they lifted the pram to the safety of the pavement. The small baby, barely a month old, jarred Amy for a second. But only a second. She never compared: it was the easiest way to avoid thinking about her own little baby.

'What an adorable baby.'

'*Obrigado.* He sleeps all the time. I catch myself checking he is still breathing, he sleeps so much!'

Amy managed a half-smile. 'Ah, newborns do that. You wait until he is older. Then you'll wish for their naps. What's his name?'

'Arthur.'

They had stood talking in the cool October air until Ernest started fidgeting and pulling at Amy's arm.

Gloria had come along just as Everest and Charlotte were leaving to go back to Bermuda. Two women, embarking on new worlds; both spoke Portuguese and they were similar ages, living near each other. Their friendship was sealed immediately.

'It must have been very difficult for you.' Winifred said. 'Working and looking after a child with so little help.'

Amy came out of her trance.

'My mam had three children and a tiny baby when my daddy was ... became ill,' Winifred said. 'He wasn't able to help on the farm and Mam relied on family and friends. Without that she wouldn't have been able to manage the farm.'

Amy looked at Winifred. *She's hiding something. I can tell. What happened to her dad?* Amy looked closer at the coiffed hair, the neat outfit and calm face. *Is it just a female trait to suffer and hide it from the world?*

'I was lucky to have friends and family around,' Amy said. 'Cambridge was full of immigrants and many were Portuguese, so we looked out for each other.'

Ernest had lived those first years in Cambridge being looked after by neighbours and friends so she could do her shifts.

'I worked hard and after a couple of years managed to move us out of the shared apartment to a smaller apartment just for the two of us,' Amy said. She didn't add that against the challenges were all her mae's letters, filled with suggestions to come home. Endless comments on how well her siblings were doing, how fine the weather was. News of friends marrying or pregnant. But Amy was determined. Better the squelch of the city.

'How did you meet my great- ...' Ellie paused, counting on her fingers, 'great-grandfather?'

'He was very handsome,' Amy said. 'And had a smile that melted me. And so kind and thoughtful.'

'But how did you meet?' Ellie said.

Amy paused. Really, she hadn't paid Joe much attention when they first met. Making eyes at a friend's husband wasn't her style.

'He lived in my neighbourhood and we knew each other through ... a friend.'

Ellie perked up. *She's avoiding the question.*

'What sort of friend?' Lotty said.

Ellie looked at Lotty. *Oh good. She will almost definitely find out.*

'What do you mean "What sort of friend?" Just a friend.'

'Well, my male acquaintances were all friends through my brothers, the church, distant relatives or the Folklore Society. I am sure I could place any friend into one of those categories. If I were so inclined to categorise my friends.' Lotty gave a high-pitched titter.

Although it wasn't a funny joke, Ellie giggled, unable to stop herself on hearing Lotty's laugh.

Amy shifted in her seat. She started tapping her dessert spoon against the table.

'Now look, things were different in 1920 immigrant America to high-society Victorian England. If you must know, Joe was the husband of a friend of mine. But we were never more than socially polite. He did help me out on occasion because he worked at a butcher's, but that was it. Just being neighbourly. But after ... well ... all that was later. '

LOTTY AND ELLIE

Lotty waited, her eyes never leaving Amy. She knew from experience that a pause and a nod was often all the encouragement a person needed to continue their story. And so it was with Amy.

'Arthur was a sweet child. Big and bubbly. Was like his mae in that sense. And nothing like James, which was a relief. Gloria and I were close. Ernest would sometimes stay with her when I had a shift to do if the woman I boarded with couldn't look after him.'

She patted her hair and fixed her attention on Winifred as she continued, 'What you've got to realise was that living in that boarding house and sharing a small apartment with another couple was not the best. One small bathroom, a tiny kitchen and noise carrying even from apartments on different floors. Gloria and Joe lived by themselves so Ernest and I would go over at weekends just to get away. It was like having a family nearby again.'

Amy nodded intently and Lotty took a sip of wine.

'And when was this?' she said.

'1920. Gloria was planning to take Arthur to the Azores to visit her family. I think her dad wasn't very well. Anyway,' her hand swept the comment aside, 'she wanted him to meet Arthur. I don't think she had seen them since she came over to the States. I remember it so well because they had to apply for a passport for Arthur. And it was all done in a rush because they hadn't realised they needed it. Being organised was not a strong suit for either of them.'

Amy smiled but her eyes were clouded.

'Gloria was worried because they had four days till they had to leave, but Joe was relaxed, said it would all be fine. Gloria would take Arthur and Joe would send the passport on. *Não há problema.* The day after they had applied for the passport, Arthur became ill. Feverish, and with horrible diarrhoea. Nothing seemed to help him. Gloria never left his side, hoping that holding him would soothe or even cure him.'

Amy stared down at the table. 'It never does. Poor little Arthur died beginning of July. Same day that the passport was approved.'

Amy was quiet for a long time. Lotty opened her mouth to say something but Winifred caught her eye.

'There are no such things as problems once a loved one is snatched from you,' Amy said. Ellie watched the other two women nod slowly, almost painfully.

'Everything else fades so fast and becomes so small,' Amy continued.

'That was what it was like for Gloria. After Arthur's funeral she couldn't stay even though she was not well. We all tried to get her to wait until she was better. But she was convinced she needed to see her dad. That if she put it off he would also be dead. So she sailed to the Azores and never came back. They said she had caught the gastroenteritis off Arthur and from being on a boat with no one to look after her ...'

No one moved. The room was quiet; the only noise was the persistent tick of the clock on the mantelpiece.

'I think Joe and I needed each other over those months. I had lost the closest friend I had, and Joe ... well, very few people have experienced the numbing pain of losing a child and a spouse together like that. It's so lonely, it hurts. In a strange way I was lucky, though, because I had had Ernest. He forced me to keep going. Joe had his parents, of course, and some siblings living in Cambridge, but they had their own lives and, in the end, they went back to them. So it was just him and me with our grief and memories.

'It wasn't a happy start to a romance, but it was a firm one,' her head nodded in confirmation, 'and in the end we both loved each other. So we married in April 1921, and when our first boy was born two years later we called him Arthur.'

Lotty ran a finger over one of her rings. She had always worn a lot of jewellery. On all but her wedding finger. She watched Winifred take Amy's hand and clasp it in her own. *I wonder if this would be an appropriate time to enquire if she received funeral cakes at any of the funerals, such as those given when my great aunt died? I imagine not, which is a shame.* Lotty let out a sigh.

'My nan talks about Uncle Arthur,' Ellie said. 'He was really into his music, wasn't he?'

Ellie twisted her hair and tried to remember what else she had been told.

'He lived in Hamilton, right? By himself, never married.'

'Now look, marriage isn't for everybody,' Amy said, pointing her finger directly at Ellie.

'My sentiments exactly,' Lotty said. 'I never married or had —'

'When I met Manuel in the 1930s back in Bermuda,' Amy said, 'I turned him down several times. He wanted to marry but I told him, "When it comes to marriage I am unlucky." So we never did. He lived on the estate he worked on, and I had Vicinity. And it worked beautifully.'

Lotty stared at Amy, her annoyance at the interruption forgotten.

'People were accepting of this ... arrangement?' she asked. 'I have heard of long engagements, indeed my sister, Alice's, lasted nine years, but to live with no intention of marriage; that is quite out of the ordinary.'

Amy shrugged. 'No, not everyone accepted it easily. My mae never liked it. But there wasn't much she could say. I was my own person. And I had saved every penny in order to build Vicinity House.'

Amy had avoided Lotty's eyes but now she looked at her squarely. 'You should have seen it. Beautiful, it was. And large: three big bedrooms, a kitchen with modern appliances and a lovely downstairs area with a large fireplace and windows looking out onto a porch and garden beyond. I designed it myself. Painted it pink, like our beaches.'

She turned to Ellie, 'Have you never seen it?'

Ellie paused. 'No, I don't think so.'

'It had red shutters.'

Ellie shook her head and looked at the table again feeling absurdly guilty for the loss of this house. Amy looked at her for a while and when no answer came, as if trying to spark a remembrance, she added:

'And Manuel had done a great job with the garden. Lots of Portuguese plants and flowers. He had so much talent. For all her comments about our relationship being against God, my mae would happily sit on our swing chair and admire that garden all day if she could. And you'd think, Okay ...' Amy nodded her head and looked at them all.

And then as if tying the strings of her conversations together, she jabbed her finger at Ellie. 'And it wasn't just my mae; plenty didn't consider it right at the time, I can tell you. But I wasn't going to be forced to do things I didn't want to do. I knew what was right for me and I stuck to it. And that is what you need to work out. What is right for you.'

Lotty watched Ellie nod at the table, as though shifting under the weight of Amy's finger. *The poor girl. Mrs Mello does not mince her words.*

'All of us here did what was right for us,' Amy said. 'But it takes courage and resilience.'

'Hmmm,' Lotty said. *I am sure that there would be few people who would put her and me together as examples of similar lives.*

'Certainly, we all had unusual lives and they are not without comparison, yet in many aspects our lifetimes were quite different from each other, Mrs Mello,' Lotty said.

Amy's eyes narrowed but Lotty ignored her.

'In 1910, I was appointed the President of the Folklore Society and the duty of delivering the annual presidential address to a learned society was, for the first time, entrusted to a woman. I regarded the honour of being placed in the chair less a compliment to myself than one to my sex ...'

Ellie felt a blush creep up at the word. *Don't be so annoying. She says stuff so weirdly, though. And she doesn't realise.*

The picture on their living room wall of 'Aunt Lotty' passed through Ellie's mind. No more than ten or eleven, sitting stiffly on a chair, a frown of concentration on her face. *What had Mum said about this Aunt Lotty? An incredible woman, smart and with a will of iron.* Ellie looked at Lotty, who was still talking about her first presidential speech. *Yeah, true.*

'Indeed, when I took the post as editor for the Folklore Society in 1900 it was also the first time that role had been awarded to a woman. I held that prestigious position for eight years until I retired due to ill health. Yet these achievements were not due to courage. Indeed not. It all came about through a lively curiosity and a love of this particular field.'

Lotty turned her attention now to Ellie, who tried hard to look fully attentive.

'As I am sure you are aware, I came from an intellectual family and Mamma encouraged our education and my writing. However, I would not have pursued it, even with such encouragement, if I had had no passion for the subject.'

Lotty sipped her wine. Faces from Edgmond slipped through her mind. Porter, the wagoner who had given her the souling song. Harriet Dowley, who sold fruit and hams and bric-a-brac. She had had a beautiful singing voice and sang ballads which Lotty had written down, Harriet always patient even in the face of requests to repeat a verse or confirm a word. Of all the faces, it was Sally Witherington with her sharp tongue and white donkey that Lotty remembered most clearly.

A remarkable woman in her way, and as firm a part of Edgmond life as the church. Underneath Sally's old-fashioned frilled cap was a mind full of songs and stories. Every fortnight, Sally walked up the hill to their house to do the washing. Those were busy, hot, long days, but afterwards Sally would sit in their kitchen with a small beer and bread and cheese and talk. It was during the pauses that she shared with Lotty ballads and songs that later entered Lotty's book.

Lotty smiled and a scene floated to her that she had long forgotten: of the School Treat, a dance and picnic put on for the village. All the village had turned out and the children from the cottages had squealed with delight, excited by the array of food that the ladies of the area had provided. Lotty had invited Miss Jackson to visit so she could attend the dance.

'It may provide you with some interesting examples of local traditions,' she had written. Miss Jackson needed no further persuasion and arrived for a ten-day visit, travelling with very little besides her trunk and hatbox.

At the School Treat, Sally barely paused between dances. Always lively, in spite of her age, Miss Jackson had commented on it, no doubt thinking of her own age as she said it.

'I don't see the good in being buried,' Sally said.

'That depends on the circumstances,' Miss Jackson retorted. How Lotty had later missed Miss Jackson's quick wit.

'If you are able to find a circle of friends who enjoy the same interests it merely increases the enjoyment you have as well as the knowledge you gain,' Lotty said, her smile assuming agreement from Ellie, but her thoughts were distracted as she noticed her empty plate.

'I wonder where the waiters are,' she said, glancing at the door. 'Dessert must surely be ready. They really are dreadfully neglectful. At least the room is clean, though, and they are nicely dressed. Unlike the garçon at the inn my aunt and uncle and I stayed at in Troyes on our way to Switzerland. Shirt and trousers only, and a dirty napkin over one shoulder.'

She shuddered, 'We were so glad to depart. But what an extraordinary tour that Swiss tour was. Another example of an experience made enjoyable by the presence of like-minded companions.

'Although I did *admire* Lucerne more than *like* it. It made me yearn for the simplicity and quiet of our own dear Cop Mere. Travelling to great lakes did nothing to reduce its loveliness.' *No doubt a bias due to nostalgia. It had been so nice to have settled into our new home with its views over the fields, free from memories, and have Jim visit.*

It had been Jim's first visit since they had moved to Eccleshall in 1877; the second move in as many years. In hindsight, a particularly special visit, as it was possibly the last time she would spend with him when it was just the two of them. She had driven them over to Cop Mere on a cold, bright day and they walked part-way around it, spotting the hardy winter feathered residents.

'You look cold and tired, Lotty. Let us turn around. Perhaps if we make good time we can stop in Eccleshall for tea.'

He gave her his arm and they walked back along the path that cut beside the ancient lake. Two swans lingered together near the edge of the water, the closest one nibbling on weeds that broke the surface.

'I have found many mythical stories referring to swans, yet I have been unable to find any pronounced belief in Shropshire or Staffordshire.'

As she talked, he bent his head close to her face. She could see his breath and hers mingling together in the cold air. A leaf caught on her sleeve and he pulled it free. It was a casual gesture, one that occurs only between friends with whom you share an unconscious ease. But it had wrenched at her breath and made her imagination swirl. When they reached the fly, he helped her in and then sprang up next to her, producing two mince pies.

'I hope Cook will not mind,' he said with a grin. 'I paid for it with a golden curl.'

Lotty had chuckled and eaten the pie in two bites. Her bodice was speckled with crumbs and she brushed them off before he noticed.

'We are losing the light,' Jim said. '"Twilight is not good for maidens, should not loiter in the glen, in the haunts of goblin men."'

Jim Vallings. Fancy thinking of him twice in an evening having not thought of him for years. If only he had not visited my family in Ilfracombe, my story might have been different. Lotty shook her head. *What nonsense I am dwelling on.* She looked at the white roses on the table.

'I am always amused by how many superstitions and beliefs are all around us,' she said. 'You might be entirely unaware as you hand a card with a robin on it that the receiver will shrink with horror at the danger you are passing to them. That is why I found folklore so fascinating.'

She gestured at the roses. 'Take these roses as an example. Are you aware that a common belief is that the plucking of a flower evokes its supernatural powers?'

Amy raised her eyebrows.

'The rose has always been symbolic of love and beauty. In ancient Greece, the rose was the emblem for the beauty of Aphrodite. So much mystery and romance cluster around this kingdom. If I may be permitted to quote Grimm: "Beneath the footstep of the goddess flowers shoot forth, as where true lovers part in sadness the grass and herbage wither."'

Ellie smiled as Amy poured more wine into her glass and gestured with the bottle at Winifred. *She really doesn't like Lotty. They can't get on about anything.*

'And did you ever have a lovers' parting, Lotty?' Amy said.

'Certainly not. I had male acquaintances, some of whom I might be bold enough to describe as close friends, but nothing beyond that. I had no interest in seeking out a mate. A woman with independent means had more to lose than gain from the institution of marriage. Unless having children was your lifetime's ambition. And indeed that ambition comes with its own uncertainties and heartache.'

Lotty took a sip of water.

'It was not so long before my time, although I am glad to say it had died away by my generation, that in the Black Country there were many authentic cases of wives being haltered and led through a turnpike gate, a toll being paid for them like cattle, and sold on the open market.'

Ellie's eyes widened as she processed this statement. 'That can't be right,' she said.

'Women's rights were as little known to society then as they still are in folklore. Folklore knows nothing of woman as the superior sex and woman is considered the "lesser man", as moonlight unto sunlight and as water unto wine. I found I could enjoy male company without the domestic complications. I corresponded regularly with those amongst my set who shared my interest in customs and calendar.'

A laugh bubbled inside her.

'A close friend of mine, Mr Vallings, created an amusing game whereby we wrote to one another using the code the Emperor Augustus was noted to have used: that of replacing A with B, B with C, and so forth. His Latin was not what he would have desired it to be; however, the letters were nonetheless very amusing.'

Winifred is looking at me with such sympathy, it is as if she knows something. Do not forget yourself. To try to distract any intuitive listener, Lotty took up the marriage and folklore thread once more.

'In humbler life, even as late as 1881, if a younger sister should be married before her elders, the latter must dance at the wedding in their stocking feet. It was regarded as a kind of penance for the elder for allowing herself to have been passed by. Fortunately, I was not requested by either of my sisters to perform such an act at their weddings.'

'What funny traditions people had,' Amy said. 'But really it's just a bunch of silly stories.' She patted her hair.

Lotty's lips thinned. *Really. This is all quite infra dig.* Amy took a sip of her wine. A trickle of red slid down the glass and lingered threateningly on its foot.

'Anyway, I got married before my sisters, so unless being a widow would've lumped me in with spinster sisters, I would've avoided that custom.'

'Widows were not expected to dance in their stockings,' Lotty said. 'There were plenty of other customs associated with death and widowh——'

'Oh, let's not talk about death any more,' Amy interjected. 'After James and Joseph, and then the months spent worrying over Joe as he got worse and worse, I have had my fair share of death.'

Ellie twirled her hair for a moment, her brows crinkled in concentration.

'Were his injuries very bad, then?' she finally said.

'What?'

'Joe's injuries. From the car accident,' Ellie glanced around, a slight blush rising on her cheeks. *I've got this wrong. I'm such an idiot.*

'You ... you said he got worse and worse.'

'Oh, yeah. I did.'

Lotty twisted in her seat and examined Amy. *Clever girl, Ellie. What a good ear she has, and quick mind. Even I had not remembered that piece of information. She continues to surprise me.*

'Yes, he ... he was in hospital for three months. Now look, let's not talk about death.'

An owl's cry filled the silence, softened by the window glass.

'How sad that bird is,' Amy said.

'It's an owl. A tawny I believe,' Winifred said.

'Yes, I would agree,' Lotty said. "'The Oule eke, that of deth the bode bringeth.'"

A blank silence followed her sentence.

'Has no one here read Chaucer? If an owl hoots near a house, some misfortune is at hand, but not invariably *deth*, from what I learnt.'

'That's just superstitious rubbish,' Amy said.

'No more than you throwing salt over your shoulder earlier.' Lotty's lips were as thin as a pencil line. Ellie watched Winifred as her eyes leapt from Amy to Lotty.

'That's just a habit. Nothing to do with superstition,' Amy said.

'I can inform you quite confidently that it is no such thing. It —.'

'I think I am should know my own habits.'

Winifred's forehead wrinkled into a frown, a gash across the calm skin. Ellie's stomach dipped at the sight. Around her, Ellie could see shadows appearing as the fire dwindled. Their dark tentacles stretched across the room. The letter by Ellie's empty place setting shifted on the table. *Who did that?* Ellie's hand shook as she reached out to keep the letter close. The owl hooted again. It was closer, its sound closing in around the room. Ellie's skin prickled. *A death is coming.* Her mouth felt dry; her ears blurred the words of the women. *Why are these women here? Where is my mum? I want my mum ...*

Gestures weaved through the air. Voices crescendoed. All the lights went out.

WINIFRED AND ELLIE

Ellie staggered in the dark. Her hip pulsed where she had knocked it against the sideboard. She reached blindly forward, searching for the door. She heard the sound of a match striking its box and then the fizz of a wick taking light once more. Muffled voices floated behind her, more candles flared up and a chair scraped across the floor.

'Ellie, darling. Please do not be afraid. It must have just been a gust of wind from the chimney.'

Ellie turned towards Winifred but couldn't think of anything to say. Winifred stepped closer and squeezed her arm and a fragrance of sweet flowers teased at Ellie's memory. Winifred barely reached Ellie's shoulder even in her court heels, but her presence was a balm and Ellie felt her fear recede.

A small smile smoothed Winifred's features as she sensed that Ellie was recovering from the scare.

'Well, that was exciting,' she said. 'Reminded me of London in the war. Streets so black you couldn't see two steps in front of you.'

She smiled conspiratorially at Ellie. 'One time, Eileen and I were late coming back to the nurses' residence and were almost locked out of our rooms because it was just after curfew. My heart was thumping anyway as we had been quite mischievous and stolen the sundae spoons at the Lloyd's café.'

Her voice tripped with laughter at the memory. 'Quite naughty and a silly thing to do, really, but we were a little giddy on ice cream at the time.'

Winifred kept the smile, her eyes never left Ellie and her hand firmly held Ellie's. Ellie was relaxing, she could tell. Winifred moved her back towards the chair but a voice sliced through the air.

'There is nothing appropriate or innocent about stealing.'

Ellie recoiled and stiffened. She pulled her arm free of Winifred's hand and crossed them over her chest. *Really, Amy. Was that necessary?*

'Well, no. Quite. I merely meant it as an amusing anecdote as opposed to a recommendation of behaviour.'

Ellie remained fixed to the floor.

'I need to go now,' she said. 'Please can you pass me my letter? I have to find my mum.'

'Yes, of course.'

Winifred picked up the letter but didn't pass it to Ellie.

'We are on your side, Ellie.'

The comment was met with sullen silence.

'We just want to help you. You have such potential, we do not want you to waste it.'

'Why do you care?'

'Because we are family.'

Ellie snorted. Winifred watched her and then stepped to the sideboard and righted the statue of the hares, which had toppled over.

'During difficult times I always found it reassuring to know that there were close friends and family to turn to.'

She looked at the hares for a while. One was in the air, mid-jump, and the other had its paws stretched out. *Are they playing or fighting?*

'My sister Kathleen found that out...eventually. Poor Kathleen. Uncle Jack was against her having to marry, but others felt that given ... well, regardless of the circumstances, the result was that they felt she needed to be married.'

Winifred managed a weak smile and looked at Ellie.

'And, at least, it resulted in two lovely, sweet boys. One

born...quite soon after she married and the other a few years later. But her husband ...' Winifred shook her head.

'In the end, Orian's husband drove across the country and picked her and the boys up and brought them back to Wales. She was so desperate, see.'

'She left her husband?' Lotty said.

Winifred didn't hear her and carried on, 'Many people were shocked by such an action: the reasons for it were irrelevant to them. People actually crossed the road rather than speak to her.'

She paused to push back the emotions from those years, then in a whisper that only Ellie heard, 'Such small-mindedness.'

Ellie shifted her weight.

'It was family and close friends who stuck by her,' Winifred said.

'Yeah, but it was family and close friends who made her marry, too,' Ellie replied.

Winifred gripped the sideboard. 'You have to appreciate that in the 1930s there were not the options for women that there are now.'

'You had options, she had options,' Ellie said, pointing at Amy. Amy moved her arms across her chest and her mouth moved, but Ellie didn't hear what she said.

'Yes, however —'

'And like you said, none of this relates to me. No one would care if I got pregnant now.'

Deep down, Ellie was shocked at what she had just said, but also exhilarated by the effect it had on the other women.

'The difference being that Kathleen ... What I mean is that that is not —' Winifred started to say.

'Yes, it is. No one would care.'

Winifred gripped the sideboard harder. It hadn't been easy to share that story, even the glossed version, and she felt tired from the effort. *Take deep breaths. She is just being a teenager.*

You have seen all this before.
'If she cared, where is she?'
'Where is who?' Lotty said.
'My mum. Where is my mum?'
Ellie felt her nails cutting into her palm. *Did I just stamp my foot?*
'I've been here for ages and she hasn't come and looked for me. She doesn't care,' Ellie went on. 'As long as her precious restaurant is doing well, she doesn't notice anything else.' *If she cared, she would have done more to help me. I wouldn't be here with a letter explaining why I'm so terrible.*
Ellie gulped, frantically trying to push the tears back. Winifred looked around at the other two, who both looked irritated by the explosion of petulant self-pity.
'Now look, your mother does a lot for you,' Amy said. 'Do you get hot meals every day? Are you clothed? Did they move house so you could go to a good school and get a good education? Do they ask about your day and take an interest in your interests?'
She counted off the answers, a finger for each question. 'Yes, yes, yes, yes.'
'Do they take you on holiday? Buy you the presents you ask for at Christmas and birthdays?'
'Not always,' Ellie said, looking at the floor.
Amy exhaled and Winifred tried to catch her eye. *This is not going to help us.*
'What Amy is trying to say is —'
'What I *am* saying is that you are a very lucky girl who is acting like a spoilt princess.' Her hand slammed against the table. The glasses rocked nervously but steadied themselves.
'Do your parents make you spend your free time doing nothing but chores? No. If you ask me, before you go to school you should make sure the floors are swept, your bed is made and the dishes are tidied away. Then the house looks clean.'
She nodded and then raised her finger at Ellie.

'But you aren't made to do anything. Do your parents disappear for days on end without seeing you or telling you where they are? No.' Her hand cut through the air.

'Are you made to work here for free? Clean toilets or mop the floors? No.' The hand swiped back again and then centred on Ellie once more.

'It would do you some good to do a bit of honest work.'

There were drops of red wine on the floor and Ellie stared at them until she was certain she wouldn't cry. Then she looked up and held out her hand. Winifred's stomach clenched at the shuttered look in Ellie's eyes. Her chin was thrust out and now pride was going to propel her out of the door.

'Ellie, darling. Don't feel you have to leave to prove something. We can help you, we *want* to help you.'

The letter was passed across.

'What would you know?' Ellie said, looking at Amy, the bitterness of the past year overriding any other emotion. 'You did all right in the end, for all of your stories. You had a big house and travelled.'

'Now look, it was not without a lot of sacrifice. I saved every penny for that house. Worked long hours, spent as little money as I could on me. And here you are with opportunities others don't have, feeling sorry for yourself.'

Ellie didn't reply but turned toward the door. For the first time since taking on this role, Winifred felt engulfed by impatience. *What was Amy thinking, talking to Ellie like that?*

'It is only when you're older that you'll understand the sacrifices a parent makes,' Amy said. 'It doesn't seem much to you, something like moving house to improve a family's situation, but it is a decision that would have been arrived at after hours of agonising and weighing up the options. Not to mention the cost. Every action has consequences and a parent understands that better than anyone because their actions impact more than just themselves.'

Ellie's hand was on the door handle. It felt cool in the

warmth of the room. She wondered what time it was. *It must be late. Too late to see if Aria is still free to work on the play. But anyway.*

'Thanks, I'll keep that in mind,' she said, and turned the handle.

Winifred finally caught Amy's eye, who sighed, paused, then stood up, her presence occupying the entire room.

'Do you know what nickname Ernest had when we lived in Cambridge?' She waited. 'Al Capone.'

The door handle stopped turning.

'As in the gangster?' Ellie said.

'Yes, as in the gangster. He was alive, you see, when we were living in the States. Alive and notorious.' Bitterness dressed the words. She took a deep breath before continuing.

'And Ernest was so spellbound by the stories of gangs and their adventures that he got everybody to call him Al.'

'So what? It's just a nickname.'

'That's what I thought, too. But I was very wrong.'

AMY AND ELLIE

'Sit down; the meal isn't over yet,' Amy said.

Ellie still felt angry and Amy's words echoed in her head: "feeling sorry for yourself". *I'm allowed to miss my friends.*

But as she thought this she realised that she hadn't been missing them as much in the past few weeks as she had pored over the German words of an obscure play so old that it had been typed out on a typewriter. As she had laughed with Aria over her impersonations of celebrities or read amusing horoscopes during their breaks, she had not once compared Aria to her old friends. Not like she did when she was with Mia and the other girls.

Something was keeping her in this room. She didn't know what, but it drew her back to her chair. As if on cue, the waiters appeared and Ellie heard Winifred let out a breath. She had been standing by Ellie's chair and only when Ellie had sat down did she take her own seat on the opposite side of the table.

The waiters went around the table organising the diminishing array of tableware. A hand moved Ellie's dessert fork and spoon to a vertical position facing one another. The waiter's sleeve was so white it seemed to Ellie to blend in with the tablecloth. *A sign that this is all a figment of my imagination?* Ellie watched Amy pat her hair as she waited for the dessert course preparation-ceremony to finish. The door clicked shut and Amy began.

'Ernest was a sweet boy. He was good with his younger siblings and Joe treated him like his own son.' Her finger weaved the air in front of her.

'Ernest never went without. None of them did. I made sure of that. We were lucky. Joe got a good job at the rubber factory and even though Cambridge was a busy, noisy place, and crowded, we had good neighbours and friends. We liked it, y'know, even though it was noisy and in the summer the smell ...' Amy shook her head '... I can still smell that putrid mix of garbage, manure and bodies. Not nice.'

Lotty frowned and scrunched her nose in agreement

'Even though I loved the energy,' Amy continued, 'the smell of horses, mixed with a driver's pipe as they passed by, could still make me want to get on the next ship home.'

'But you never did?' Ellie said. 'Visit Bermuda?'

'What you need to remember is that Bermuda wasn't all wind through palm leaves; those tree frogs and kiskadees could make an awesome racket, too.' She smiled at her joke. 'When Ruth was born we moved to a bigger place just the other side of Hampshire Street. Nice area. Things were going well and it felt like I had a proper family again. And then Joe died and I couldn't afford to keep such a large house. I moved us to a smaller one, just up the road from where I had lived when I first moved to Cambridge. Ruth and Arthur were young; Arthur was just four and Ruth two. They coped with this new change.'

That isn't quite true. There had been déjà vu about it: a little boy asking after his daddy. But this time it had been so much more drawn out. The reassuring lies had gone on for longer. Arthur understood and heard more than she had thought. Soon after Joe was taken to hospital, a close friend had called when the children were in bed.

'I've brought a pot of tea,' she said, lifting up the base of her basket to reveal a compartment underneath.

'You really shouldn't have. You could've been caught.' Amy said.

Hattie had laughed, a short dry laugh. 'Who would catch me? Besides, I think you need something stronger tonight.'

Amy sniffed the contents of the teapot; it was strong.

'How do you know if it is any good? There are stories of people going blind.'

'This is good quality. Trust me.'

Hattie poured the gin into teacups and they sat in Amy's little front room, sipping it tentatively and talking. The next morning, Arthur sat quietly, letting his hair be brushed without any shouts of protest.

'Mommy. What is a hospital?'

The hairbrush paused mid stroke.

'It's a place where sick people go to get better.'

'Is that why Daddy is there? To get better?'

'Yes, I hope so.'

But for all the questions, Arthur and Ruth were still young enough to be distracted. Amy sat a little straighter in her chair.

'But Ernest. To lose another person. He had taken it hard. And it was soon after we moved out of the house that the trouble began. He would sneak off without telling me where he was going. And then come in late, long after he was expected back. He was fourteen and perhaps a bit rebellious.'

She smiled, 'He got that from me, I guess. At first, I figured it was just hanging around with friends. And it probably was. As he got older, though, the behaviour got worse. He stayed out longer, sometimes all night. I thought he was just being a bit wild, needed to get that part out of his system. Go on some dates, sow some oats.'

'Hmmm, but who was he sowing his oats *with*,' Winifred said.

Amy patted her hair. 'Yeah, well. It wasn't that. It turned out that he had taken on more than just a nickname. He was part of a gang ... bootlegging gin.'

As she talked, she toyed with the dessert fork and stared at the marks the prongs made in the tablecloth.

'They were young, just boys thinking it was an easy way to make some money. It was Ernest who had had the initial idea. He had read in some old *Farmers' Bulletin* about how to distil fruit to make alcohol.

'But it was others who made the jump to then combine the alcohol with other ingredients to make it taste vaguely decent, and therefore sellable. They did it all from the bedroom of a friend with less curious parents. Even smuggled in a bath for the operation.'

Amy shook her head.

'This I assume was during Prohibition? I recall it had come into effect in the United States of America towards the end of my life,' Lotty said.

'Yeah, I found out about it in 1929.'

'We also experienced a temperance movement in England,' Lotty said.

'And elsewhere,' Winifred said. 'Mam signed the Pledge.'

'Indeed?' Lotty said. 'It was never something I entertained although one of our washerwomen, Mary Porter, attended a temperance fete. We said to her, "But you are not teetotal." She replied, "Oh yes, but I was for the day".'

Lotty chuckled. Ellie would normally have laughed but she wanted Amy to continue.

'How did you find out? About the bootlegging?' she said.

Lotty shifted in her seat and Amy suppressed a smile. But then a sigh escaped her.

'How had I found out? They came to my house. Dressed in their finery. Ready to attack. Me and Hattie called them the Archangels. Three of them, standing in my front room, declining tea and looking around as if unsure whether it was safe to sit down.'

Amy shut her eyes but the story tumbled out anyway.

'Is Ernest in?' Archangel Two had said.

'No, he's out right now.'

Someone had sniffed as if this confirmed something.

'Just as well, as it is about him we are here,' Archangel One said.

Amy said nothing. Let them talk if that is what they want. After a silence, Archangel One continued:

'We are sorry to have to tell you this, Mrs Mello, but it has been brought to our attention that Ernest is involved in bad company.'

Amy stayed still, her face impassive.

'He's a kid,' she said. 'Whatever he gets up to it is just what you would expect from a boy of his age. Thanks for your concern but I know his friends. They aren't bad kids.'

Archangel One had simpered at this. 'Oh, I am sure they weren't bad kids but they are young men now. You don't know what they do together, I take it?'

Silence.

'They are making alcohol.' She said 'alcohol' as if the mere use of the word could conjure up this evil.

'Yes,' Archangel Three said, keen to get in on the moment. 'Making alcohol and selling it. Illegally.'

Amy had looked at her, taking in her clean gloves, hat and polished shoes. The mother of three girls who went to church dressed identically, a spindling patter of short smocks and ribbons.

'You have made a mistake. My Ernest is a smart kid and wouldn't get involved in anything illegal.'

'Doesn't he like to be called Al?' Archangel Two said. 'Sees himself as a bit of a gangster, doesn't he?'

'That doesn't mean he's bootlegging gin,' Amy replied.

'We never said it was gin,' Archangel One said. Amy looked at her.

'Thank you for your concern. But you've made a mistake.'

'Well, l do hope so,' Archangel One said. 'I am sure the Reverend would be most concerned to learn of such goings on. He is such a law-abiding man. He might feel he had to tell the authorities.'

Amy gritted her teeth. 'And so he should if such things are happening in his church.'

They had left then. And Amy had sat up waiting for her oldest child to come home.

Everyone listened to her in silence.

'I had had my suspicions. Of course I had. But I thought they were just making it for home use, small quantities. I mean, you could buy brewing kits, for crying out loud. There were adverts on how to make grape juice, with a bunch of steps on what you need to avoid doing as otherwise it turns into wine.'

Amy gave a harsh laugh and shook her head. 'But to have those women come into my house and judge me like that. I never went back to that church.'

'Often it is the most Christian people who do the most un-Christian things,' Winifred said, and Amy nodded in agreement. 'It was the final straw. Within a year we were back in Bermuda.'

Ellie tilted her head, her eyes betraying her curiousity, 'Wasn't he mad at you for getting involved like that?'

Amy shrugged. 'Maybe, but I wasn't there to be his friend. I'm his mother and my role is to do what is right for him and it doesn't matter whether he is pleased about it or not.'

'But why do you think you knew better than him? Maybe his friends weren't bad. Maybe you just didn't know them.'

Amy gave her a look. Ellie had seen a similar look from her nan when they had last talked about Mia and the other girls.

'*Dá Deus nozes a quem não tem dentes,*' Amy said, and then added, 'God gives nuts to those who don't have teeth.'

'What? I don't get it,' Ellie said.

'Ernest had his whole life in front of him,' Amy said. 'So many opportunities. But he didn't know what to do with it. He didn't place the right value on his future. He was too close to see what sort of trouble those boys were making for him.'

Ellie thought about conversations with her nan, and her

parents' barely suppressed dislike. *Is that the same? Are Mia and the others 'bad company'.*

'Bermuda wasn't an easy decision but it was the right one,' Amy said. 'For all of us. The factory was cutting back on jobs and reducing the wages of those who were left. The Depression was beginning to hit and it was only going to get worse. In one move, I could avoid joining soup queues and take my son away from the wrong sort of crowd.'

ELLIE

What is that? It looks like an upside down cake but that doesn't look like sponge. And what's that on top? Pears?

The dessert had interrupted Amy. A large round plate hosted a carefully prepared creation of pale creamy white and winter green. The whole mound glistened as vanilla, cinnamon and fruit scented the room; a decoration made of food.

Winifred picked up the large silver spoon that had been placed next to the display.

'Who would like some dessert?' she said.

'What is it?' Ellie said

'Poires condé,' Lotty said. 'The French version of our rice pudding. A hotel near my apartment in London served it in the autumn. It was quite delicious.'

Ellie scrunched her nose up. *Rice pudding?*

'I agree, kiddo,' Amy said, laughing at Ellie's reaction. 'Nothing beats Portuguese desserts in my opinion. If it doesn't have custard it isn't a real dessert. Now, my Ruth, she could bake. The most delicious pies and cakes. She did all my baking after I lost my leg.'

'You lost your leg?' Ellie said.

'How very careless,' Lotty said. 'Did you ever find it again?'

'It was amputated. I was the first woman to have a leg amputated in Bermuda.'

'How odd to see that as something to be proud of,' Lotty said.

'I still got around, got myself upstairs without help and was very active,' Amy said, looking at Lotty. 'That *is* something to be proud of.'

'Well, this dessert looks lovely,' Winifred said. 'It smells just like the ones my mam used to make, although hers weren't as fancy as this. It was such a treat to arrive home to the smell of rice pudding baking in the bread oven.' She spooned a portion onto a plate, passed it to Amy and reached across for the plate Ellie held out.

'It's sad that we can't eat it without ruining it,' Winifred said. 'It now looks like a quarry cutting into the side of a hill.'

Lotty accepted her serving and cut the stewed pear with her spoon.

'"Come buy our orchard fruits",' Lotty said.

Ellie didn't say anything; she was getting used to Lotty's unusual ways.

'*Goblin Market*,' Lotty said. She took a mouthful and a noise of appreciation emanated from her. '"I ate and ate my fill, yet my mouth waters still."'

No one replied. Winifred took a spoonful and ate it slowly. Ellie glanced across the table, unsure if she wanted to eat this strange gooey pile of rice. Amy was halfway through her helping, the spoon moving with a fast grace between the plate and her mouth. She was telling Winifred about how she had taught her daughter how to bake.

'Not sure how much of a cook she was, other than pies, though. She always told me she didn't need to cook 'cause she had me!'

Ellie considered this. *Nan never cooks either.* Ellie had once asked why Nan and Pops never cooked and her dad had laughed and said, 'if your nan had her way, she wouldn't have a kitchen.'

Ellie took a tentative spoonful of her dessert. *Pretty good.*

'I wonder if Aria is translating *The Burgomaster's Guest* right this moment,' Lotty said.

Ellie looked at her. Lotty seemed to be listening to the other two women, who had moved on to comparing dishes that had been favourites in their families.

'Until she was unable to, Mamma would make Bury Simnels every year for Mothering Sunday. A recipe that was from my grandmother's book of recipes,' Lotty added to their conversation. 'Quite different from the Shrewsbury variety, where the cakes are boiled before being baked. Folk etymology says the name derives from an imaginary old couple named Sim and Nell, who disputed whether to boil or bake the remains of their Christmas pudding, and finally agreed to do both.'

Winifred started to give a reply and Ellie took another spoonful of rice pudding.

'The play has such humour and some quite interesting characters,' Lotty said.

Ellie looked up again. Winifred was still talking. *Did Winifred hear Lotty? It's not like she speaks quietly ... No, she didn't. Was it just me then? Is she talking to just me? How? Does she know I can hear her? She has to know. Wait, can she hear me?* Ellie watched Lotty but her face remained passive and polite. As she watched her, she heard Lotty's voice again. 'It has been a surprisingly interesting dinner and it is far from over.'

AMY AND ELLIE

'That was how I knew that Joe wasn't right.' Amy waved her spoon at Winifred. They were still sharing family recipes.

'He stopped eating. Pushed away a bowl of porridge. I made a *great* porridge.' She nodded and leaned towards Winifred, 'The secret is lots of cinnamon and nutmeg.' She sat back and smiled. 'Joe would eat two bowls of it. And then one day he pushed it away. Said he wasn't hungry. That's when I knew that it was more than just a common cold.'

It hadn't been the only symptom: for over two months Joe had complained of not feeling well and had had a cough that wouldn't shift. But refusing to eat had been the warning sign for Amy.

She nodded her head and waited for Winifred with her nursing background to confirm the accurateness of her diagnosis. But it was Lotty who spoke first.

'Mrs Mello, Joe was your second husband, was he not? It is only that I believe you said he died in a car accident.'

Amy put her spoon down and turned to confront this truth. 'No, that's not right.'

'Not correct that he died in a car accident, or that he was not your second husband?'

Amy could feel the scowl surfacing. She tried to relax her jaw, which was beginning to protest. 'This was after that. But I reckon the two were linked.'

'How so?'

Would this woman ever stop? Amy patted her hair.

'Now look, Cambridge had a real go get 'em attitude to it. But that energy had problems. Lots of people and traffic. Kids were often hit by vehicles and there was a tram that you always had to watch out for. I used to tell Ernest ——'

'It is a simple question, Mrs Mello. Was Joe in a traffic accident?'

Amy opened and shut her mouth trying to relax her jaw, her eyes narrowed as she faced Lotty.

'He almost was. He wasn't watching where he was going, was crossing the street and almost got hit by the tram.'

She turned to Winifred for support. 'He was normally so careful. People who saw it said he seemed in a daze.'

She picked up her spoon and watched it move some of the pudding around the plate.

'Soon after that he started to spend longer and longer in bed, saying how tired he was. He got so thin. Then suddenly he got really bad. They said there was nothing they could do. They could try to make him comfortable ...'

'Why did you say he died in a car accident?' Ellie said.

Amy took a deep breath. 'Because he died of TB. A poor person's disease. And we might not have been grand and rich like some, but we weren't poor either.'

The anger shot felt like it hit Ellie in the chest and all her questions dried up in the glare of that emotion.

'It must have been very hard for you,' Winifred said.

'Yeah, well, you just get on it with it, don't you? What choice do you have?'

She scooped a sample of the pudding onto her spoon but left it on the plate.

'Joe was in hospital for three weeks and we did what we could. It wasn't like we didn't know about TB. They had a hospital built specially to treat it 'cause it was so bad. But we still hoped it was just a cold. Right up until he got the fever.'

'What a shame you did not go to see a doctor sooner,' Lotty

said. 'They might have been able to do more for him.'

Lotty casually placed a mixture of rice and pear onto her spoon. Amy blinked at Lotty, too surprised to find a suitable retort. In the silence, Lotty leaned towards Ellie and added.

'I am not without some experience of tuberculosis, or consumption as it was commonly known. A girl from Edgmond, whom I stood for as godparent in my teens, was admitted to Brompton Hospital suffering from the disease.'

Lotty tilted her head to the side and looked at Amy. 'I wonder what the standard of medical care was like in the United States of America? Brompton Hospital was quite new and a fine example of a hospital and dedicated entirely to diseases of the chest. She had excellent care.'

'Well, TB was a very difficult disease to cure,' Winifred said. 'There were few cases of recovery.'

'I looked after him very well,' Amy said, her teeth grinding as she said it. 'The doctors said there was nothing we could've done.'

A draft gusted from the fireplace. Amy tried not to look at Lotty but she couldn't help it. *I don't like how she's smiling, all sympathetic and caring. She really thinks she knows everything.*

'What would you know about caring for others?' Amy said, holding Lotty's gaze for a moment longer than she knew she should. 'You said yourself you don't like it.'

Lotty's hands momentarily clenched her spoon and fork. She placed the cutlery on her plate before replying, 'Mamma and Frances were excellent with invalids; however, we also knew when to show a person the doctor.'

'I grew up on a farm, I was well aware of how to look after things,' Amy said.

'Yes, of course.'

The candles flickered. Ellie realised she was holding her breath. The mirror over the fireplace took on a dark hue and the picture of the crows became hard to make out.

'Joseph and Joe were very different people but they were both healthy and young. And decent men. They didn't deserve to die like that. Alone, away from home surrounded by strangers.'

'It is fortunate that you were so resilient; widowhood does not suit everyone,' Lotty said.

'What would you know of that? Of having no choice but to live without someone you loved?'

From the corner of Ellie's eye she saw something move across the mirror. *A shadow? No, there was no one else in the room.*

'To have had to work all your life just to keep those who depend on you fed and clothed,' Amy went on. 'To smile and look in their innocent eyes and tell them it will be all right when you are wracked with hunger pangs 'cause you've given up your meal.'

'I assure you I am well aware of what hunger pangs feel like,' Lotty replied. 'Mamma sent us to a dreadful boarding school where they barely fed us and I resorted to smuggling bread in my petticoats to share with my sister and brothers.'

'Our corsets were tightened each week,' she added. 'All to make the young pupils achieve a "narrow waist and lady-like elegance". Torture and hunger. We were miserable.'

Amy's jaw sawed her teeth. She forced herself to smile. Ellie glanced at the mirror again. *Is there something inside? Don't be stupid. But what was that? And why did the mirror darken? It's my imagination. That's all.*

'You do not own the rights to grief and misfortune, Mrs Mello. I too have suffered from losing those who were dear to me. And they were much harder to replace than a husband.'

'Nothing is harder to replace than a child,' Amy said.

'I can assure you that losing a sister, and suddenly, is a heavy loss. Or watching a father dwindle away year after year. You are not the only one to have had to carry on after death. To feel the blank of their absence, yet continue to be outwardly cheerful, all the while wishing you could sit still and stay in the company of ghosts.'

'I think money and connections would soften any blow,' Amy said. Her hand pulled her whole body forward and registered each syllable she said.

'You've never had to make sacrifices or worry about how you will put a simple scrap of food on the table while grieving that they died alone while you were comfortable and asleep.'

'I have never heard such impudence.' Lotty stood up, sweeping the chair to one side as she did.

Ellie shuffled closer in to the table as the skirts flowed past her. Winifred started to say something but Ellie didn't hear what she said. The room seemed yet darker, the candlelight fighting against shadows. Something moved in the mirror and Ellie felt as if she saw a face glance her way. *Is someone watching us?* Red flickered across the mirror's face. Amy crossed her arms, Winifred stood up, Ellie jumped to her feet.

'That is enough.'

'Stop!'

The shouts stunned them. No one moved.

'There is no hierarchy to grief,' Winifred said, her voice calm and controlled. 'You two should know that. We all have the scars of loss. We all have our stories. My brother-in-law died alone in an Army hospital in a strange country. His family didn't even know he had been injured, let alone had died, for five more days.'

Ellie noticed Lotty stiffen at the reference to Roger. But it was a fleeting thought interrupted by Winifred telling her to sit down again.

'Yeah, sorry,' Ellie took her seat again.

Her foot knocked against her fork and she leaned down and picked it up.

Lotty looked at the fork and then at the room, her hands resting on her stomach, her chin tilted up.

LOTTY AND ELLIE

Lotty looked again at the fork. *If a fork falls it means a woman is coming.*

Ellie carefully put it down on the table and watched Lotty. *She looks like she's surveying us like we're her audience.*

Lotty's initial desire to leave had been replaced by a feeling unfamiliar to her: embarrassment. She looked at Ellie, so young and keen. Her chest tightened as memories laughed at her. *So much like Frances at that age. I should make amends.*

'Mrs Mello, I owe you an apology. Mamma taught us, if you have done wrong do not be awkward to own it; my comments were ... insensitive.'

Amy's face didn't change, her eyes narrowed as if waiting for the catch to this apology.

'I informed you that I am not without my own experience of hospitals; however, what I omitted to mention is that poor Kitty died there far from any home she knew,' Lotty said, her fingers intertwined tightly as she spoke but she didn't move them off her stomach.

'I am sure the hospital was the most appropriate place for her as she could not be cared for at her home, yet it was a large, imposing building and I am glad that I knew no one else who suffered enough to pass through its doors.'

She allowed the comment to be absorbed in the room before continuing, 'My dear papa became very poorly having twice fallen from his horse whilst hunting a few days after my sister Agatha was born. The second fall was from an immense height and he did not come to his senses for two or three hours.'

'Was that why he died?' Ellie said, then bit her lip as Lotty's cool gaze landed on her.

'They were very concerned for him,' Lotty said, 'so in 1858 Papa was taken to the specialist, yet there was nothing that could be done. Mamma was told there was undoubted mischief on the brain, and resulting from it a parietal paralysis. There was no hope of recovery.'

Lotty paused, remembering the letters she had received at that time as she, Sambrooke, Frances and William were passed from one family member to another, barely ever at home, kept away so they would not be an extra burden on their mother or have to witness their father wasting away. Her mother would never write anything other than 'Papa is still unwell.' But they were encouraged to write to him. Sitting in the drawing room in Ilfracombe, Grandmamma Goodlad had watched her open the latest letter from Mamma.

'Read it aloud, my dear,' she said.

'My Dear Lotty, You do not know how much pleased I am with your present and letter to Papa. He was so pleased when I was reading the letter to him that do you know the tears quite came in his eyes and he likes to have it on the chimney piece to look at every now and then ...'

Lotty had stopped and turned puzzled eyes to her grandmamma.

'Grandmamma, why does Papa cry? He is always so merry.'

Her grandmamma's face was turned away and Lotty wondered if she had heard her. Eventually she replied, 'People cry for many different reasons.'

'Even men like Papa?'

'Even men, my dear. But it is best not to discuss such things in public. This is a family matter.'

Lotty glanced around. It was just her and Grandmamma in the room but the statement was heavy with meaning and she felt very grown up. She could hear Sambrooke and William on the lawn, and although she couldn't hear her, she knew Frances was with them. Their laughter and games seemed silly in comparison to the power of the words in her lap.

Later in life, Lotty saw the irony of her younger self sitting there feeling superior for not playing outside when all her father had ever wanted to do was have fun and play. *Enjoyed life too much*. Her thoughts returned to the moment and she looked at Amy.

'Mamma had to care for him, my sister Agatha, and then, later, the baby. Papa grew worse and worse over the next three years before succumbing in 1861, a few months before his own dear father died.'

Lotty stopped. She had never shared the details of her father's death and although she was quite used to talking in public, this was speech different.

'It was a very difficult time for Mamma; however, they were thankful for being spared yet greater miseries during his care, for he died amongst his own people.'

Lotty looked at Amy, sitting still, pale and pristine against the backdrop of a dark window.

'So you are quite correct in your statement that I do not know what it is like to have a loved one taken away from home to die. However, I do know something of losing those you love and not being there when they died.'

She took a shuddering breath and breathed out a smile. 'I do hope we can put our differences aside and resume the purpose of our gathering.'

Amy's mouth slightly opened at this last sentence and she was silent a moment before replying, 'Thank you, Lotty. And yes, let's get back to Ellie.'

Amy reached across the table and served herself a second helping of rice pudding.

'Is there anything you might wish to say?' Lotty said; after all, her sacrifices might seem trivial to some but that did not stop them from being sacrifices for her.

'Oh, sorry. Anybody else like seconds?' Amy held the serving spoon aloft and Ellie heard Lotty sigh. A sweetly sour odour passed over her as Lotty glided back to her seat. Ellie looked at the window. *I wish I could open that, just a tiny bit.* She scooped a mouthful of rice and pear onto her spoon.

'What do you mean "get back to Ellie"?' she said.

'Ellie, no one requires a vision of the inside of your mouth full of partly chewed food,' Lotty said, stretching her napkin across her lap.

'Sorry,' Ellie said, still chewing.

Lotty sighed but she couldn't suppress the smile.

'But seriously, why are you here?' Ellie said, swallowing the spoonful of dessert. 'I mean, what is this' — she waved her spoon at the room — 'all about?'

'Now look—'

'An excellent question—'

Lotty and Amy paused at the same time, then both waited for the other to take over and then, in the stuttering pause, both resumed their thread.

'Lotty, why don't you start?'

Lotty's eyebrow twitched and she willed her face to hide some of her surprise.

'Thank you. Through my association with the Girls' Friendly Society, where I was the Head of the Literary Department for the Lichfield Branch, I have assisted and provided guidance to many young women of the poorer classes. We would encourage them to read and better themselves through our guidance as Associates.'

She shifted her gaze to Ellie as she continued, 'They all needed to realise that they had been entrusted with bodies, souls and minds and that self-improvement was their duty. In many respects, our presence here is very similar, viz: providing assistance, guidance and encouraging you to make good decisions.'

'I can make good decisions,' Ellie said.

'Missing lessons does not suggest a person who is making good decisions,' Lotty said.

'It's only History,' Ellie said.

'So you have said. Perhaps you do not fully appreciate the importance of history, if you take such an uninterested attitude to it.'

Lotty didn't wait for a response. 'It is through history that we learn who we are. It is by learning what races peopled a country, to what external influences it has been subjected, and under what conditions its people have lived and died from generation to generation, that you may learn the influences of a modern country.'

Lotty hand darted from her lap towards Ellie before settling back in its home, 'You are more than just your name, your livelihood or situation,' she said. 'Although, interestingly, your name suggests you have ancestors who came from the village of Hardwick. Are you aware of any such connection?

'No, I don't think so.'

Ellie marvelled at this woman's style. She seemed to feel no embarrassment about being clever. *In fact, she loves it.* Ellie watched Lotty's face turn from haughty to enthused as if on a switch.

'More's the pity; however, I digress. You are made up of your history, your parents and the history of the country you live in.'

She raised her voice a little, looking at each of the diners in turn.

'To understand a person, you must understand their history. Folklore, in fact, is the expression of the psychology of early man and presents features common to the world at large.'

Ellie stared at her mesmerised. Lotty seemed so comfortable and confident being in the centre of the conversation.

'Their worship of fire and water,' Lotty said, 'observations of the solar year and feasts at the change of the seasons; these customs and beliefs are held still by their descendants to this day.'

Lotty gave a swift gesture that took in all three of them. 'Take Winifred's ballads made up during the scourge of wartime, or Mrs Mello's insistence on throwing salt over her shoulder. Both of these stem from times we would consider unrecognisable to our present thinking and lives, but the actions and ideas would be as familiar to our ancestors as they are to us.

'Did you, Ellie, as child play ring o' roses or hide-and-seek?'

'Yeah, of course,' Ellie said.

'Then you were taking part in history,' Lotty said. 'By missing lessons and choosing instead to idle away that time, you are throwing away the privilege of debating the question man has grappled with since time began: *Why are we here?*'

'I'm not being idle. I'm just not at school,' Ellie said. She knew her face gave away her sullen conviction that they were being unfair to her.

'What are you doing?' Winifred said.

'It's not been years or anything — just the last few weeks. The first time, I went to the river and made some sketches. I love drawing birds but they aren't easy because they move. At the river you can get them floating or standing still, so it's a good place to go.'

She toyed with the corner of her napkin. 'Other times, I just went and did some homework.'

Ellie looked at the three women, her eyes landing on Winifred last. 'When I saw you today I was on my way to the train station to go and see an exhibition on bird drawings at different stages of completion.'

Winifred jumped; her eyes blinked, her mouth gaped. For a second, Ellie wondered if she had been wrong about the woman's identity from earlier but something told her she wasn't. She was about to ask if Winifred was okay but a colony of waiters appeared. With brisk efficiency they cleared the plates and the remainder of the pudding and brushed the crumbs off the table.

'What a shame to take the pudding before we finished it,' Amy said as she watched it leave. 'I really liked that. Nothing on a custard, of course, but still very good.'

The waiters came back with small finger bowls of warm water and a large bowl.

'Oh good,' Amy said. 'Perhaps this is the custard course?'

Ellie wasn't sure if Amy was joking, but when the bowl revealed peeled and sliced pineapple, Amy waved it away. The rest ate the pineapple although the leftover slices remained untouched in the centre of the table. Lotty was silent as she ate, watching Ellie, weighing up the facts and balancing them against her opinions. *Why am I here? That was answered easily over sherry, but now ...*

'You are quite a surprising young lady,' Lotty finally said.

Ellie kept her glance moving, her lips bunched, unsure if this was a compliment or the start of a lecture.

'I was certain that you had little about you that I would find interesting. A silly girl who preferred the company of other silly girls and their sporting pursuits.'

Ellie's stomach churned at this description and she blinked fast to keep her eyes from watering.

'Yet I find a clever, capable young woman with a variety of interests who has the ability to attract clever and capable friends. All she requires is the ability to value those qualities.'

Lotty's storm-blue eyes never left Ellie's face. They analysed the tiniest muscle tweak and seemed to know the meaning of the smallest of gestures. Ellie's blush moved down her throat, her lips quivering into an embarrassed smile. She wished there was more on the table to create a distraction.

'As a girl I also enjoyed taking notes and doing sketches, although Alice was a much more dedicated sketcher than I.'

Lotty dipped her fingers into the little bowl, nudging the lemon slice up against the side as she did.

'Frances and I used to search out birds' nests and make a note of the number of eggs and where they were,' she said. 'I recall being about your age when we found a new robin's nest with four warm eggs in it. We were quite surprised as it was September.'

Lotty paused, remembering all the times that she and her sister had wandered through meadows looking for flowers, birds and insects.

'I always loved writing,' Lotty said, her voice soft for a moment. 'Words can be so interesting, do you not think? There are occasions when drawing is more appropriate, though. When I was twelve, I asked to be permitted to study church architecture, so Mamma arranged for me to read *Bloxham's Handbook of Gothic Architecture* in the school room.'

Her governess's pretty face appeared before Lotty. The patient smile, as they looked at drawings of architecture and Lotty read aloud passages from the books. *Dear Miss Mitchell did not have any interest in the subject but she patiently endured.* Lotty looked at Ellie again.

'What you require is passion.'

———

Sitting in that room, surrounded by the flow of history, Lotty's words didn't sound out of place.

Ellie looked at the three women. *Did they all have 'passion'?* She wasn't sure. *Ambition, determination, yeah. But passion? Seemed a bit of an exaggeration ... Another Mum word creeping into my language: 'Don't exaggerate: you don't* need *that top, you want it.'* But Lotty's statement clung on, like a person's perfume after they have left a room. *Do I have passion?*

It had a vintage chime to it. *Do I need passion?* Ellie wasn't convinced.

'Yeah, but ...' Ellie paused, unsure whether she wanted to sound like she was contradicting Lotty. 'I enjoy tennis but it doesn't mean I am good at it.'

'We are not talking about tennis,' Lotty said. 'I was referring to exerting yourself in *subjects* that you are passionate about.'

Ellie took another deep breath. 'Yeah, I get that but just because you are ... passionate about something doesn't mean you are going to be good at it.'

Ellie looked up from her lap and caught Winifred's eye.

'Very true, darling,' Winifred said with a smile. 'I was never very good at playing cards although I did enjoy it. What I believe Lotty is trying to say is —'

Lotty frowned. *Trying, indeed.*

'Do not assume that you can only be passionate about things you are naturally good at,' Lotty said. 'There is always hard work that is required in order to achieve high standards. As William Shakespeare's Ophelia says, "We know what we are, but know not what we may be".'

Lotty allowed a pause for the others to consider this point. Amy nodded in agreement and leaned forward so Lotty hurriedly continued, 'My brother, Sambrooke, understood that just in time to pass his exams at a second sitting when at Magdalen College. He was no scholar, of course. If rowing had been a subject he would have achieved the highest awards.'

She chuckled and, in her good humour, patted Ellie's hand.

'No, my dear, having natural talent will not be enough, you must challenge yourself to excel. There were many people within my acquaintance who had natural talent yet never applied it, male and female.

'I was fortunate to have a mother who encouraged my writing and interests despite having little interest in folklore herself. I dedicated my life to the pursuit of folklore and found it deeply fulfilling; however, it came with its own sacrifices.'

Lotty glanced at Amy. She was still leaning forward, tapping a finger to her lips as she listened.

'I was always very fond of children,' Lotty said. Amy sat up and tilted her head as if considering this.

'I was,' Lotty said earnestly. 'I would happily entertain my nieces and nephews with stories and play games with them. I would often use stories that Frances had made up when she was younger. She had been such an excellent storyteller.'

She paused. 'I did enjoy having my nieces and nephews to stay when they were involved in studies. They were so interesting to have about. So enthusiastic and energetic.'

'Words often used about puppies, too,' Amy said with a wry smile.

'They are not for everyone, however,' Lotty said.

'Also true for puppies,' Amy said.

'Both also have a clever habit of being able to find their way back home,' Lotty said, smiling as much at her joke as at the surprise on Amy's face. Then with a short laugh added, 'Sambrooke once bought his three to visit when Mamma's sisters, Atty and Emily, were visiting us.'

'Puppies?' Ellie said in confusion.

'No,' Lotty chuckled, 'boys…The aunts were quite progressed in years by then and Aunt Emily looked at the boys as if they were vipers. They both declared them very plain. They were unused to children and their ways, of course.'

Lotty paused and recollected her thread. 'My dedication to collecting stories, the travel involved and the time required to write them down and search them out meant that I did not have the time for such family considerations.'

She held Winifred's eye as she said, 'It would have been a very understanding husband indeed who would have allowed his wife to seek such an existence when there was a household to run.'

Amy raised an eyebrow.

'There were such unions. My friends Mr and Mrs Gommes, perhaps, would be an example of such a husband and wife. However —'

'So you never met anybody you wanted to marry?' Amy said.

'No, I was perfectly content without such distractions.'

Amy frowned. Lotty could feel her scepticism from across the table.

'You yourself referred to marriage as unlucky.'

'No, I said I was unlucky to marry. That's different.'

'Indeed. Nevertheless, you managed to have a successful life without the distraction of marriage. My family did not have a strong affinity with the state of marriage; the majority of my aunts remained spinsters their entire lives.'

She leaned forward still looking at Amy, 'And happy and fulfilled lives they were, too. One could surmise that to be happy in marriage was lucky.' She chuckled and watched Amy smile back but then sighed.

'My papa was funny and kind,' she said, 'but was particularly fond of hunting and shooting. His behaviour was quite a burden on Mamma. They had a marriage of love but not always of happiness.'

Lotty paused, recalling the silences that had hung over most of her life when it came to her father. Small mysteries such as the inheritance of Loynton, her Burne aunts' dismissive attitude to her mamma, and Papa's accidents, had only become clearer as she grew older.

'Even more unlucky are those who indulge in activities only meant for those with a marriage bed.'

Ellie choked on the water she had been sipping. Lotty glanced at her but carried on, 'It was 1874 and we were still living at Summerhill in Edgmond. I remember it quite clearly as it was our last winter there. I had a terrible cough and had sent Elizabeth, our maid, for some linseed. She had taken so long about it that Miss Roessel, Alice and Agatha's governess, and I went in search of her. We were standing in the kitchen when Elizabeth came down and unlocked the back door and out appeared one of our maids, Anne, looking dazed and caught.'

Lotty looked at the women sitting around her. The kitchen had still been warm from the oven but everything had been in darkness and so quiet that the click of the key had echoed across the scrubbed tiled floor. Against the light of her candle, Anne had seemed ghost-like, her blonde hair a dishevelled halo, her blouse hastily pushed into her skirt.

'Lovers, I thought, and went to look, more for the satisfaction of knowing than anything else.'

'I'm sure,' Amy said.

Lotty glanced at her. Amy looked innocently back.

'There was a man in the laundry, who said when I asked him who he was: "a friend".'

Lotty's eyes glittered and she felt the same adrenaline she had experienced when she had written the details to Frances, too ill to be moved from Loynton but well enough, at that point, to correspond.

'Then he added that he was John Bailey and came from Stafford. I ordered him off the premises. He was sober enough to know I was a lady, and spoke civilly.'

'What happened to Anne?' Ellie said.

'Of course she was sent away.'

'You fired her for that?' Amy said.

Lotty sat taller and raised her chin, 'At the time, being locked up with a man after prayers was a very bad thing indeed. But who was the accomplice who locked the kitchen door? We never did discover.'

They fell silent, each analysing the story and coming to different conclusions. Ellie wanted to ask what had happened to the girl. But she wasn't sure she wanted to know, even if Lotty was able to offer an answer. The silence was interrupted by the clink of cups. Two waiters appeared and cups with saucers, spoons and a plate of small chocolates were carefully put in the appropriate places. A large pot of coffee circled the table, followed by sugar and milk.

Ellie didn't mind tea but coffee she had always found too bitter. Unlike her mum, who was permanently attached to a coffee cup, with almost worshipful views of the murky brown stuff.

'Could I ... do you have any mint tea?' she asked.

The waiter nodded as if he had expected this question and produced a teapot. He stood between Ellie and Lotty as he placed the teapot, with delicate blue birds floating around it, on the table. He slid out of Ellie's view but she could still feel him near her. She reached for the teapot, hesitated, and looked around. Just behind her, standing perfectly still was the waiter. Lotty sat absolutely still as well, her face turned down to her plate, her cheeks turning redder with every passing breath. Ellie looked again and realised that the waiter's sleeve was caught in Lotty's hair bun. She looked at Amy and Winifred, who were talking and hadn't noticed. Ellie hopped up.

'Let me help,' she said and reached for the sleeve. As she stretched out her hand, her fingers went through the material. Ellie shook her head, feeling slightly dizzy from the sensation, and tried again; but the sleeve came free and the waiter hurried out.

'I am much obliged,' Lotty said.

Ellie sat down, unsure whether she had done anything, and concentrated on pouring her tea, but her hand shook a little and she put the teapot down with only half a cup poured.

The silence grew and then Amy struck, 'I guess, never having had love yourself, it is hard to understand why anybody would do such risky things for it.'

Amy stirred milk into her coffee and reached for the sugar cubes. It took Ellie a moment to realise Amy was talking about Lotty's maid in the kitchen.

'The presumption that I never loved because I never married does you no credit, Mrs Mello. Indeed, my heart was as capable of being turned by a gentle face and kind manners as any other lady's.'

Lotty paused, not wanting to dissect her heart. *Mr Vallings. How often I have thought of him during this dinner.* Ellie caught Winifred giving Amy a look.

'Is that right?' Amy said, still stirring her coffee. 'Who was the man with a gentle face and kind manners? A Mr Vallings, maybe?'

Lotty looked at her in surprise.

'You mentioned him earlier. I wondered.'

Lotty sighed inwardly. *How foolish I am.*

'He married ... the daughter of an acquaintance of our Goodlad aunts. They met ... they met when he was visiting us in Ilfracombe. Of course, I did not know at the time that there was a mutual interest; I discovered it later, quite by accident.'

A mahogany table, paper laid out on it, black words marking the creaminess of it, took Lotty back to 1879. When she had found out that he was writing to Miss Chanter. When she had known for certain that his heart lay elsewhere.

Barely aware that she was speaking out loud she began to recite a poem she knew well.

> '"I hold a letter from my love; writ by his own dear hand;
> how fair upon the shining page; his characters here stand.
> But not for me, oh, not for me; for other eyes t'was meant;
> his playful wit; his gentle heart; on others were intent.
> No thought of me, no thought of me; in his regrets finds place;
> in all these kindly friendly words; nought of myself I trace.
> Hush. Hush, proud heart.'"

'That's beautiful,' Winifred said. 'Who wrote it?'

'I did,' Lotty said. She smiled sadly. 'Silly, really, to have thought it could have been anything more, however I hoped at one point it might be.'

She brightened at a memory. 'I visited my brothers at Oxford for a couple of days and Jim was good enough to find some time to spend with us. He had not been sure if he would have time, but in the end he took tea with us. Sambrooke said it was a great dissipation but I enjoyed it.'

The cobbled streets and spires of Oxford and a table laden with gingerbread, sponge cakes and, bread and butter swirled before her.

'Did he mean the tea or the man?' Winifred said.

Ellie frowned, unsure what 'dissipation' meant but not wanting to admit it. Lotty's mind was still in Oxford and she didn't hear Winifred's question.

'After studying, he joined the Church and I would not have suited the life of a vicar's wife. Besides, if he had loved me, I am sure he would have lost what I held dearest: his dignity of mind.'

She smiled and everyone smiled back, all of them trying to soften the moment. Ellie blew on her mint tea and the noise of her slurping the tea as she took a tentative sip sounded loud in the quiet of the room.

'Sorry,' Ellie said. 'It was hotter than I thought.'

No one seemed to mind; Lotty didn't seem to have even noticed.

'Only a fool would have swallowed it,' Winifred said.

Lotty jerked at the phrase. *Strange to hear my own family quotations spoken by future generations.*

'Were you ever prescribed spectacles, Winifred?' Lotty said.

Winifred looked surprised for a moment but answered without any hesitation: 'Yes, although not until much later in life. I must have been almost seventy when I finally decided I needed them.'

Lotty waved her hand at this. 'Seventy! Why, many people I knew did not live to see such an age. And seventy does not count as needing spectacles. That is a simple conclusion of old age.'

Ellie watched Winifred raise her coffee cup to her mouth, the small hint of a smile escaping behind the barrier. Lotty turned to Amy next.

'Did you require spectacles at a young age, Mrs Mello?'

'No of course not. I had excellent eyesight.'

'Mmmm. I imagine factory work does not strain the eyes.'

Ellie winced but Amy didn't seem to notice the comment.

'I was provided with spectacles and told to rest my eyes in 1881, when I was barely in my thirties.' Lotty turned those same eyes on Ellie now. 'It was due to the book, of course. Writing and reading late at night with nothing but candlelight put too much strain on my eyes.'

She went to take a sip of coffee, noticed the colour and put the cup down.

'However, if I had not been prepared to do this,' she continued, stirring some more milk into her cup, 'the book might never have been written. It did give me such headaches, though. Some days I could not leave my bed or would spend my time on the sofa flat on my back. That is why Mamma insisted I go to an occultist.'

Lotty tried her coffee again and allowed herself a moment to enjoy the assault of bitter smoothness.

'To rest my eyes, however,' she said, 'was not a feasible option, for Miss Jackson was relying on my industry being, herself, gravely ill and unable to undertake the task. So I was anxious to produce the complete manuscript; and although I grieved at the end of the interest of so many years, I was thankful that she whose brain projected the work was spared and saw it completed ...'

Ellie took a braver sip of her tea and watched the light from the three candles in the candelabra dance across the tablecloth. It had been put at Ellie's end of the oval table but even with its proximity it would be almost impossible to read in this light. Ellie was still thinking on this as she began to register what Lotty was saying.

'I was also never particularly devout. That might have been a hindrance to being a vicar's wife: not truly believing.'

Ellie smiled even though she wasn't sure if Lotty had meant it as a joke.

'When your family are unquestioning of the importance of church and attend regardless of any inconvenience, my own doubts made me stand out from them,' she said. 'I went to church, of course. And would even say prayers. Yet over time I did not find the same consolation in believing in His will.'

Ellie squinted into the fading light; she could see Lotty's eye's reflecting the candles' glow as she continued to expound.

'We discussed earlier the enduring nature of folklore in the world we experience, yet folklore offers more than just murky glimpses of the past. Its source is to be found in the first crude attempts of mankind to account for the wonders of Creation. The originators of folklore were, in fact, the first natural philosophers.'

Lotty leaned forward as she spoke, the animation increasing in her voice. 'Their many inconsistent theories, accepted then as facts, are the foundation of an unwieldy structure to which the history, circumstances and habits of life of each individual nation have made continual alterations.'

Ellie rested an arm on the table, her head turned sideways as she tried to keep up with what Lotty was saying.

'The introduction of Christianity has been the greatest of these later influences, as we discussed, with the natural death of the belief in fairies and goblins. Herein was my struggle,' she said, almost in a cry.

'For good or ill, the main endeavour of the Church was whenever possible to turn heathen customs to Christian uses; to give them a new meaning, rather than utterly destroy them.'

A quote came to Lotty from the depths of her knowledge and she eagerly carried on.

'"You cannot cut off everything at once from rough natures", wrote Gregory the Great,' she said. 'He desired that the heathen temples were consecrated to Christian worship and that festivals in honour of the saints held around them in place of idol-feasts.'

Lotty leaned back from the table, her posture once again resuming its upright position. The movement allowed Ellie to catch the now familiar scent of body odour and, involuntarily, she moved away.

'Despite my family connections to the Church, the knowledge I gained simply created more questions, as it is wont to do,' Lotty said. 'My extensive knowledge of history and the origins of such concepts as Christianity reduced my conviction and I felt a divide, albeit a silent one, between myself and my family. If I had not found a purpose I so enjoyed, it might have been too great a compromise.'

'How did you —' Ellie began, but Lotty was already talking again and she picked up her teacup pretending she hadn't wanted to say anything in the first place. Amy caught her eye and they shared a smile.

'And then came a rather unpleasant experience with our clergyman in Eccleshall, Mr Allen,' Lotty said. 'He started such a feud with Mamma and put about lies and false accusations that were most upsetting. He was a wicked man and acted in quite an infra dig manner for one in his position.' *And his daughters were incredibly vulgar.*

'That experience leads me to agree with you, Winifred, when you say that the most Christian people can behave in the least Christian way.'

Winifred looked startled and a little uncomfortable. Lotty took a sip of coffee, unaware of Winifred's silence, and began speaking again before the cup was resting back on its saucer.

'When we remember that the Egyptians abstained from work on the seventh day for fear of ill luck, we cannot venture to blame Pope Gregory.'

She smiled at this remark and received a smile back from Ellie.

'But to this day we see the effects of the policy which he and other Fathers of the Church before and after him pursued, in the sometimes foolish, sometimes pleasing and poetical, customs connected with Church festivals adapted from the old pagan ceremonies for Christian use. When you analyse the evidence of the origins of Christianity, it is not easy to sit that against unquestioning faith.'

She took in all the faces around her but didn't notice their reactions. She had always loved moments like these, sharing and debating the stories and history of folklore. *Dining always lends itself so well to such discussions.* She realised she had been reciting the words she had written in her book, as if she was no longer in this strange room with strangers but sharing her work with family and friends. *Words procured through extensive reading and collecting, no less.* The thought took her to her writing desk, looking out over fields, disconnected from the household sounds and movements around her, fully absorbed in a text or letter.

'Take today,' Lotty said.

'Halloween?' Ellie said.

'No, Wednesday. Before it was translated to English, Wednesday in Anglo-Saxon was pronounced "Woden's Day", that is the Day of Woden.'

The sudden feeling of dreadful satisfaction she had had when she had first read *Northern Antiquities* washed over her and the myths of the ancient world sprang up in her mind.

'After all, Woden, the victory bringer, the war god,' Lotty said, 'is the supreme god of our heathen forefathers. In his original character as the Teutonic representative of the universal storm god, he rides on the blasting wind and scatters clouds as a victorious general.'

Her hand flew through the air as if impersonating Woden, a jewelled-sparkle of light flowed from her fingers. 'Then the storm sinks to rest – yet the storm god is not dead but sleeping; he will return.'

She said these last words slowly to emphasise them. Winifred shifted in her chair.

'Stories such as that of Woden,' Winifred said, 'is just that: a story from ancient times when people were trying to understand natural phenomena like storms.'

Lotty leaned forward savouring the promise of a debate and fixed her gaze on Winifred.

'And yet, when all is said, the steadfast searching for a deliverer is so deeply rooted in the traditions of every nation that the story of Woden can hardly be regarded as a myth about nature,' she said.

'On the other hand –,' Winifred said.

'Remember,' Lotty said, too engrossed in her argument to stop, 'how the promise of the Great Deliverer was given ere the gates of Eden closed on our first parents and that their descendants have everywhere carried with them the knowledge of how He hideth His face for a season and shall one day come again.'

Lotty stopped as if coming up for breath. She radiated satisfaction, pleased at the delivery of her argument.

'History can uncover the journey of our beliefs just as melting snow reveals the grass underneath,' she said as she carefully topped up her coffee, which was beginning to go cold. 'No, no. I would not have been suited to a vicarage.' She said this as a murmur as she watched her spoon swirl milk into the coffee.

Ellie had listened closely. It hadn't been easy to understand everything Lotty had said; her way of talking was elaborate and strange to listen to. But the sentiment had been felt. It was only now, in the pause, that Ellie noticed the strained silence. Amy reached for the plate of chocolate truffles and put two on her saucer. She passed it to Winifred, who shook her head. Lotty's jewelled hand reached for the plate as it swung back in her direction.

'It is quite a decadence to have chocolate of high quality,' she said. She held the chocolate truffle for a moment in admiration. 'We cooked and baked often at home. We always had Seville orange marmalade as well as jams. Preparing the fruit, especially the oranges, was one of dear France's tasks but later the responsibility fell to me. We would spend a full day cutting the fruit, stewing it and pouring the mixture into jars. Chocolate, however, was not something we ate.'

The noise of Birmingham's streets came to Lotty's mind.

'I recall that there was a firm called Cadbury's in Birmingham who sold tea, coffee and cocoa and then later, I believe, concentrated on just chocolate.'

'Cadbury's is every–,' Ellie said.

'On occasion, normally near Valentine's Day we might purchase a tray of chocolate for Mamma,' Lotty said, too absorbed in nostalgia to hear Ellie.

'This must have been after 1869, when poor Mamma was confined to a chair, unable to move without assistance due to her illness. She would protest that the chocolates were an unnecessary expense but Frances and I were in agreement that the trays of chocolate were a well-deserved treat.'

Lotty turned the truffle over in her hand, admiring its crumpled folds of chocolate, and then, delicately bit into it. She passed the plate of chocolates to Ellie, who took one and immediately popped it into her mouth.

They tasted different to the ones her mum would buy at Christmas or on a whim. Those ones tended to come in a variety of shapes and flavours. Ellie's favourite was a square one with a crunchy chocolate shell and smooth caramel inside. These were hard balls of dark chocolate with the bitter strong flavour of dark chocolate.

'I ran a candy store in Bermuda,' Amy said. 'They used to sell all sorts of candy and chocolate bars, and at Christmas I'd give the lady who did my ironing a box of candy. Puffs always reminded me of her.'

'How so? Were hers often dirty?' Lotty said.

'What?'

'Why did they remind you of your ironing lady?'

''Cause she loved them. She would be happy with just the traditional peppermint, y'know. But she also liked the different-coloured ones.'

'Different-coloured? She would have different-coloured ones?'

'Well, yeah, sometimes.'

'And this did not look odd?'

'Look odd? No, lots of people chose the assorted ones.'

'For their blouses?'

'What about their blouses?'

'You said cuffs always reminded me of her.'

'What? *Puffs.*'

'Puffs of what?'

Amy exhaled.

'I do not need a demonstration, Mrs Mello. I am quite aware of the definition of a puff of air.'

'They're candy,' Amy said.

'Puffs of air are candy?'

'No, I mean puffs are a type of candy. They look like —'

Winifred, who had been staring into her coffee cup, suddenly interjected, 'On the other hand, I was always very supportive of the Church and the good works that it does.'

Everyone stopped and Ellie saw the same look of surprise etched on Lotty and Amy's faces.

'We attended church every Sunday as children and I kept that up throughout my adult life. It was not just an opportunity for reflection and humility but also an important lifeline for a rural community to come together and support each other.'

She let the hold on her coffee cup lessen and said, as if to lighten her tone, 'Even so, in 1943, when I was engaged to John, I received a wonderful religious New Year card and suspected someone thought I needed reforming.'

'And did you?' Lotty said.

'I did not think so.'

'Are we the best judges of ourselves, do you think?' Lotty said.

'Some would argue that only God can judge.'

Lotty didn't reply and Winifred continued, 'I saw for myself the wonder and delight children and adults took in celebrating the Christian festivities when I organised my church's first Christingle service. There was a magic to it and a kind message of love, inclusion and hope.'

As she spoke, faint colour rose to her cheeks and Ellie wondered if Winifred was embarrassed by her little outburst. As if aware of this speculation, Winifred hesitated before speaking with careful emphasis.

'The Church Family provides help to people in times of need; not always financial, of course, but food deliveries, visits, assisting the bereaved with funerals, or on happier occasions, weddings and baptisms.'

Ellie reached for her second chocolate truffle. 'My mum says Christianity prays on the vulnerable and that you can find religion behind any war or atrocity,' she said. She wondered where that interjection had come from and put the truffle on her saucer, but Lotty smiled at her.

'I do not disagree with you, Winifred, that the work of the Church is meant to be that of good,' Lotty said. 'The Girls Friendly Society, which I was much involved with, was an organisation set up with the support of the Church.'

She sipped her coffee.

'No, I spoke merely of the origins of Christianity,' she continued, 'and the foundation that that faith is based upon and mention it now to make the point that in order to succeed at one's passion, there may be unforeseen sacrifices to face,' she said.

'I could not satisfy my desire for knowledge, even that which others might not wish to know. However,' she chuckled, 'there is solace for me: as Shakespeare says, "ignorance is the curse of God; knowledge is the wing wherewith we fly to heaven".

'I chose a different path that did not allow for the social conventions of marriage and children due to the demands of writing and Folklore Society council meetings. I deemed it worth those sacrifices.'

She turned her steely gaze on Ellie, 'That is what you must understand, Ellie: regardless of what you choose to pursue there will be sacrifices. But things sacrificed in the pursuit of a passion will never give you cause for regret. That is why I say you must find *your* passion.'

'There's no catching trout with dry breeches.' Three faces looked blankly at Amy.

'A Portuguese saying. It means things worth having aren't always easy or without sacrifice.'

Lotty's hand twitched, desperate to be holding a notebook and pen.

Mrs Mello must have many beliefs and tales to share, even if she doesn't realise it.

'I could not have put it better myself,' Lotty said.

WINIFRED AND ELLIE

Who would have thought that of all of us, it would be Lotty who would break through? In some ways I am not surprised. My father-in-law always spoke fondly of her and of the help she had given him. And she didn't stop at him. She paid for his sisters' education, housed Agatha's eldest when she was training for her medical doctorate in 1907, and Rachel even travelled from Canada to look after her in those last months. She might seem haughty, condescending and imperious but she also attracts huge loyalty.

But did she have to bring up the subject of religion? Basic dinner rules: don't talk about religion, politics or money. Never mind, Ellie didn't seem to care. Nice to see how relaxed she looks now. Her arms aren't crossed anymore and she makes eye contact and smiles. A transformation.

And yet ... There was something strange about Lotty's behaviour over dinner. If I was being unkind I would call it erratic.

Winifred studied Lotty for a moment until Lotty caught her eye and smiled at her. *Probably just my imagination. At any rate, I am very glad the meal is ending in a much better place than I thought it might. After those moments earlier, I did not think I would be up to the task. Such negative energy. Why? Where did it come from? And now such calm and warmth. What changed?*

Winifred glanced again at Lotty trying to be subtler in her eye contact. Her eyes flicked over Lotty's face to the high-necked bodice with its lace collar and large pearl pendant. The bodice itself was blue velvet, decorated with sequins. It was so dark, the blue looked black and only the glossy shine of it revealed its true colour. Even though it was of higher quality than anything Winifred had ever worn, it reminded her of another velvet dress. Her eyes rested on the velvet but her mind was on a journey taken decades ago: the outward trip filled with excitement and hope, the return route shrouded in misery and sorrow. She shook her head to bring her back. *Strange, the little things that can set me off.*

It hadn't been a lie to say that education had given her a way out. But that hadn't been the full extent of it. After all, she left the nursing profession within three years of qualifying. School had given her a release; a distraction from the deprivations of home and a noise against the silence.

She watched her great-granddaughter and tried to remove the tentacles of worry from her mind.

This is going better than I thought. But will it be enough? What else can I do?

Winifred took in Ellie's features and mannerisms in a way that she hadn't before. *I wonder how much she resembles her mother when she was this age.* From Ellie's current age onwards, Winifred's memories of her granddaughter were hazy. She knew she must have seen her, and recalled a family dinner when she was still living in her home in Dartford, but it was a blurry memory. With some effort, Winifred realised she had been asked a question. Her hand adjusted her necklace as she blinked the room back into focus.

'I'm so sorry. I missed what you asked,' she said.

'What brought you to nursing?' Amy repeated. 'I'm curious. Lotty's road to writing and folklore could be put down as much to chance as circumstances.'

Winifred glanced across the table as Lotty made a noise that sounded like the beginnings of a refute, but stopped herself mid-word.

'Ellie was just saying,' Amy continued, 'she didn't have a passion and I was telling her that sometimes it doesn't hit you. You've got to remember that what you are interested in at fourteen isn't necessarily what you enjoy at thirty-three. So, did you always want to be a nurse?'

Winifred thought about the trudge through snow to school, collecting water from the stream behind the farmhouse, the dampness and cold. But there were things she later missed: the smell of pies mingled with baked bread, the smoky reassurance of the parlour, the calves' puddle-brown eyes and soft muzzles, the bottomless source of laughter that was her mam.

'No, I did not always think to be a nurse. That came out of the subjects I found I enjoyed the most. It seemed a good choice and my uncle was able to assist in finding me a place to start training, which was a great help in deciding the route.'

'Why did it seem right?' Amy said.

'Oh ... I suppose because of ... being on the farm. Animals getting sick ...'

'Then why not be a vet?' Ellie said.

That wasn't an option for most women back in the 1930s,' Winifred said.

'Now look,' Amy said, 'it was hard to do things out of the ordinary back then, for sure. But it could be done. You just had to want it enough.'

'And have the right opportunities present themselves,' Winifred added, hearing the sharpness in her voice but not caring. Kathleen had been as smart as her. Everyone had said so. And probably more talented. "Her singing voice could charm angels", their Uncle Jack had said more than once. If not for being the firstborn and family circumstances, she might have been the one carving a life away from servitude and ... *him*. Winifred was aware of Lotty's stare; it felt unblinking and all-seeing.

'We tried to avoid paying the fees for a veterinary surgeon,' Lotty said, 'preferring to use home-created remedies, our own knowledge. Of course, when cattle plague struck it did require us to rely on external expertise, for all the good it did, as we still lost several cows over the years. A big blow given that we relied on the heifers for their milk, butter and cheese.'

No one said anything to this. Winifred looked again at the fine velvet. Ellie poured some more mint tea. She wasn't that thirsty and the tea looked much stronger than before but she wanted something to do against the awkwardness.

'Mmm, all relative I suppose,' Amy said. 'So Winifred, what was it about nursing? And don't say it was the easiest path, as you don't strike me as the type.'

Winifred smiled and swirled her coffee cup watching the coffee grains dance in the small pool of water.

'That is kind of you, but ...'

Ellie leaned one elbow on the table and stifled a yawn. She felt full and the room felt warm. She licked her finger and collected the chocolate crumbs that had fallen from the truffles and settled on the tablecloth. The women's chat was a gentle background buzz.

'Come, come, Winifred, do not be coy,' Lotty said. 'There was a greater meaning to it. I can tell from your reluctance that there was.'

'I can assure you —'

A loud hiss caused Winifred to pause and then Ellie shouted.

The dark shape thudded against the window. The noise of the collision was followed by scraping and scratching just below the windowsill.

Ellie instinctively ducked. Lotty cried out, her hands clasped at her chest.

'What was that?' Amy said, so alarmed it came out as a shout.

Winifred jumped up and stepped up to the window. Amy moved her chair and tried to peer out of the window without having to stand up while Lotty sat still, her hands still clasped together. Ellie swivelled out of her chair, her sleepiness and inertia forgotten. She and Winifred peered into the darkness, looking out onto the small Juliet balcony.

'I think I can make out a shape. A cat, maybe? Or a squirrel?' Winifred said. She went to open the window but Lotty's cry stopped her. Amy was still leaning around in her chair, although it was clear from her position she couldn't see anything beyond the reflection of the room in the window.

'It's hard to tell,' Ellie said, pressing her face against the glass and blocking out the light with her hands. 'I think it's a cat, though. Do cats jump into windows like that? And a first-floor window?'

She turned back to the room, the glow of excitement still radiating. A scuffle and a crackle of branches and the black shape disappeared. Winifred opened the window to listen in case she could hear a noise but it was silent. The cold burst of air that had greeted her now threatened the candles and she shut it, to the relieved exclamations of Amy and Lotty.

'Maybe it missed the balcony railing,' Amy said.

Lotty scoffed and shook her head. 'It was far more likely to have been an unfortunate bird or a squirrel than a cat.'

'But the sound it made. Like a hiss and shriek all at once ...' Ellie said. 'Sounded like a cat.'

'Aren't cats lucky?' Amy said. 'Maybe we should take it as a sign.'

'A sign of what?' Winifred said as she sat down.

'Well, that we are in for good luck.'

'It's just if they're black, I think,' Ellie said.

'The cat – domesticated, yet not tamed – is the subject of many superstitions,' Lotty said, settling herself into the conversation. 'There seems to be a curious diversity of opinion as to the luck of black cats. Black cats seem to be considered lucky possessions from Shropshire as far south as Lincolnshire. But at Ford, Shropshire —'

'Listen,' Ellie said. The noise she had just heard was different to before, less animal-like. A mewling, sad noise which seemed to whisper through the glass pane.

'I don't hear anything,' Winifred said.

'There it is again.' Ellie skittered to the window and peered out even though she knew it was too dark to see anything.

'It was probably the same creature again but further away,' Winifred said. 'There's bound to be a reasonable explanation.'

As she said it, she too heard the noise: a pitiful cry of sorrow and pain. She had heard it before, she was certain, and something began to rise from the deep caves of her memory. Her breath caught and she resisted the urge to tell Ellie, who still peered out into the darkness, to sit down.

'What *is* that?' Ellie said.

Through the reflection in the window she peered at the faces around the table. No one said anything.

'A fox, perhaps. They make strange noises that sound as if from another world,' Winifred said.

'Or a ghost?' Amy said. 'Don't look at me like that, Winifred.' She leaned forward and looked pointedly at Winifred. 'We all have our ghosts lurking nearby.'

Winifred froze and then shook it off. *That is not going to help move this conversation on. I really wish we had discussed our plan for this dinner in more detail: agreed what to say and what to avoid. I would certainly have put discussions about ghosts on the latter list.*

'We wave our farewells from the shore and they depart, and come no more, or come as phantoms and as ghosts,' Lotty said. 'Mmmm, discontented ghosts. I mentioned that even as I wrote *Shropshire Folklore* there were areas of Shropshire where poor children, and sometimes men, would go souling for a dole of cake, ale, apples or money. There were other practices preserved by Christian nations, too – France, Austria, Germany – where the belief still held in ghosts roaming on this evening, Hallow'een.'

Ellie stepped back from the window.

'Observe, for instance, Tyrol,' Lotty said, 'where the poor

souls released from purgatory's fires for the night have cakes left for them on the table and the room is kept warm for their comfort. In Brittany, a supper must be left for the souls to come and take their part.'

Winifred could feel Ellie standing behind her, her hands gripped the back of her chair.

'And at last,' Lotty continued, 'as the inmates retire to rest, there is heard at the door a doleful chanting – it is the souls, who, borrowing the voices of the parish poor, have come to ask for the prayers of the living.'

Winifred tried to control her annoyance. *This is the sort of superstitious nonsense I would have expected to hear in the parlour of my childhood, not here.* She glanced up at Ellie. Her eyes were wide open, any teenage cynicism left behind by the enthusiasm and elegance of the storyteller.

'Do you think that was a ghost? A cry from a soul?' The question escaped her before she could check it. Lotty smiled but Winifred cut in.

'No, darling. Of course not,' she said with more conviction than she felt. 'Such practices were ways for people to make sense of their worlds and tales to tell children to make them behave.' She held the edge of the table to stop the shake of her hand.

'But you can't tell me there are no such things as ghosts,' Ellie said.

'Well ... not the types who come knocking at your door asking for food,' Winifred said.

Amy gave a loud laugh that ended in a partial snort and said, 'As interesting as it is to speculate on the different types of ghosts there might be, let's just agree that it was probably a squirrel.'

A branch scratched at the window. Ellie let out a cry and jumped back to her seat. *Oh God, that was too dumb. So embarrassing.*

'Shush, Orian. Stop rattling that grate,' Winifred said.

Ellie shot her a look, too surprised to feel embarrassed any longer. Winifred's face took on a strange, angry look and her voice was pitched like that of an irritated child.

'It was not the grate, Winifred,' Lotty said, 'Nothing but a branch scratching at the window.' Winifred stared at her hands, wondering what had just happened.

'I am so sorry. How foolish of me. Too many ghost stories.' She smiled and twisted her necklace.

'It was super-spooky. But Mum says I have a vivid imagination,' Ellie said, still thinking of her reaction to the branch. Lotty's hand covered her own for a moment.

'I always said it was my sister who was the leader in make-believe,' she said.

'Now look, make-believe or not, I think we've had enough of superstitious tales for one evening,' Amy said. Her face had paled a little.

'Besides, I am sure it was a squirrel,' she continued. 'Y'know, I missed squirrels when I went back to Bermuda. There weren't any there, but plenty in America. Even in the cities. You'd see 'em scurrying about, always doing something. Such fun animals.'

A small memory bubbled inside Ellie. 'My granny has red ones at the cottage that are really cute.'

Winifred smiled at Amy. *Good. Getting back to safer ground.*

'Winifred, the excitement is over and I still want to hear about you,' Amy said.

Ah, not so safe. Amy jabbed her forefinger towards Winifred. 'You can't be silent forever.'

Winifred watched Amy's finger move through the air and it felt like she was slicing away the warmth with every action. *I disagree. I was silent for a lifetime.*

———

That silence had kept Winifred safe from well-aimed questions and intrusive curiosity. Few people had broken the seal, even John. *It was better that way.* She toyed with her necklace, feeling her hand steady with every twist. *And safer.*

But the sad, moaning noise wouldn't leave her and slowly the memories that had sunk and been covered for so many years began to rise until before her stood her dad. She had few early memories of him: a kind man with a smile that everyone said she had inherited. What childhood memories and knowledge she did have, her mam had given her.

A dad who was good with horses. A dad who loved his children. A dad who had wanted to have a large family to replace the orphaned only-child upbringing he had had. Never did he want *his* children to sit at a train station at four years old with only a little chair as a keepsake of the parents and grandparents who had loved them. He had wanted the best for them. That is what Mam had always said.

Winifred had batted away questions about her family all her life. She was good at redirecting the conversation, encouraging others to speak. She knew she had taken refuge in John's enthusiasm to tell stories. It ensured she didn't have to. But now, as she looked at Ellie, the strange, negative sensations that had been mingling on the edges of the evening seemed to close in once more.

That pitiful noise. Is that what made me shout out like that about Orian? Where had that fear and anger come from? Perhaps it is time to tell what I remember. How can we gain her trust if we do not share some of our own secrets? Perhaps it will keep the ghosts at bay.

Winifred took a deep breath and found herself back in 1925, in the depths of childhood and in an experience that she had never allowed to be re-lived. Until now.

Winifred held tight to the doll Uncle Jack had given her. It was the first, and only, doll she had ever had, and even though she was beginning to lose the stuffing in her left leg and her hair was now a bird's nest of blonde string, Winifred still loved her. Kathleen had laughed when she saw Winifred clutching Gwen against her chest.

'Let's brush Gwen's hair, then. She looks too messy to go to town,' she said, a smile of gentle mockery twitching at her lips. Winifred had just held onto Gwen tighter.

'Let her be, Kathleen,' Mam said. 'It'll be a long day; if the doll helps her, let her have it.'

Maggie smiled at Winifred. Orian skipped out of the front door, shouting for them to wait. She stumbled on a small patch of ice and landed on her knees.

'It's fine Mam, I didn't tear my stockings,' Orian said, crouching to check. She wiped her hand across her face leaving a small smear of mud on her cheek. Kathleen walked over to Orian and, in a gesture that mimicked her mother's, rubbed the mud off her younger sister's cheek.

'Aye, can't have the smart folk of Talgarth thinking us scruffy,' she said.

Maggie smiled at the comment that was clearly parroted from adult conversations. Winifred smoothed her dress for no reason other than to feel the soft velvet. It was a beautiful rich red colour and she had never had anything like it before. Her Aunt Catherine had posted dresses and new stockings for this occasion. Mam had read out her card to them over supper.

'Dear Maggie, I hope you are all well. We thought the girls would like to wear something nice for the trip. It may make the whole thing nicer and less ...' Her mam's voice trailed off.

'Less what, Mam?' Orian had asked.

Kathleen moved around and read the card over Maggie's shoulder. Her lips moved as she read but she didn't say what was written.

'Nothing important,' Mam said to Orian and Winifred with a smile. She had patted Kathleen's hand and suggested that they go and try on their new outfits.

And now, today, Winifred was finally allowed to wear the dress. And go on a bus. And see Daddy. Butterflies fluttered in her stomach. It had been a long time. He had missed her birthday and Christmas, but Mam said he couldn't visit at the moment. *Maybe he will have a present for me.* Maggie adjusted the sling and kissed the baby's head. Arthur gurgled and waved his hands at his sisters, happy to be involved in the excitement.

'Time to go,' Mam said.

Maggie herded her girls down the lane just as the morning sun began to hit the edges of the fields.

A wail interrupted Winifred's story and the diners all glanced at the window. Ellie swallowed nervously and glanced at the others, Winifred shut her eyes, and for a moment they waited. Nothing else was heard and Winifred's story continued.

The day was cold, the threat of snow lurked in the March air. But the girls ran up the paths, racing each other and shouting at the wind. The purpose of the journey was forgotten in the thrill of being away from school and chores. Maggie followed behind, baby tied to her and grasping a basket filled with food for the visit.

Winifred trotted along next to her older sisters, refusing to fall behind. They walked past her school with its grey slate roof and two second-floor windows that Orian had told her were the school's eyes. A solitary light flickered in one of the windows. In an hour, it would be alive with children's voices and the stove would be surrounded by cold wet boots and coats.

'What are you waving at, darling?' Mam asked.

'Just in case Miss Morgan is looking outside. She knows I won't be there today, doesn't she Mam?'

'Aye, that she does.'

'Oh good, I don't want her thinking I'm late.'

Mam smiled and ruffled Winifred's hair. They walked on.

The sun was gaining height and the birds greeted the morning, echoing the girls' excitement about the day ahead. They were early for the bus and waited for twenty minutes at the bus stop. The warmth was still not in the air yet and Winifred could see her breath. Maggie started a game of I spy to help pass the time, and the girls were allowed to choose between spying for what colour something was (Winifred) or the letter the word began with (Orian and Kathleen).

'I spy with my little eye something that is brown,' Winifred said.

'The road,' Orian shouted.

'Sticks,' Kathleen said.

'Oh wait, no it's not brown it's ... grey,' Winifred said.

'No changes,' Kathleen said.

'No changes! No changes!' Orian said, jumping up and down.

'But it's not fair. It flew off.'

'Doesn't matter!'

'Yes it does – it's not —'

'Girls, mind. The bus is coming,' Maggie said, gathering them next to her.

Happy to be out of the worst of the cold, they clambered on, forgetting their game. There were only a couple of other people on the bus and Maggie nodded and said hello but didn't start talking to them. This seemed strange to Winifred, as Mam talked to everyone.

'We're going to Talgarth to see Daddy,' Winifred told the people.

The two women glanced at Maggie. 'How nice,' one of them said. 'How is he, Maggie?'

'Doing better, I'm sure,' Maggie said.

'Do you know —' Winifred began.

Kathleen nudged her.

'Ow!'

'We don't talk about it,' Kathleen said in a loud hiss.

Winifred rubbed her arm. Ever since Daddy had left, Kathleen had started acting like she was all grown up. Kathleen laid a blanket over her and Winifred's legs and put her arm protectively around her youngest sister. Winifred shrugged off the dead arm and cuddled into Kathleen. She watched the fields and hedges zip by, absorbed in wonder at the sight.

'The bus goes really fast, doesn't it?' she said.

The three older women shared a smile. Maggie unwrapped a parcel of oatcakes and passed them around. A few more people got on the bus and by the time they arrived at their stop, the little bus was full. The family got off and stood for a moment getting their bearings. The town was busy compared to the sleepiness of Beulah. The main road had horses and carts trundling down it, and even a couple of cars. Winifred and Orian followed behind the others, staring at everything.

'Come along, you two,' Maggie called. 'We have to cross here. Daddy's ... staying up this road.'

They left the town behind them, walked across a bridge and headed up a lane that twisted into the hillside. On either side the huddled houses began to be replaced by the more familiar sight of fields and trees. The river copied the path of the road, twisting here and there but following the same course. They came to a turn-off and Maggie stopped. She looked at her three girls, who looked back at her with wide, open faces. Arthur's head drooped in his sleep.

She sighed and smiled at them, 'Now, girls. Don't be sad if Daddy isn't his usual self. He has gone through a very tough time and is very poorly. He may not remember everything, see, or be ... as happy as he has been. We are almost there now so just wanted to remind you. Oh, and no worrying if other people seem a little strange or do odd things. They are also sick, mind, and are being helped by the doctors and nurses.'

She started to walk on and the three girls followed in a row behind her.

'Almost there now.'

Buildings appeared on their right, long rows of low, grey

buildings with slate roofs. A little further on a large building stood alone, imposing itself on the landscape. It was three times as long as her school building, and although only two storeys high, the middle section's peaked roof was topped with a clock tower and weather vane. This ornate pinnacle reminded Winifred of a bishop's hat, a mitre, that she had seen in a picture. It gave the building a sinister feel.

The windows of the second floor looked down on five-year-old Winifred and glowered at her. She stood in front of the stone steps and the large front door and hesitated. *Does this building let people out?*

———

A fire burned in a small grate but gave no warmth to the large hall. The room was poorly lit and the multicoloured floor tiles of grey, black, brown and cream didn't improve the sombre air that hung like an invisible, heavy cloak.

Arthur had woken up and was crying for food as Winifred entered the hall. The noise echoed around the room. Winifred's feet dragged across the tiles and Maggie looked up from the basket, the parcel of biscuits half opened. She smiled distractedly at Winifred as she settled Arthur on her lap and gave him a biscuit. The crying stopped and immediately the hall fell back to its natural silence. Winifred stood in the middle of the hall unsure what to do. She clasped Gwen tight to her chest and half buried her face in the doll's hair. Kathleen caught her eye and patted the wooden bench she was sitting on.

The noise of Winifred's boots pinged around the hall as she dashed across it. She pulled herself onto Kathleen's lap. And waited. Finally, they heard footsteps approaching and the door at the other end of the hall opened. Light framed a woman dressed in a white apron and white hat.

An angel.

The angel walked over to Mam and said a few words. Winifred couldn't hear the whole conversation but certain words drifted across the tiles: 'confused ... his mind ... blank ... the doctor says ... restless.' They meant nothing to Winifred but her mam was clearly listening closely.

Maggie asked the angel a question but the white-capped head shook her head; then she smiled at the three girls and, in a voice that was soft against the harsh surroundings, beckoned them to follow her. They followed without questioning.

Winifred trotted just behind the apparition, trying to keep in step with her. The angel looked down at Winifred. She had a round face, brown eyes that seemed to absorb all of Winifred's fears, and a smile that promised all would be fine. Winifred reached out to take the hand of this safe person.

The angel's mousy-brown hair was curled and clipped back off her face but a strand had broken free just above her ear and she released her hand to tuck it back under the cap. The corridors became less grand, the tiled floors replaced with simple slate ones. She led the family along corridors and through more heavy doors, all the time holding Winifred's hand and talking quietly to her. Her lilting voice added to her charm.

She suddenly stopped outside a wooden door and, taking a set of keys from her belt, unlocked the door and invited them in. The room was sparsely furnished with just a table and some chairs. There was a fireplace but no fire was lit. Winifred's eyes struggled to adjust in the dimness produced by the small amount of light coming in from narrow windows too high even for Mam to look out of properly.

A cloud moved out of the sun's way and more light filtered in as a criss-cross shadow stretched across part of the room. Winifred moved her arm over the shadow, watching the black lines dance on her hand. The angel said a few more whispered words to Maggie and then left.

'Mam, why are there bars on the windows?' Winifred said.

Maggie said nothing. She sat down at the table with Arthur

and focused her attention on keeping him smiling. Kathleen leaned against the wall just by the window, her eyes fixed on the door. Orian climbed onto a chair and sat kicking her legs out in front of her and fiddling with something in her hand.

'I made a card for Daddy, Mam,' she said and waved the crumpled piece of paper.

'I wish I had something for Daddy,' Winifred said, her bottom lip beginning to tremble.

Orian gave her a serious look, looked at her picture and then back at Winifred.

'You can give it with me,' she said. Winifred nodded solemnly and came closer to look at the picture.

Footsteps again: the firm steps of someone familiar with their surroundings. In the shadow of these assertive steps, she could hear a different, shuffling step. And then into the room walked Daddy.

———

He looked around, his face still familiar but his eyes flickering from face to face, not lingering long enough to make contact. His clothes were ones that Winifred hadn't seen before although they looked similar to the overalls and shirts he had left at home. The angel gently guided him to the table. She spoke quietly in the same tone she had used with Winifred.

'Sit down, Pryce. Are you comfortable? Your family has come to see you. That's nice, isn't it?' She looked around the room and smiled at Winifred.

'Daddy, I made you a picture – I mean, me and Winnie made you a picture,' Orian said, and waved the paper again. 'It's got all of us on it together. Look, that's Mam and Arthur and me and Kathy and Winnie, and there's you with Shep.'

Pryce looked at the paper but didn't pick it up or say anything. He just nodded.

'That's pretty, isn't it, Pryce?' the angel said. The picture lay on the table.

Maggie was sitting next to him and he looked from her face to the baby in her lap. A frown grew across his forehead.

'You remember Arthur, don't you darling?' Mam said, holding Arthur up for Pryce to get a better look at. Arthur gurgled away, happy to be centre of attention, and reached across the table for the picture.

'No!' Orian cried. She snatched it up and held it tightly to her chest.

Pryce nodded but he didn't look at Arthur.

'It's good to be home,' he said, looking earnestly at Maggie.

'Oh ... Aye, home is very nice.'

'This isn't home, Daddy,' Orian said.

The angel moved closer to Pryce.

'I think he means he is comfortable here,' she said, looking at Orian.

'Aye,' Maggie said. 'He knows this isn't home, darling.' Orian's lip quivered and she moved to stand close to Maggie and pushed the picture across the table, staring intently at Pryce as she did. Pryce stared at the window without seeming to take it in. Suddenly he let out a low sob and buried his face in his hands. Maggie reached over and put her hand on his back, startling him. He sat up and looked at her.

'I don't want them to famish,' Pryce said, wringing his hands and moving upon his chair as if to stand up. 'I am ruined. Ruined.' He mumbled this over and over until the mumble merged into a pitiful moan.

Maggie held her smile and put her free arm around Orian. She glanced at her oldest daughter standing against the wall, arms across her chest, eyes cloudy and unfocused.

'We won't stay,' Maggie said to the angel.

As if at the sound of her voice, Pryce stopped moving. He looked around in confusion at the faces before him, stopping last on Arthur, who was oblivious to the tension. Arthur stretched a hand towards this unfamiliar face and Pryce let him take one of his fingers. He clasped his father's finger with all his baby strength and for a moment Pryce smiled. Encouraged by this, Winifred moved around the table and grabbed her daddy's arm. He looked down at her and stroked her back.

'Soft as lamb's wool.'

Winnie did a twirl.

'It's new. Special for today,' she said, the pride glowing through her words. 'I wanted to wear it to school but wasn't allowed. Oh, and Daddy, I brought Gwen to show you,' she said, and ran back to where she had dropped the doll on the floor. She dumped Gwen on his lap and stood at his side, waiting for the attention she had once been given so willingly by him.

'She is very nice. Lucky girl.'

'Uncle Jack gave her to me. Look, you can take her dress off and her shoes; but I don't because then she would get cold.'

Pryce nodded and repeated: 'Jack.

'It is good you visited. You're being looked after?' he said to Maggie.

'Don't be worrying yourself about us, mind. We can manage,' Maggie said.

Winifred held his arm and played with his hand, twining her hand through his fingers.

'Daddy, your hands are all dirty. Just like at home,' she said.

'Home?' he said. There was a pause and Winifred realised she was holding her breath without understanding why.

'I help on a farm here,' he said, releasing Winifred.

'What do you do here?' Kathleen said, arms still across her chest and refusing to leave the security of the wall.

'I look after horses, do some field work,' he said. 'No sheep or cows, mind.'

'Why are you working on this farm, Daddy, and not ours?' Winifred said.

'Winnie, dear, I've told you why,' Mam said.

'But ... but ...'

The angel interrupted and said they would have to leave soon.

'Your daddy gets tired quickly,' she said to Winifred. 'But don't worry. We are taking good care of him.'

They all stood to leave and the angel went out of the room to summon an orderly to take Pryce back to his room. Suddenly, Kathleen bolted to him and clung to his waist, her arms wrapped tightly, her head buried in his stomach. He patted her head but didn't say anything. Kathleen bit back tears. Winifred and Orian stood nearby, waiting for Kathleen to move away. The orderly arrived and without any further words Pryce allowed himself to be led out of the room. Maggie slid her hand across the table and, with a deftness that comes with being used to working quickly with your hands, put something in her basket.

'Come along, girls. Time we were leaving,' she said.

'Mam, my picture,' Orian cried, running back to the table. She stopped when she saw the table was clear. 'He must of took it, Mam!' she said, her eyes filled with childish joy.

Maggie smiled and nodded, unable to say anything but thinking of what she had hidden in her basket.

———

No one spoke as they retraced their steps to the entrance. They passed a room in which Winifred could see three men sitting at a table. There were pieces of material stretched out on a table and the men were quiet as they cut and sewed. The scene gave off a peaceful silence.

One of the men looked up from his cutting and saw Winifred peering into the room. The man's face became distorted and he let out a low moan which grew into a yell. He pushed away from the table and clutched at his sides, rocking and yelling, all the time staring at Winifred. A flash of white appeared and a nurse was at the man's side, holding and talking to him.

The nurse rushed out into the corridor and called for an orderly, who rushed in, and together they half carried, half walked the man out of the room, down the corridor and then disappeared behind a large dark door.

Winifred spun around with the realisation that the others hadn't stopped. The corridor was empty, the remaining men had barely missed a stitch and were still focused on their work. A door slammed somewhere and hurried footsteps brought Winifred's angel back. Relief swept away the worry for both of them. The angel knelt down by Winifred and peered into her face.

'Are you all right?'

'A man started yelling.'

The angel glanced into the room.

'Ah, yes. Mr Thompson. He ... gets upset very easily. But he doesn't mean any harm.'

'Is he sick like Daddy is sick?'

'In a way.'

'Will he get better?'

'I hope so.'

'Will you make Daddy better?'

'We are going to do our best.'

'Mam says you should always do your best.'

'Your mam is a very clever lady.'

They walked back into the hall with the multicoloured tiles, small fire and large heavy door. Winifred kept a tight hold of Gwen as she went down the stone steps. At the bottom she turned and waved at her angel.

Only words of necessity were exchanged on the way home. Lunch was eaten waiting for the bus, the bustle of the little town a stream of movement that happened around them, not with them. The familiar paths of their valley were walked without enjoyment. The excitement and novelty of the day was behind them, leaving room only for the sadness of the

UNEXPECTED COMPANIONS

reality. Winifred curled up on the bed she shared with Orian and threw her blanket over her head. She stroked the velvet material of her dress.

'Soft as lamb's wool,' she whispered.

An hour later, Maggie found her asleep, still curled up, and tried to undress her, but she wriggled out of her grip.

'No, Mam, no!' Winifred said, alert even in her sleepiness. 'I don't want to. I want to wear my dress forever.'

She sat up and pushed Maggie away.

'Daddy liked it, I won't take it off.'

Maggie moved a lock of hair out of Winifred's eyes.

'All right. You can sleep in it, Winnie.'

Winifred snuggled back into the blanket and Orian climbed in next to her.

'Mam, will the angel bring Daddy home soon?'

Maggie's hand stopped stroking Winifred's hair.

'Angel?'

'The angel who looks after Daddy. With the white dress and nice smile.'

'Ah, Nurse Roberts ... She will do her best, I'm sure.'

'That's what she said.'

Maggie kissed her youngest daughter's forehead.

'Mam, what's a nurse?'

'Someone who helps people get better.'

'She was really nice.'

'Aye, now get some sleep.'

Maggie took the candle and Winifred watched the light disappear down the narrow staircase until all that was left was darkness and silence.

———

'Mam never spoke of it. Of why he was there, his state of mental well-being, when he would be back. Never. So neither did we,' Winifred said, staring at the tablecloth without really seeing it. 'Until I heard that cry and it all came back again.'

Ellie had forgotten about the strange noise that had snatched her attention earlier. She listened now but she couldn't hear anything.

Winifred had also been listening and, with a mixture of sadness and relief, now said, 'It was an unspoken fact and we locked it away. He sometimes came for visits but they never lasted longer than a few weeks. He would be so quiet and seem to become more withdrawn, and then would start doing strange things: disappear for hours on end or not move from one place and just sit there muttering and crying pitifully. He looked so sad and dejected. But I was a child and assumed that that was just who he was. Sometimes I would ask Mam why Daddy was always so sad, but she would just pat my head and change the subject.

'Only years later did I fully understand why people had given sage nods if they asked after Daddy and were told, "gone to Talgarth". Everyone knew what *that* meant. So his presence was something of the past and the stories were all of golden years gone by. People stopped asking after him and life moved forward, interspersed on occasion by one of his visits.'

'But it explains so much, don't you think?' Amy said, 'Your strength of character, your own values. All down to the difficult circumstances with your dad.' She nodded her head to confirm the validity of this declaration.

'I think it is too simple to say "it shaped who I am"; that sounds like the sort of nonsense I heard my teenage children come out with.'

Winifred looked at Ellie. 'But everyone has their obstacles to overcome and it is very easy to use them as your excuse for not accomplishing all you can rather than as a justification for striving for better.'

Ellie bit her bottom lip but curiosity took over and she said, 'What happened to your dad?'

205

'He was finally released in 1939,' Winifred said, 'because my cousin, as a doctor, was able to put pressure on the hospital. He had been better for a while, you see, but they liked having him there. He was good with animals and an excellent farmer.' Winifred smiled. 'Just like Mam said. However, by then I had already moved to Swanley. So I never really knew him at home. John never knew. He only knew Daddy as a kind man who did not speak a lot. The opposite to the Burnes!'

She threw Lotty a smile and sat a little straighter as she added, 'And my mam's side of the family, come to think of it.'

Winifred paused ready to stop talking, then a fonder memory broke through. 'John always loved telling the story of his first visit to Troedrew, when a man in a horse and cart came and without saying anything took his luggage, put it on the cart and drove off. We walked the six miles from Garth station to the farm, and when we got there, who was sitting by the fire but the man with the cart. His future father-in-law.'

Winifred smiled and the old twinkle came back.

'Your husband never knew about your dad's time in a mental hospital?' Amy said.

'No.'

'How? I mean why?'

'It was not something we spoke about. And then Daddy died in 1947, six months after our first child was born. John had only arrived back from India the previous year. He had been stationed there for two years. We had other things to talk about.'

Again, that soft smile.

'That must have been tough, to lose your dad when you had just got him back,' Amy said.

Winifred shrugged. 'Yes, perhaps, but "if pots and pans were ifs and ands —"'

'There'd be no need for tinkers,' Lotty said. 'You said it earlier. Do you think it is a Welsh saying? I would love to write it down.'

Ellie was still mulling over Winifred's story and didn't hear Lotty. 'And that's why you became a nurse?' she said.

'Maybe. It's romantic to think so but there were also practical reasons for the choice. Like I said, my uncle was able to get me a place to start training, which was a great incentive.'

Winifred looked at Ellie, who was twirling a piece of her hair and seemed deep in thought. Winifred felt exhausted from her story. It had dredged up a lot and she felt a hollow sadness at what had been lost; or never found. She looked at the others. *But then, we could all say that.*

ELLIE

Ellie wrapped the hair around her finger and then let the hair slip free. She repeated this action, unconscious of what she was doing. She was lost in a muddle of thoughts, all scrambling for prime position but none of them winning through. She watched Amy listen in firm concentration to something Winifred said and tried to imagine this middle-aged woman as a girl. *Did she really live in America during the glamour of the twenties?* Ellie didn't know much about the twenties. Only what she had seen on TV. And that didn't look anything like the twenties Amy talked about. On TV it was parties and clunky cars. Ellie watched Amy's fingers tap against each other and then at her lip as she readied herself to say something. But Amy's America hadn't sounded that much fun. Hard work and grit.

Oh God, grit. Sounding like Mum again. I should ask Amy about America. Mum's always going on about taking an interest in the country I was born in. She heard her mother's voice now: "It's important you learn about your citizenship and where you are from." *Where I'm from ... What* do *I want to do?* Same questions, different crowd.

Ellie sighed. Family gatherings were getting boring now that her GCSE years were beginning. All anyone wanted to know was what was she going to do after her exams. What A Levels? And then the unwanted advice: "Study something you enjoy"; "Do something you're good at".

Winifred stood up and replaced one of the candles, which had begun to splutter. Amy leaned across the table and lit a taper that she then used to light the new candle. Ellie watched Amy, admiring how her make-up and outfit were as neat as when they had sat down. Her mum always complained that by the end of the day her make-up had vanished and her clothes normally had some or other mysterious mark on them. But not Amy. Not a smear of mascara or a half-wrinkled skirt. And definitely no wine stains.

Ellie glanced at Lotty as she thought this, remembering the spilt red wine and the shadowed look that had sent her back to that bridge. Ellie traced a finger over the stain which divided her and Lotty. *Weird about the play. Mum would say that coincidences are signs that you are on the right path. Lotty would probably want to write that down.* Ellie smiled and watched her finger run around the stain again. *You could say that Lotty has led a neat life. No children, off on her own, doing what she wanted. First woman president of a society. That's pretty sick. And it all came through doing something she loved. But oh my God she talks funny. Why use ten words when a hundred would do?*

Ellie smiled again and felt her fingers tingle with the need to text Aria. *She would love this gathering.* Ellie looked around, trying to remember the details to recount to Aria: Winifred's crisp, clean look and kind smile; Amy's wispy hair against her neat profile; Lotty's bejewelled, pudgy hands and her glossy, shimmering dress which rustled so much it was like the dress was talking as much as its owner. *I do like her, though. She's loud, opinionated and self-absorbed but she's nice, too. Although the whole bridge thing was weird. And her telling me to leave. As if she didn't like me or want me here. Not the first time that's happened.*

Ellie looked at the letter, which seemed to lie on the table as an accusation. *Eventually I will have to give this to Mum.* She sighed. *Better have an explanation. I will tell her that I just don't like the teacher. That isn't a lie. Mum will tell me to grow up and that in life you have to work out how to deal with people you don't like.* Ellie looked again at the letter. *Maybe I should open it first and read it so I know what it says. I could say I opened it by mistake. In the scheme of things, this isn't really a big deal. I mean, it's not like living through bombings or collecting your water every day from a stream.*

Ellie heard Winifred's voice replying something but didn't register the words. She was too busy in her mind creating a world for Winifred in a World War Two book. The main character, with a secret past of rags and mental hospitals, recreates herself in a faraway city, the wartime life an easy cover for her lack of clothes and need to mend rather than buy. Ellie saw Winifred running down cobbled roads, wearing smart chunky shoes and a full-length coat. *They always wear long coats in these films. Probably had a hat too.*

Overhead, planes droned by and sirens screamed. And then the book would take the reader into a hospital: people sitting patiently, glancing up at the ceiling now and again as they wait to be seen; a baby cries. And there she would meet a tall, handsome doctor and she would fall madly in love. But the war would rip them apart and they would write romantic letters. He is sent abroad and she paces, paces, waiting impatiently for him to write, just as Anna does in *The Burgomaster's Guest.*

But there must be a misunderstanding. Like Sparrow thinking he is engaged to Anna, Winifred's character should have her love tested. She didn't mention any specific problems, but all good books have a problem the heroine must overcome. Ellie's hand took up its habitual twirl as she dug into her imagination for a suitable storyline.

Outside, the owl began its call again. Ellie snapped out of her thoughts and listened. The owl hooted again. *It must be in the tree outside; it's closer than before.* A scrambling noise, a rustling of wings, or maybe leaves, and a tiny squeal. Then silence. Ellie's hand stopped. *Oh, wow. What was that? I hope it wasn't a squirrel. I like squirrels.*

There was a red squirrel at her granny's cottage in Canada

that Ellie loved. He, or she, was considered 'cheeky'. It would come up onto the deck and scamper about searching for any crumbs left by messy eaters. It was brave, too. Ellie had sat on a blanket and it had run right over her feet in its attempts to fill its stomach.

Her granny couldn't stand the creature and shooed it away whenever she saw it. But Ellie loved watching it and would leave morsels out and wait for it to come and feast. Perhaps it was because it was different to the other squirrels she'd grown up with in England. Those were all grey and large, while this animal was smaller, with a rusty orange coat; like something out of Beatrix Potter.

A couple of summers ago, she had started drawing it and creating stories for it. She had named it Nutty. Not very original but it suited her, because this brave, cheeky squirrel had to be a girl.

When Ellie got home – her previous home – she and her friends had started drawing other animals and birds and adding them into the stories until Nutty lived in a mongrel world of North American and European species. A few zoo animals had been thrown in after they visited London Zoo, so the mongrel world also had a monkey and a lion.

They had loved the mongrel world, as it became known, and became so fascinated by it that their teacher asked them to read out one of the stories. They wrote one specially for the occasion, each spending time carefully drawing the characters and sharing ideas about the story. The four of them had then stood in a line in front of the class and read out their short story. It was about a teacher and a class, with enough similarities to their own school for it to be recognised. The antics of the make-believe class and the silly behaviour of the teacher had had everyone (including the readers) in giggles. At the end, their teacher asked them to put their drawings up on the wall as a display for the last few weeks of term. They debated for ages which ones were good enough to be displayed and finally chose the monkey with a love of chocolate, a bluebird whose blue chest was drawn as a waistcoat, a Labrador who carried a stick and had a flat cap, and last but not least, Nutty.

Ellie sighed at the memory and reminded herself that that had been ages ago; she had been twelve and as far as Ellie was concerned she hadn't known anything. Barely had the next school year begun before her parents wrenched her away to Richmond. She had left her friends and with them her interest in drawing and stories. Until the Cupboard Incident.

LOTTY AND ELLIE

Ellie's thoughts mingled into the conversation. Something about the wish to know some people better.

'Or not as well,' Winifred said with a wry smile.

'What you've got to remember,' Amy said, 'is that there is no point in worrying about what might have been. You just have to get on with it.'

She waved her finger in Lotty's direction. Ellie was surprised: Lotty didn't strike her as the sentimental type. She glanced at the lady sitting to her right. Lotty's hands were in her lap, her spine straight as a pole, but she was smiling.

'I share your sentiments entirely, Mrs Mello,' she said. 'I was referring to Winifred's comment that it is hard not to consider what might have been if her papa had spent less time in the ... hospital. I had not realised what similarities we shared in our childhood, my dear.'

Ellie looked at Winifred, trying to imagine what Winifred and Lotty had had in common as children. She imagined one in smart petticoats, with governesses and three meals a day cooked by a servant; the other in simple dresses, walking two miles to her primary school and eating the scraps left over after the best produce had been sent to market.

As if reading Ellie's thoughts, Lotty said: 'We had to sew our own clothes. I was never strong at sewing; however, my sisters were.' She waved her hand as if to justify her inertia for the task.

'Alice enjoyed sewing and undertook embroidery all her life.

She would work tirelessly on gowns for balls and was often head costumier during festivities. Frances was also very capable although she never could darn stockings. We were also, of necessity, brought up on the system of "what you have not got, you must manage to do without", and indeed we did. Mamma did not approve of waste. We cooked every part of the animal and, as children, were never permitted to draw or scribble on the bought stationery.'

Lotty paused as a childhood memory of their neighbour, who lived in the manor house came to her. Whenever they visited, they were given bought stationary to use to scribble on. *How rich those neighbours had seemed.* She smiled but it faded with her train of thought.

'We were both raised in female households. Managed and run by capable women without the constant influence of a male presence. Not for the same reasons, of course, yet our primary male influences were both men who were deeply troubled. Your father with his depression and mine who could not find a role for himself and thus required endless enjoyment to the extent that Papa had to finally agree to a reduction in his stable and to restrict himself to two glasses of wine a day.' *Not that it helped poor Papa.*

'Perhaps it was this female environment that proved to be our greatest strength.'

Lotty leaned forward as she said this, fixing her eyes on Winifred. She did not want a reply but waited for Winifred to acknowledge the accurateness of this point.

'The tragedy of your sister ... Catherine.'

'Kathleen.'

'Yes, Kathleen also reminds me of my dear Frances, who was lost to me when I was not even twenty-four years of age.'

'Well, that is not —'

'Of course, an indiscretion with a young man is hardly comparable, I agree; however —'

'That is not quite how I would describe it.'

Winifred pronounced each syllable of the word, making Ellie and Amy both look at her.

'No? I assumed that the quick wedding and appearance of the child was the result of —'

'No. It wasn't like ... she was ...' Winifred stopped, her hand rotating the beads on her necklace. She looked at her hands and then back up at Lotty.

'I assure you, you have it quite wrong.'

Lotty felt her cheeks grow warm under Winifred's firm gaze.

'I do apologise for any misunderstanding,' she said. 'Let us discuss such unhappy subjects no longer.'

There was an awkward pause until Amy filled it. 'But what were you going to say?'

Lotty frowned.

'About your sister?'

Lotty paused and Ellie wondered if she was going to answer Amy. When she did speak, she turned to Ellie and gave her the full force of those grey-blue eyes.

'Do you recall we spoke of a little play called *Margaret's Marriage*? Using the proverb, What the snow conceals the sun reveals?'

Ellie nodded, feeling a little ashamed at the memory. *When I get home I'm gonna find it and read it.*

'I published it posthumously for Frances twenty years after she died. I found I was unable to do so sooner. Frances and I were so close and very similar in many respects; however, she was the gentler, more compassionate one. Losing my sister when the threat of childhood illnesses was behind us and our adulthood stretched invitingly in front of us was quite a blow.'

She stopped and when she spoke again her voice had a quiet sadness to it. 'I should have suspected that not all was well with her, yet I refused to see it.'

'What was wrong with her?' Amy asked.

'She complained of tiredness all through the summer of 1873. We all suffered with headaches and coughs and were often in ill health, which my Aunt Whitelegge attributed to the house not being very warm; yet Frances was the most active of us all. By Christmas that year she was in a desperate way and had barely been out. Sambrooke and Alice accompanied her to Buxton to take the waters. I stayed in Edgmond to care for Mamma.'

'That must have been very ... remedial,' Winifred said.

'The *table d'hôte* was rather awful by their accounts,' Lotty said. 'I recall Frances describing an old man who was very bad; he had no brogue but a very vulgar accent. He wore a shawl and had no sleeves to his coat and his arms were swathed in flannel.'

Lotty shuddered at the thought and didn't notice Amy roll her eyes. Ellie suppressed a giggle, aware that this story was going to have a sad ending and that giggling would not look good.

'By the end of January Frances seemed better and came home.' Lotty said. 'A couple of days after, she went to dine and sleep at Loynton. It was decided she should stay for a few days. This was then extended as she became increasingly tired and took up invalid habits. In her last letter she wrote that all she did was eat, go out and lie down. She had made up a Valentine card for a family friend but was then too tired to complete it so she asked that I puzzle it out.'

Lotty sighed. 'She was still cheerful and thinking of others even then. Later we learnt that she had written this last letter lying on the drawing-room sofa, and did it with great difficulty.'

Lotty stopped. She was in a different room from the rest, a room with gilded mirrors, good quality, but old, upholstery and rugs. Large windows looked onto a lawn where peacocks pranced. On one of the sofas lay a young woman with features as familiar to her as her own. Balanced on her sister's lap was a portable writing desk. The room was quiet except for the stilted scratching of pen against paper.

'The next day she took to her bed.'

————

Ellie glanced at Winifred. Her face reflected a sadness. *She already knows this story. Of course she does. Mum and Granny are always referring to these dead relatives. I've never bothered to really listen. Just a bunch of people who have nothing to do with me.* She glanced at the women in the room. *Until now.* Lotty's comment on her past as a reflection of her present suddenly made some sense.

'Frances remained at Loynton, where she could be so much better nursed,' Lotty said. 'Agatha's rheumatism and my cough were still bad and kept us both in the house. It meant I did not see as much of Frances as I would have liked.'

The fire crackled, filling the silence of her pause.

'Mamma was excessively uneasy,' Lotty continued, 'despite the accounts from Loynton that all said she was progressing favourably; that the doctor, Mr Lindop, expected her to get up her strength again.'

Her eyes shone momentarily with the memory of the hope those assurances had provided.

'However, in reality she was slowly worsening with slight improvements which we used as evidence to reassure everyone, including ourselves, that it was only a matter of time before the laughing, light-hearted Frances returned. I believed, anyway, that it was likely to be long business.'

Lotty stopped. She could feel her throat closing, and a weight so heavy it made her feel she might stop breathing pressed at her chest. *After all this time, it still can hurt.* She looked at the others.

'I do apologise; I have never spoken of this to anyone. We did not discuss our trials and tribulations, even with family.'

Winifred and Amy said nothing but Amy reached across the table and squeezed Lotty's arm. The move surprised Lotty and her arm flinched as if to remove itself from the contact.

'Yes, well, well. I am thankful at least that Mamma arrived

the previous day in the rectory carriage and that we were both with her at the end.'

Lotty was still, trapped in memories: Mamma being helped out of the carriage, propped up with cushions in her chair, her face drawn and anxious. Lotty had not seen her this worried even when Sambrooke had scarlet fever. Lotty felt the same churning sensation in her stomach as she had had watching her mother being slowly wheeled into the house. Her mamma's presence at Loynton made Frances's condition more real, more final.

With an effort, she carried on, 'On the day Mamma arrived, Frances had been restless and uncomfortable but had eventually slept. She worsened during the night and sank gradually until about seven thirty in the morning without suffering at the last.'

Lotty stirred the small remains of her coffee and stared into the cup.

'She was a heavy loss for all of us. Perhaps the others found ways of colouring in the sad vacancy, but I never managed to fill it. Fifty years later I would still catch myself wishing for her advice and humour.

'It leaves a question, does it not? What would they have said and how would they have acted? In the years after she died, I worked tirelessly collecting folk tales and travelling the county, but she was always there, in an empty seat of the train carriage, or sitting in a kitchen or parlour. Always there, the shadow in the mirror.'

Ellie instinctively glanced at the mirror but there was nothing unusual in it.

'When I published *Shropshire Folklore; A Sheaf of Gleanings*,' Lotty said, 'I wished so much that she could see it. And again when I became the first woman editor of the Folklore Society. Later, as its president, I did so miss her counsel. I fancied that I saw her on the night of my second Annual Address, amongst the white-bearded, grey-haired heads, but that was simply fanciful. It is not well to mourn long for the departed.'

She looked about the room. She could feel the thoughts of the other women, themselves thinking on those who had left too soon. She looked at Ellie. Her straight brown hair, which refused to stay behind her ears no matter how often she pushed at it, almond-shaped eyes and the concentration on her face were all echoes of Frances.

———

'You were close with your sister,' Amy said. 'That's good. It's good to have a close relationship. Important, you know.'

Lotty looked at her. *A peculiar comment considering what I have just said.*

'She was only twenty-one years of age when she passed away.'

Lotty spoke slowly, pronouncing each syllable, and Ellie wondered if she was trying to control herself.

'So sad. But maybe there was some good that came out of it.'

Lotty felt as if she had been hit by a coach. *Good?* Winifred started to say something but Amy sat forward.

'What you've got to remember,' she said, 'is that if your sister hadn't died so suddenly maybe you wouldn't have done so much with your writing and fairy stories and stuff.'

Ellie stared at her hands. She couldn't look at Lotty, whose simmering anger she could feel even at an arm's length. She risked a look at Amy, who was nodding urgently at Lotty. Sensing Ellie's movement, Amy turned her attention to her.

'Maybe that's what *you* need,' Amy said.

'What, a death?' Ellie said. She bit her lip; it had sounded funnier in her head.

'No, a kick-start. Something to get you on the right path.'

'If I may correct you, Mrs Mello,' Lotty said, raising her great body to its full seated height, 'my sister's death did not *get me on the right path.* I was already much engaged with Miss Jackson's project before my sister fell ill.

'And I am sure I do not need to remind you that I had spent my childhood collecting folklore stories and had made notes of local folklore for the Severn Valley Naturalists' Field Club, which I gave permission to the secretary of the club for Miss Jackson to see. If Miss Jackson had not become ill herself I would not have presumed to take on such a task. It was her brain that projected the work.'

'So that was what kick-started you,' Amy said. 'This Miss Jackson's illness.' Amy sat with her arms crossed and nodded her head.

Lotty spoke slowly, willing herself to keep calm, 'I am sure I do not understand what you mean by "kick-start"; however, if you mean that Miss Jackson's illness was the reason I became the sole editor of our endeavour, that is correct; however, it was not what —'

'But that is what Ellie needs, something that makes her realise her own value. Or something that gives her the confidence to do well.'

Ellie slunk lower in her chair, her eyes darting from Lotty to Amy. She hoped this conversation would move on; any other subject would be good.

'If she had that, then maybe we wouldn't be here. She wouldn't be spending time with the wrong sort of crowd and skipping school because she doesn't like the teacher,' Amy said.

Ellie sat up as if she had been prodded by a hot stick. 'That's not fair!' she said. 'It's not just the teacher. It's ... it's ... It's *them.*'

———

The envelope tapped at the table and Ellie watched it as she spoke.

'I had just wanted to fit in, you know? I mean, it was so annoying changing schools and not knowing anybody. I missed my friends. Mum kept saying I would meet new friends but I didn't *want* to meet *new* friends. I wanted to stay where I was. And I didn't meet new friends. Not really. I mean, I met Aria but I thought she was just being nice because my mum had met her parents and basically *forced* me on her.'

Ellie rolled her eyes. Her mum had had Aria and her parents over soon after they have moved in because 'they are neighbours and she goes to your school'. Ellie had become a pity project.

'But Aria wasn't in many of my classes and I didn't really see her. And then I met Rosie and she introduced me to the others and they let me join them playing tennis. It was cool. I thought my dad would be pleased because they all play tennis and squash really well, you know? But he didn't seem to like them. Ever since we moved here it's like I can't do anything right.'

Ellie gulped and reached for her tea. Her hand shook a little as she took a sip. She hadn't talked about this before. She had built walls around her to avoid her parents' looks of concern and comments. And now as she began to dismantle it, brick by brick, she realised how much she had locked up and how miserable it had all been.

'It was my fault that it all started to go wrong. I'm not a very good tennis player so they don't really like playing with me unless someone else isn't there. I just can't get the coordination right. But I don't mind watching. Mia said it was a good way to learn. And if that wasn't enough, I failed at the dares as well.'

'Dares?' Amy said.

'Yeah, they would play these games where one of us would have to do a dare. Although really it was just me who did the dares. I guess because I failed with the first one, I had to try again. But the last one was scary and stupid and I wouldn't have done it if Beth hadn't also said she would. And she's only young so it wasn't fair.'

Her eyes darting from one face to the other, pleading for understanding.

'And I knew they wouldn't forget if I didn't. And my balance is good so I thought that I would be okay. But then the train, and shadows ...'

Winifred and Amy looked confused. Lotty went very still. *The bridge. The train.* She remembered. *What did Ellie mean by the shadows?*

'The train and shadows?' Winifred said.

'Yeah,' Ellie said. 'There was this thing that happened on the footbridge over the railway and I ... I fell off the wall. It was so dumb and pointless. But — don't you remember, Lotty?'

'I am sure I do not know what you are referring to,' Lotty said, and brushed imaginary crumbs off her skirt.

'Oh.' Ellie frowned in confusion. *It was definitely Lotty. Why is she pretending she wasn't there? Maybe ghosts have short memories.*

'Anyway, after that they started to ... ghost me.'

'To *what* you?' Lotty said.

'Ghost. Ignore. Pretend you aren't there.'

'And so the work of folklore continues,' Lotty murmured.

'It wasn't so bad. I mean, Aria and I had become closer as she was helping me with languages and I was helping her with maths. And we had the play we were doing together. But we didn't really hang out together, you know?'

She took a deep breath. 'But when Rosie started chatting to me before History I was really glad. I liked being part of their group. They were cool and did fun things and I guess I wanted that. But afterwards, even though they were nicer, I still felt ... they would sometimes still ...' Ellie remembered that afternoon and waving to them to wait.

'The next week I was allowed to go to Mia's house after school because we were doing a school project, Amelia, Mia and me. I was on Mia's iPad with Amelia when she said to me to look at the screen 'cause Mia and Rosie were messaging and they were talking about me. It must have been connected, you know — her phone and the iPad — 'cause a message flicked up and they were saying some mean stuff about how I had cried when the teacher came in. Which wasn't true.'

'Did you confront Mia and Rosie about it?' Amy said.

'No. Amelia told them I was reading their messages and Mia got really mad and I went home.'

'The next day was a Wednesday and in History Rosie and Amelia passed a message to me. Just a picture of me with really big teeth, because I have ugly teeth – they're too big for my jaw.' Her hand covered her mouth for a second.

'I'm getting braces to fix it. I could hear them laughing as I opened it. They'd called it a "self-portrait", which was clearly wrong because I hadn't drawn it.' She let out a cold laugh.

'Did it happen again?' Winifred said.

'Yeah, the next week as well, but this time another girl in the class refused to pass it on. Which was super-nice of her. But still ... just seemed easier to not go.'

Ellie looked at her hands. Her eyes had begun to sting and she concentrated on the mole on the back of her hand. Her hair framed her face, hiding a tear that escaped and rolled down her cheek.

'Why pursue a friendship with these girls if they are so mean-spirited?' Lotty said.

Ellie shrugged and brushed at her face. 'I don't know anybody else. And they were fun to be with and I liked playing tennis with them.'

'You know Aria,' Amy said.

Ellie nodded. 'But we don't hang out at school. She's in different classes to me so I don't really see her.'

'Now look, you will always meet people that aren't ... nice and others that are, kiddo,' Amy said. 'It might seem easy to stick with the false ones but that doesn't mean you should.'

Ellie wasn't listening. 'I was getting really good at tennis and was gonna surprise Dad with a game.'

'Are you sure your parents put so much importance on sport that it's worth demeaning yourself with these people for?' Amy said.

Ellie shrugged and looked at the space behind Amy. 'All my family are really into sport, and are good at it.'

She looked suddenly at Winifred. 'Mum used to represent Jersey for horse riding ... and ... and my uncles on Dad's side are all really good at racket sports. Everybody has either represented their university, county or country at something, and I can barely run for a bus.'

'And you felt you needed to fit in at home?' Winifred said.

Ellie shrugged again. 'I just didn't feel I fitted in here, in Richmond. I was happy that people wanted to hang out with me and then I thought it would help if I could be good at something. Maybe then they would like me and Mum and Dad would be impressed, too. I could forget about my old friends and home. I guess being good at tennis, or any sport, hadn't mattered before. But I was younger then.'

'What would *you* like to be good at?' Amy said.

Ellie started to say something but Amy's hand swiped at her words.

'I don't want you to tell me tennis or any other rubbish,' Amy said. 'What do you want to be good at? Not what you think other people *want* you to do. That's no good.'

Ellie played with the letter, tapping each corner of the envelope against the table.

'I really enjoy wildlife – that's why I like drawing birds. They have such amazing colours. And I like reading.' Ellie paused, thinking of the fun she had had drawing those characters with her old group of friends and how much she had enjoyed picking up her sketchbook again.

'I wouldn't do drawing as a job. But I am good at maths and science ...' She trailed off.

'A budding scientist, perhaps,' Winifred said.

Ellie shrugged. 'I guess ... But not sure my parents would think of that. Neither of them are interested in science ...'

'Mamma had little interest in folklore,' Lotty said. 'It was to encourage and support my interest that she subscribed to the *Folklore Journal* — the predecessor to what became the *Folklore Society Journal*. Your mother gave you *Margaret's Marriage* because she knew of your interest in reading, even if it was not a book to your taste.'

Lotty saw Ellie wince at her words and deep down couldn't help but be a little satisfied by this reaction.

'You may not have appreciated the gesture; however, I have no doubt it was offered as a way of supporting you. There is no reason to believe she would not do the same if you said you wished to learn about the sciences.'

'Yeah, well, when she gets this letter and is told what a disaster I am she isn't going to care about helping me,' Ellie said, still tapping the envelope on the table.

'Urgh. Now look, kiddo, all this feeling sorry for yourself is not going to get you anywhere.' Amy leaned forward, elbows on the table, her eyes fixed on Ellie. 'You don't know what that letter says and you don't know what your mum will say. You *do* know what you can do about it. The only thing you can control is yourself.'

Her finger stayed in the air pointing at Ellie. 'Ignore those girls that are no good and do what is right for you. That is how you will succeed,' she said.

'Easy for you to say,' Ellie said.

Amy fixed her with a look and Ellie stared at the tablecloth. Suddenly, she looked up and looked at them, curiosity flashing in her eyes.

'Do you know that because you can see the future?' she said.

'What?' Amy said.

'All that you've said — is it because you know what will happen if I don't?'

Amy made a sound but didn't manage to create words. Lotty

watched Amy open and shut her mouth and a small smile danced at her lips despite the dangerous path Ellie was leading them down.

'We are here to help you,' Winifred said simply.

'Yeah, but why now? Why all together?'

Lotty picked up the coffee pot but put it down again.

'Did they not provide extra hot water?' she said, not expecting a reply. 'I believe we have put our case forward, Mrs Mello, Winifred. Perhaps now would be a good moment to retire.'

'No, you can't leave.' Ellie's hand hurt from slamming it on the table. The noise echoed in her ears but she ignored the looks of surprise from the women.

'You have to tell me. *Why now?*'

AMY AND ELLIE

Amy looked around her; Winifred looked concerned, Lotty uncomfortable, Ellie determined.

It's only fair, I suppose. I'd want to know. But what to tell her? This was always the danger with this plan.

'Instinct,' Amy said. 'That's why now. It seemed the right time.'

Ellie's mouth held its frown and her chin jutted forward as if expressing that this was not a good enough answer. The look reminded Amy of the time she had caught her oldest granddaughter — Ellie's grandmother — stealing cookies from the jar Amy kept in the kitchen. They were meant to be have been outside playing while Amy finished watching her soaps. But a noise had distracted her from the TV and she had found Kay, in her school uniform with grass-stained knees, hurriedly replacing the lid of a jar from the candy trolley. When Amy had scolded her for not asking, Kay had jutted her chin out just like Ellie, and, with a little stamp of her foot, exclaimed that it wasn't her fault; she had been *too* hungry. Amy would have allowed a smile at the memory but knew Ellie would think she was being patronised.

'If you consider that these are important and formative years, it should be no surprise that we are here,' Lotty said.

Something in Lotty's manner caught Amy's attention. Lotty's face had taken on a dismissive air that had a whiff of something else about it. *Anger? Irritation? No, not that. Defensive? Maybe ... Guilt?*

Winifred moved closer to Amy and a puff of lilies and vanilla floated in the air. It reminded Amy of being at her dressing table applying the body lotions her sister used to send her from Macy's.

'I believe the best plan would be to keep our answers brief but truthful. A short answer is always best when you don't want too many questions to follow,' Winfried whispered.

'Absolutely,' Amy said, but her thoughts were in Bermuda, at a dressing table that overlooked a garden full of plants and flowers. Her favourite had been the tall bulb flowers that lined the pathway, because they were so beautiful when they flowered in the spring. *Manuel had such talent. After everything I'd gone through early in life, those years at Vicinity House with my kids and grandchildren were very special.*

'... and that is really it, darling. Think of us a guides.' Winifred's voice prodded at Amy and she came back to her present reality.

'Exactly: guides,' Amy said. 'We are called upon when needed to help and provide advice.'

She nodded. Ellie's eyes sparked with renewed interest.

'Called upon? Who calls you?' she asked.

It sounded as if Winifred had just sighed but Amy couldn't be sure. She patted her hair.

'Well ... not so much *someone*. Just ... we just ... it's instinct. We act as a ... presence. Yes, a presence. Your conscience, almost.'

'My conscience?' Ellie said. She looked at Lotty, the bridge coming to mind again. *Why didn't she stop me from walking along that wall if she's my conscience? And the time I shouted at that girl and made her cry? Were they there afterwards making me feel bad?*

'So why don't you stop me from doing things that are wrong rather than making me feel guilty about them afterwards?'

'No, what Amy means is that we are *guides*. We are not your conscience,' Winifred said. Her right hand rubbed her neck.

'What you've got to realise is that we can be there in the background to steer you if you seem to be in difficulty, but we can't stop you from doing something if you really want to do it,' Amy said.

'Steer?' Ellie said. 'You can read my mind?'

'No, of course we can't,' Winifred said. 'We are simply a positive influence, albeit from far away.' She smiled and reached for Ellie's clenched fist. 'We do not read minds, nor do we reprimand you when things go awry. We are merely guides.'

Winifred squeezed Ellie's hand and Ellie felt calmer. *Guides; that doesn't sound that bad. Nice to know you have people on your side. But still something didn't seem right. Why scare me with spooky visions and voices from nowhere? Why not just remain hidden?*

'Do other people have ... guides?' Ellie asked.

'Oh, do you know, I am not sure,' Winifred said.

'It is likely that they do,' Lotty said. 'The worship and appreciation of ancestors and their powers is quite an ancient one. Since the time of Confucius, the idea that great men – rarely women – retained after death their interest in their own clans and were still able to watch and influence their descendants gradually gained force.'

Winifred tried, unsuccessfully, to catch Lotty's eye, desperate that they didn't lose Ellie's attention right at the end. *Please keep this short.*

'Hence, reverence and affection for the departed developed,' Lotty said, 'and the belief that those poor souls who are not properly cared for after death — through neglect or lack of descendants — become ghosts. These unhappy ghosts are considered to cause mischief such as bringing ill luck and poor health; however, those who are tended to and cared for through the ancestor tablets steer a family to happiness and prosperity.'

'How do you care for a ghost?' Ellie said.

'They have sacred festivals where they honour their ancestors by tidying graves, picnicking and offering ancestors their favourite foods. My nephew, Arthur, and his boys used to clear the graves at Norbury. Did you and John do something similar?' Lotty said to Winifred.

'Yes, we did; every time we visited Arthur and Christine.'

'I wonder if your children carried on this tradition,' Lotty said.

Ellie thought there was an edge to her voice, as if she knew the answer to her own question.

'What food do you think they would offer me if my family did a picnic?' Amy chuckled at the thought of her two boys preparing anything.

'Ruth would've prepared something,' she said. 'Like I said, she was an excellent baker. I taught her how to bake bread and cakes and Portuguese desserts. Her favourite was lemon meringue pie. Not my first choice but the one she made was excellent.'

Amy thought of the family meals, lunch always at one p.m., dinner at eight. She never changed those times and everyone kept to them. She loved those family occasions: everyone gathered around the dining-room table with the scents of garlic, onion and spices flowing from the large pot of fava beans she did for winter gatherings — her mother's recipe. And always a cut of meat to go with it. Her favourite was spare ribs marinated in an allspice and paprika rub.

'Mmm, salt cod fritters. Now they would be good picnic food,' she said. 'Homemade, of course,' she said with a decisive nod.

'We would occasionally picnic at Cop Mere,' Lotty said. 'I do enjoy sandwiches and meat pies yet they are not my favourite foods. I recall an exceedingly good lunch in Basel composed only of bread, cold meats, salad and Bavarian beer.'

'What about you, Winifred?' Amy said

'I was partial to a good curry,' Lotty said, not noticing that she had interrupted Amy. 'And jam pudding. I was very fond of fruit puddings. We had a new cook in 1873 — Anne Jones;

a little Welsh woman, clean and brisk. She was a good cook but did not catch what Frances or I said very well. However, she made an excellent jam pudding.'

Lotty licked her lips and Amy took the moment to jump in. 'What about you, Winifred? What would be your preferred meal?'

'A roast dinner,' Winifred said without hesitation. 'I loved a roast dinner: a large piece of meat, roast potatoes, buttered cabbage or beans, glazed carrots. All the family together and leftovers to see you into the next week.'

'Not easy for a picnic,' Amy said.

'True, although favourite *picnic* food is surely a different question.' Winifred smiled briefly and Amy realised it was nearing time to go. *But will she let us go?*

WINIFRED

Winifred watched the waiter appear with a silver tray, ready to take away the cups and pots. *Is it my imagination or does he look surprised to see us still here?* Winifred put her napkin on the table. *It is time to leave and yet we cannot. Where is she? If she is not coming then we cannot have done enough.*

"For I dip't into the future, far as human eye could see, Saw the vision of the world, and all the wonder that would be."

If only I could. Although if Tennyson is right, I might not want to. Maybe we should have done it differently. We are all so different and with strong views. Did we complement each other or were our various styles too much of a distraction? Nothing to be gained by thinking about that.

And I feel exhausted. Such an unfamiliar feeling these days. But to have focused on such sad memories was bound to have an effect. Not even memories, really; events that had been absorbed and buried.

I wonder how the others are feeling. Amy looks as poised and elegant as when we arrived. Lotty looks a little tired, but at least Ellie looks thoughtful. So perhaps we have done enough.

Give positive advice; that was our goal. Who knows if that is what we have achieved.

It is time to leave. The dinner is over. They are even taking away our coffee cups.

Our efforts are completed. Yet we stay. What is keeping us here? Why is she not coming? There is a question that hasn't been asked ...

ELLIE AND LOTTY

'I should probably go,' Ellie said, watching the waiter pick up her teacup.

'Yes,' Winifred said, but the word disappeared, leaving no impact.

The waiter balanced Lotty's cup on top of Ellie's and she heard Lotty tut. He headed to the door, the cups rattling in protest at the casual treatment. They waited until he had left but the door creaked ajar behind him and Ellie stood up and pushed it into its frame. There was darkness beyond their room, as if all the lights were turned off. Not even the glow of street lighting seeped into the corridor. *Is it always this dark up here? They can't have locked up already.* Ellie's stomach churned and she twirled her hair as she returned to the table.

'This has turned out to be a very pleasant evening, Ellie,' Lotty said. Ellie stood by her chair, unsure if she should sit or instead say goodbye and head home. Seeing her uncertainty, Lotty stood up. *It would be best if we finished this now. Winifred is beginning to look puzzled and I would be foolish to under-estimate the workings of the mind of either of those women.*

She moved around her chair and the noise of material brushing furniture interrupted Ellie's thoughts. Amy pushed her chair from the table and stood up, patting her hair and brushing crumbs from her dress as she did. Ellie looked at Winifred, who stayed where she was, her hands clasped together on the table. Her eyes glanced from Amy to Lotty to Ellie and back.

'It is time to depart.' Lotty's voice floated through her, and

Ellie's stomach did another somersault.

'Why do you do that?' she said. Her voice hit the quiet of the room like a hammer. Lotty turned to her, her face twisted in surprise. But Ellie could see something else. Her eyes, previously so direct and penetrating, now moved up and down Ellie's face, refusing to settle.

'Ellie?' Winifred said.

'If you are all here to help me, then why didn't you?' Ellie said, her eyes on Lotty.

Lotty remained very still.

'We are only guides, darling.' Winifred's voice, calm with authority, tapped at Ellie's thoughts.

'Yeah, I get that,' Ellie said. She couldn't get her breathing to relax and it continued in short bursts as she spoke. 'But why don't you stop me from doing things that any grown-up would obviously know were wrong ... or dangerous? What type of guide lets me walk across a footbridge wall?'

Amy and Winifred looked at Ellie and then at Lotty, their heads moving in unison.

'You are over-excited, Ellie,' Lotty said. Her voice was controlled and she stood a little higher although Ellie still towered over her.

'No! I am not over-excited,' Ellie said. 'I saw you on the bridge. In the shadows. And ... and you just *watched* the whole thing. And then I fell and nobody helped me.'

Ellie experienced the sensation of the fear she had had at the time and closed her eyes to it but the sounds of a train rumbling, and running feet, found her anyway. She opened her eyes to see Lotty still looking at her.

'It was you,' Ellie said, her voice now a whisper.

'You saw Lotty?' Amy said. 'That's impossible.'

'Yes,' Winifred said. 'Under normal circumstances, you are not meant to be able to see us.' Her tone lacked the surprise of Amy's; instead she sounded thoughtful. 'It is only because we three are here together that we have the power to appear to you as we have.'

'Well, I did,' Ellie said. Her hand shook slightly as she pointed her finger towards Lotty. 'She was younger and had on a green dress. Or it could've been brown; she was in the dark. But I saw her. It was a really long dress and looked old-fashioned, which is why I remember her. She was standing on the other end of the footbridge. I wanted to wait until she had passed us but then Beth said *she* would do it instead. They said I was too scared to.'

'Did the others see her?' Amy asked, glancing at Lotty, who hadn't moved, and refused to look at any of them.

'No. I don't think. They said I was just making it up to get out of doing the dare. But I wasn't. She was there and she didn't help me.'

Lotty raised her hand and Ellie stopped.

'Ellie is correct, I was there. I had not arrived earlier partly as I felt that this girl who was prepared to pursue such damaging friendships and trivial pastimes did not deserve my attention. After all, she showed no interest in family history; in the successful endeavours of those who had come before her or how their sacrifices enabled her to live as she did. *Light come, light go, my Faither got it a-throshing*, as they are fond of saying in Pulverbatch. I thought, if she was prepared to waste her life on a dare then let her. In the end, however, I did not funk and how fortunate it was that I arrived when I did.'

Lotty looked at the other women now, her confident stare taking in their expressions.

'I arrived too late to remove Ellie from the nonsense of the dare, which was to walk across a narrow wall that spanned the length of a railway bridge. The height of the wall was certainly over five feet and the distance to the ground was considerable. It was a remarkably foolish enterprise. Ellie was sensible enough to refuse and I hoped that my intervention might not be required, when that silly girl piped in with her willingness to undergo the task.'

'Beth,' Ellie said.

Lotty waved a hand to indicate that the girl's name was irrelevant.

'She did not strike me as a girl of athletic prowess. She also looked much younger than the others and I feared that the worst would occur and that the repercussions for Ellie would be severe.'

'What, more severe than me falling off in front of a train?'

Lotty sighed but continued to focus her attention on Winifred and Amy.

'Of course, there were risks; however, I felt that my strength of mind and focus could help Ellie across safely. Which is exactly what happened until a train came under the bridge. The speed of it was quite a surprise to me and I lost my concentration for a moment, which is when Ellie's foot slipped. I had the presence of mind to tell her to look for the footbridge, which she did, and thus moved her balance away from the drop and onto the safer, albeit still painful, floor of the footbridge.'

'So you can control my mind,' Ellie said.

Lotty finally looked at her, taking in the pinched lips and furious stare, and smiled.

'No, dear, we cannot. We can propound thoughts among the millions that swirl around in your head already; however, whether ours are taken into consideration is up to you. When I instructed you to look to the footbridge, we were in close proximity, which did aid the process, I am sure, and you had few other thoughts to be distracted by, given the situation.'

Ellie paused. She remembered clearly balancing upon the wall and how slow everything had gone when she had lost her balance. But now Lotty said it, she did remember a voice encouraging her to fall onto the footbridge. Mia and Sam had laughed when she had told them afterwards that was what she had done.

'You fell off on purpose?' Sam had said.

'Why not just get your balance back? Would have hurt less,'

Mia had added.

Aria had shaken her head at the story and told her that it was better to fall onto the footbridge then risk falling onto the tracks. 'You should've just told them to get lost,' she had added, but hadn't said whether she meant for their comments or the dare itself, although Ellie thought the latter.

'So you can see us?' Amy said. 'You aren't meant to be able to. That's kinda the point.'

'Is that the only time you have seen one of us?' Winifred said.

'No. I saw you today outside school.' Ellie felt a wave of confidence fill her now that she had been right about Lotty.

'Yes, I thought something was strange at the time because you spoke as if I had spoken directly to you,' Winifred said.

'Well, you had, hadn't you?'

'Yes ... I mean, no. I had spoken but you should have heard it as a thought of your own. Did you hear my voice or yours when I spoke to you?'

'Yours.'

Winifred nodded. 'I thought so at the time, but with all the preparations for this dinner I did not have time to reflect properly on it.'

'Have you always heard us?' Amy said.

'I ... I don't know. I know I've heard you since I moved here.'

'This is remarkable,' Winifred said.

Ellie shifted her weight and leaned against the back of the chair.

'Why?' she said.

'Quite simply, what we say to you as thoughts are meant to sound as if they come from you yourself,' Winifred said. 'Our presence nearby allows these so-called thoughts to be at the front of your mind and take precedence over others, although it by no means guarantees that you will adhere to them.'

'So I am not meant to hear you? Does that mean I'm weird or something?'

'Quite the contrary,' Winifred said. 'It means you have an unusual gift.'

'That's normally a nice way of saying *weird*,' Ellie said, but she stood a little taller and struggled to stop the grin that was breaking through.

'It is a human foible to not appreciate the skills you possess and to wish for the talents of others,' Winifred said.

Amy pointed her finger at Ellie and said, 'Appreciate what you're good at, kiddo, and don't worry about what others think.'

Winifred murmured something but Ellie wasn't listening.

She shook her head, 'This is sick ,' Ellie said, her face beaming.

Lotty shifted her weight, wishing to go. 'It is time to depart,' she said looking at the others.

Amy didn't turn to her but was still studying Ellie. 'Do you hear us all the time?' she said.

'How often are you around?' Ellie said, suddenly wondering if they watched everything she did.

'We have no interest in prying into your daily routine,' Lotty said as if reading her mind.

Ellie narrowed her eyes at Lotty and gripped the back of the chair. The feelings from the bridge were still simmering, clouding her thoughts, and she struggled for words, so she just blurted out what she could.

'You don't seem to of had lots of interest in me at all.'

'Ellie, please keep calm and reserve the dramatics for the stage,' Lotty said, sighing inwardly at Ellie's loss of grammatical control. She shook her head. *Emotions so often bring out the worst in people.*

At the edge of Lotty's vision, Winifred cocked her head and looked at her. Lotty could sense Winifred's eyes sharpening as she spoke, and her voice — previously so calm and tranquil — now took on a different note.

'You were not going to help Ellie on the bridge. Was that the only time you have hindered our efforts to help our ward?'

Ellie remembered Lotty's words from earlier, encouraging her to leave the dinner.

'Yes, of course,' Lotty said. Her thumb swivelled the ring on her forefinger but she stopped when she saw Winifred watching it.

'Or at least, I've never done it over anything important. Perhaps once or twice I missed the moment or was too far away to be effective, however —'

'Lotty! Really,' Winifred said.

Lotty turned and faced Winifred; her dress glowed dark and together with her grey hair it gave her the look of a jackdaw. Winifred remained sitting.

'How sad that all our hard work was being undone by you,' Amy said.

Lotty's lips became a tight line but Winifred spoke first,. 'We do deserve an explanation.'

Lotty's steel-blue eyes flashed back at Ellie and a chill swept over her.

AMY AND ELLIE

Lotty brushed her hand over the sideboard and glanced at the small statue of swans, their necks intertwined. Amy frowned at the swans. *Weren't they a pair of hares earlier?* She looked around the room but the hares weren't there. *Swapped when a waiter came in? How strange.* Lotty still didn't say anything.

'Now look —' Amy began but she was cut off mid-sentence by Lotty.

'I have reflected often of late on the melancholy history of one whose evil life and pretended sorceries made her deserve, as far as anyone can do so, her reputation as a witch. "Nanny Morgan", as she was commonly called, was still well remembered by many people at Wenlock in my time. She was supposed to practise witchcraft, and to have the evil eye.'

Lotty switched accents and it took Amy a moment to realise this was probably a Shropshire one.

'The Wenlock people say, "Everybody was frightened at her and no one durst refuse her nothing, for fear she should do something at them. And she kep' a box full of live toads in the house, and the place fair swarmed with cats."'

Lotty cleared her throat and continued in her usual voice, 'At last, in her sixty-ninth year, Nanny Morgan came to a shocking end. On the 12th September 1857, she was found lying dead in her house, stabbed on face and neck and wrist, and just as she lay, they tell us, she was buried. No one was found to perform the last offices for the detested witch, and not even the shoes were removed from her corpse.

'On the day of her death, a young man who lodged with her was seen leaving the house with blood upon his clothes. He was arrested, and tried for the murder at the spring assizes.'

Amy tapped her fingers together in impatience as Lotty talked. Ellie looked over at her, her face a swirl of bemused interest, and Amy gave her a swift smile which she hoped looked reassuring.

'It appeared that the woman had had a violent affection for this man,' Lotty said, 'and that he often wished to escape but he believed that she could by her arts force him to return to her. On the day in question he had returned home and was greeted with a storm of abusive taunts. It was urged that, maddened with rage and fear, he stabbed her recklessly and repeatedly. He was condemned to death, but many of the jury and of the county magistrates petitioned for a commutation of the sentence and it was not carried into effect.

'Wenlock folk had not lost the art of legend-making. At the time of which we have been speaking, transportation had already been abolished; nevertheless they tell us that the criminal was sentenced to be transported, but that the vessel in which he sailed went down on the voyage, and the man who so narrowly escaped hanging could not escape drowning.'

Lotty pulled the chair out a little and sat down. She looked at them all with an air of satisfaction, as if this story explained everything. The silence crept about and Lotty absent-mindedly rubbed at an ink stain on the side of one of her fingers. Ellie wondered if Lotty was going to say anything else.

'Just a wonderment, but ... where is this going?' Ellie said.

Lotty looked at her in surprise. 'Going? I am not aware that we are travelling anywhere at present.'

'Yeah, I get that. But ...'

'What's the meaning of the story,' Amy clarified. 'That's what she means.'

'I would have assumed the meaning of the story is perfectly clear.'

Amy stared at Lotty, who let out a sigh. 'At the time, the popular verdict seemed to be like that of the people of Melita: *"Surely this man is a murderer, whom Vengeance suffereth not to live."'*

Amy tapped her fingers. *Oh, for Pete's Sake.*

'No, Lotty, that doesn't make it clearer.' Amy continued to stare unblinking at Lotty, who gave a slight laugh and said, 'I fear the superstitions I dedicated my life to studying and understanding have infiltrated my reasoning. Or perhaps there was more truth in the beliefs of uneducated people than we allowed.'

'Lotty, please: how is all of this relevant to Ellie and our role as guides?' Winifred said. Her arms were stretched towards Lotty as if trying to reach her. Lotty looked at Winifred and adjusted her skirt folds, keeping her hands at a safe distance from Winifred's touch.

'The relevance may become clearer if I start at the beginning,' Lotty said.

Amy took a deep breath and settled down into her chair. *This could take some time. I hope Winifred has allowed for this in her planning.*

'This is not my first experience as a guide. If only it had been, for I then could have approached it with a lighter heart. My first ward was also a family member. One that I had met in life although could hardly say I "knew" as he was a mere child when I saw him. He was a dear child and lacked the gravity his younger brother betrayed even at a young age. In many ways, my ward was suited to being a younger sibling and not the oldest child with the responsibilities that entailed.'

Winifred sat up a little and pulled her arms in. Amy sensed a shift in Winifred's mood. *Does she know who Lotty's talking about?*

'When I became his guide he was sixteen years of age. It was quite surreal, I assure you. However, it also felt natural. I had lived my life as either a niece to my aunts or an aunt to my nieces and nephews, so I was perfectly suited to the role. And I had had such an affection for his father — another who had a questioning mind and whose interests spanned folklore and history — that I committed myself fully to the task of guiding this boy to adulthood as I had done in life for his father, uncles and aunts.

'Those early years of my guide-ship were enjoyable. He was finishing his studies and doing quite well. Shrewsbury suited them, I believe, with the lovely buildings bordering the river — a delightful change after the dreary primary boarding school; I really do not know what his father was thinking in sending them to that school in the middle of Wales. At Shrewsbury, he did well and I thought that an aspiration for the Law would best suit his mind and his future as Loynton's heir. His efforts suggested he had taken my thought to heart.'

'Sorry — but who are we talking about?' As Amy said the words, she had the sense that the others knew; that she was being included, out of politeness, in a private conversation in which the other participants were fully aware of the characters and the back-story.

'Roger,' Ellie and Winifred said in unison, confirming Amy's thoughts.

Lotty nodded and beamed at Ellie, 'She listens. She appears not to listen or care but then will surprise you with what she has learnt.'

Ellie fidgeted against the unwanted blush.

'Indeed I am of course referring to Roger Sambrooke Burne,' Lotty said. 'The eldest child of my dear nephew, Arthur. Arthur, who had inherited Loynton and yet could not reside there until his mother's death. My brother — Arthur's father — had died in 1916, yet in 1934 the family were still residing elsewhere. Bestowing on Julia a lifetime tenancy at Loynton prolonged her life, I am sure.'

Lotty chuckled but the sound faded as she recalled Winifred's earlier comments about the fate of Loynton.

'It was not an awful home Arthur and Christine had created for themselves in Stafford. In the summer they would
draw lines on the lawn and make a tennis court. It reminded
me of the summers of my youth. Both boys were good sports-
men although Roger was the more athletic of the two. They
had so many interests, even as boys. Arthur was a keen bird-
watcher and the boys would trick him by making bird calls.
They were too old for such games but the laughter it would
bring as Arthur stood looking through binoculars trying to
identify the kestrel he had just heard was sufficient to forgive
them these childhood pranks.

'*You* must have been very good at bird calls, Winifred; a
childhood spent in the countryside does that, I am sure. As a
child I would note down any species of flora or fauna I discovered. I made a note of hearing bird calls as well.'

Winifred looked at Lotty for a moment before answering.
'Growing up in the countryside I took bird calls for granted,'
she said after a while.

'You were probably too busy to care about what kind of bird
it was,' Amy said.

'Well ... perhaps ...' Winifred carried on quickly: 'However,
there was such a variety of birds in Arthur and Christine's
garden it is no wonder they enjoyed watching them.'

'They all seemed very happy,' Lotty said, picking up on her
earlier story. 'Although I did think Arthur and Christine doted
a little *too* much on Roger. He could do nothing wrong. I tried
to counter that influence and remind Roger of his duty to his
family. It was I who encouraged him to join the Territorial
Army. His father had served in the Shropshire Regiment in the
Great War and his grandfather, although never a professional
soldier, had been in charge of the Shropshire Territorial Force
Association at the time of death.

'Not to mention, it was part of one's responsibilities as the
head of Loynton Hall to perform certain military tasks, albeit
most were ceremonial in nature.' Lotty looked earnestly at

them all as she said this, warming to the story.

'I was sure that experience in the Territorial Army would be invaluable to Roger. Sadly, I was quite correct although not in the way I had expected. At the outbreak of the war, Roger was immediately moved to the Regular Army and awarded the rank of officer.'

She sighed. 'I was greatly disturbed by his enthusiasm for Army life, however, I recollected the successful Army careers of his father and uncles. And for most of the war he was perfectly safe. His regiment was stationed across the United Kingdom and by the time you married, Winifred, he had been in more danger from the cold and wet weather in Northern Ireland than the guns of France.'

'Yes, that is true,' Winifred said.

'So often a person is only good,' Lotty said, 'in the sense of being "good to their own kind"; however, Roger was generous to anyone regardless of station. And thus more like his mother than his father. I loved Arthur, although in many ways he was quite conservative and cared little for the progress of women; they should know their place, so to speak. With the exception of myself.'

Lotty shook her head and Ellie realised that Lotty would have been alive when some women, including she herself, were first given the vote. *I don't think she was exactly throwing bricks through windows, though.* Ellie smiled at her comment as she looked at Lotty. *And being chained to a barrier would be super-tricky.*

'Now, where was I?' Lotty said.

'The war,' Amy said, still sitting with her arms folded across her chest. *Does this story justify what Lotty did to Ellie? Not one bit. That's the end of it. But just let her carry on so the others realise this as well.*

'And then, in June 1944, his regiment was sent to France. He was not in the first waves of that attack. He arrived in the middle of June, and as he was now a Battery Captain he was responsible for the advance party of his battery. They were camped just inland from the beaches and during July they marched further inland through pretty villages and cornfields. One could not avoid the realities of war, even if you were away from the enemy. Abandoned tanks and trucks, burnt or dismantled, shell craters and ruined buildings. Life met death. How true T.S Eliot's words were: "I was neither living nor dead, and I knew nothing, looking into the heart of light, the silence".'

Lotty paused. Amy couldn't decide if Lotty was lost in the memory or just trying to remember the rest of Eliot's lines. Her lips twitched but she checked it after seeing Winifred and Ellie's expressions as they listened to Lotty.

'... at times it was hard to be understood.'

'Didn't you speak French?' Amy said.

'I am referring to the crowds and noise. So many souls, the thunder of bombs and crackle of gunfire. So loud. I had never heard such an uproar. The streets of London, even the bombing in the Great War, did not prepare me. And I had heard nothing as loud, or startling, since, until that day on the bridge.'

Winifred gave her a curious look with that last comment, and Amy wondered what she was thinking.

'I could not communicate as easily as I would have liked. I have wondered, since, whether, if I had been able to ... However, speculation of that nature is futile.'

Lotty smiled weakly and looked around, her eyes fixing on Amy's. Amy adjusted her arms and moved a little forward in her seat.

Lotty continued: 'Roger's regiment had been in France for six weeks on the fateful day. By the start of August they were just outside of Monts-en-Bessin. It was warm and sunny, beautiful countryside; a criss-cross of fields, orchards, copses and narrow country roads. Trees dotted the landscape and the hedgerows were scattered with the colours of summer.

'He had persevered with his CO for a chance of being Forward Observation Officer and was thrilled when it was approved for the attack on Noyers-Villers Bocage Road. He was right to want the task, as he was suited to the position. It was a dangerous role: often the artillery could not see what they were firing at as they were too far away. The FOO was responsible for being their "eyes". He was required to be closer to the enemy lines and his task had been to silence the German anti-tank guns. Precision was paramount and Roger's talents for accuracy and speed made him a valuable FOO.'

Amy felt herself soften as she heard the glint of motherly pride in Lotty's voice.

'That is why I did not discourage him: I knew he would be excellent. After all, it was this talent which had first made me direct him towards the Law. I was compelled to stay near to him once he arrived on French soil. Although I wanted him to excel in the Army as his uncle Alfred had, I felt responsible for him. It was I who had encouraged the Officer Training Corps, which had directly led to his zeal for Army life.'

'You cannot blame yourself,' Winifred said. 'Roger was young and able-bodied. He would have been drafted sooner or later if he had not volunteered.'

Lotty stared beyond Winifred through the blackness of the window.

'He got out of the tank. I heard him say he wanted a better look. He climbed down and he and another boy crept forward. There was a tree; I remember thinking it looked as if it was guarding him. Roger peered through the binoculars and then whispered something to the boy with him and looked through the binoculars again. They could have been tracking a rare bird or stalking deer. They were crouched by the tree and its branches stretched out towards them, scattering shade. Roger took one last look. There was a distant spark of light, Roger's lips said "Fire" and the tree above him exploded. He was wounded in the head and never regained consciousness. Shrapnel from the German bomb. Died in a strange land far from home, all because of me.'

Lotty dabbed at the corner of her eye but any other sign of emotion was checked. 'I disappeared after that. I had failed in my duty and had guided him into danger.' 'Yeah, but ... didn't he have other guides? I mean, how do you know it was all your ideas that he was following?' Ellie said.

Lotty frowned as she thought about this. Amy smiled at Ellie, amused by her innocent directness.

'I was not aware of other guides for Roger,' Lotty said, and then, in a voice that sounded as if she was thinking out loud, added, 'However it is quite likely that there *were* others.'

She adjusted her position and pulled her hands together on her lap. Ellie watched her hands cement themselves together.

'I was quite undecided over the next wardship. However, I decided that I owed it to Roger. The initial experience was not to my liking; this later generation, diluted as it was from the Burne and Goodlad blood, seemed to lack potential.'

Amy shook her head and tried to catch Ellie's eye but the face of the youngest diner was staring at the floor.

'Now look, the Mello blood may not be as "blue" as yours but we have plenty to be admired for and there is a lot to be said for not always marrying your cousins. That's how you get webbed feet.'

Lotty smiled. 'Of course. I am merely explaining how I perceived the situation on first glance.' She waved away any unsaid words and continued: 'This ward seemed to be grappling with such silly issues; many of them of her own making,' a glance at Amy, 'I thought at the time. It made me quite carnaptious to think of Roger sacrificing his life so this foolish girl could worry over whether her shoes were the right kind of shoes or whether certain other girls who were anything but fascinating would like her more if she could hit a ball well.

'I thought: is this worth it? Those young men and women giving up their chance of a future so others could waste theirs so frivolously? Roger would have studied law and helped the community —'

'Well, you do not know that,' Winifred interjected. 'I was incredibly fond of Roger but he was not perfect. Decent and kind, yes; but not a saint.' Winifred smiled at Ellie. 'Unlike the rest of us, of course.'

Ellie managed a smile but the words 'silly' and 'foolish' were biting into her.

'I realise I behaved in quite an infra dig manner ... I believe I may have recalled things more fondly than they were in reality. The bitterness of my failure obscured my perception.'

Amy leaned forward and patted at her hair, surprised at what she had heard. *I wasn't expecting that. To admit she was wrong, again.*

'I did not observe the qualities that were there all along. Intelligence, wit and a good amount of assertiveness. It has taken me a while to realise that to judge a person by their youthful personality is not to do them credit. Indeed, when I came to be Roger's guide he was only a few years older, although they are such critical years, do you not think?' She looked at Winifred and Amy. Amy softened a little bit more at Lotty's keen look.

'When I recall my own early-adult phase,' Lotty said, 'some might have described me as wise beyond my years; however, I am quite aware that others, particularly some of my Burne aunts, felt that Frances and my behaviour was not ... very *lady-like*, and they would have preferred it if our mamma had checked us on more occasions. My Aunt Sophia wrote once that I was full of self and would turn into a most ordinary and disagreeable young woman.'

Lotty laughed, 'Later, she overlooked my younger self and we always were on good terms when I was older. This dinner has made me realise that I was in danger of following my aunt in being too harsh a judge on a young person.'

Lotty squeezed Ellie's hands, which were curled over the back of the chair. The contact surprised Ellie and she felt a rush of embarrassed pride. Ellie sat back down and looked earnestly around the room.

'But ... how am I gonna know if what I am thinking is a good thing or if it is just ... Lotty in a bad mood?'

Lotty chortled loudly as if the tension of what she had just been saying had been released. Winifred chuckled and said, 'The best thing to do is not keep big problems to yourself. Discuss them with someone you can trust.'

'And go with your instincts, kiddo,' Amy said. 'If it feels wrong, it probably is.'

Ellie nodded and toyed with the envelope, which had lost its fresh whiteness during the dinner. She wondered where the tea stain on it had come from and how one of the corners had become dented. Amy and Lotty both turned to Winifred, who had sat up and cocked her head as if listening to something, her eyes narrowed in concentration. With a nod, she turned her smile upon Ellie.

'I believe our dinner is almost at an end. I do so hope it has been an enlightening experience and given you some food for thought, as it were.'

She smiled again and Ellie saw the same look of finality settle across the faces of Amy and Lotty.

'Where will you go after —' Ellie's question was interrupted by the sound of crashing plates.

'What was that?' she said, spinning round. 'It sounded like it was right outside the door.'

Without thinking she ran over and opened the door. She peered into the corridor but it was thick with darkness and she couldn't see anything. Her hand sought a light switch but without success. A breeze swirled around her legs and pushed past her into the room, snuffing out the candles.

Ellie heard the candles whisper as they were extinguished, and she turned back.

'I can't see any ...' The sight in front of her was difficult to process; gone were the candles, the curtains, the long table, tablecloth and silver rose bowl, the fireplace. Gone were the three women. The room was plain; electric lights glared down at her, a simple wooden table with six chairs stood in the centre of the room, and where the large mirror had hung there was now a picture of two swans. Ellie stared at the swans, their necks entwined as they floated along calm waters. She could feel her mouth opening and closing but didn't think to stop it.

'Ellie?' Her mum's voice, which she had longed for earlier, was a sharp disappointment now. She turned around and looked at her mum, who stood in the doorway, the brightness of the corridor behind her another stark reminder of the difference from a moment ago.

Ellie whirled back to the room. 'Did you see them?'

'See who, darling?'

'The ... the *women*. Who were here, just now. Did you *see* them?'

'No. I haven't seen anyone else up here. Are you okay?'

'Ummm, yeah. Yeah ...' Ellie stared at the chairs, willing the women back.

'Ellie? I said, shall we go?'

'Oh yeah, of course. It must be really late'

'Not really, darling. It's just past five. You hungry?'

Ellie didn't answer as she picked up the envelope that lay on the table. The writing scrawled across it was her teacher's, the school logo in the corner was her school's. It was the envelope she had been given earlier that day. She ran a finger slowly over it; the tea stain was gone, the corners were sharp. It was as crisp and bright white as when she had been given it.

ELLIE

They left the restaurant together. Ellie carried a box of Halloween costumes and she only partly listened to her mum's monologue that stood in for conversation: a stream of worry over being late and missing the trick-or-treaters.

'Did you know that ages ago people used to go around asking for apples or money on Halloween? I always thought it was an American thing, trick-or-treating, but it actually isn't.'

Her mum glanced her. 'Yes, I have heard that. Did they teach you that in History today?'

The question sounded strained and Ellie felt the rumblings of irritation.

'No. Mrs Milvern doesn't teach anything that interesting.'

Her mum said nothing and they turned onto their street in silence. They reached their house and Ellie waited for the door to open. She put the box and her bag down and then with a deep breath handed her mum the letter.

'What's this?' her mum asked, looking at the envelope with cautious curiosity.

'It's from Mrs Milvern. She gave it to me at the end of class.'

Her mum glanced at her again and then back at the envelope without saying a word.

'You'd think she would just email you but I think she likes the drama of a letter,' Ellie said. Her mum made a 'hmmm' noise as she read the note but didn't comment on Ellie's dismissive attitude to her teacher. Ellie frowned. *It must be bad if she isn't going to tell me to be more respectful.*

She waited, concentrating on breathing. Her mum's lips moved silently as she read, and then she looked at Ellie with a strange expression. Ellie tensed and shuffled under the look. *Why does Mum look nervous?*

'Now, what I am about to tell you may upset you at first, and I am sure you will say we have meddled and should have Minded-Our-Own-Business, but I feel that what we did was for the best and that even if you don't agree now or even later we, as your parents, have to do what we think is best for you rather than what you would like.'

'What is it, Mum? What have you done?'

Her mother sighed and handed the letter to Ellie. For a confused moment, she just held it. She'd made so much of this letter, but now she wasn't sure that she wanted to know what it said.

Dear Mrs Hardwick,

Further to our conversation yesterday, I have spoken to the Head of History, Mr Mason, regarding Eleanor.

I put to him our suggestion that she move class and he has agreed that as long as she is able to maintain the level expected of the pupils in that class, she can move.

I assured Mr Mason that Eleanor was a bright pupil and would no doubt be an asset to the class.

I hope you will agree that this seems the best course of action and, although it doesn't solve the bigger challenge, it should give her the opportunity to concentrate on her learning in a friendlier environment.

Yours,
Celia Milvern

Ellie kept her eyes down, staring at the piece of paper. *Never knew Mrs Milvern's name was Celia, she doesn't look like a Celia.*

'Ellie?' Her mum's voice floated up through her thoughts and Ellie noticed that her mum was chewing her bottom lip. For a brief minute she wanted to be annoyed at her for getting involved. *I want her to be interested, sure. And for her to help. But not to go and do stuff without me knowing it.*

'People will know I'm getting special treatment,' Ellie said.

'Possibly, although Mrs Milvern assured me that it was quite common for pupils to move classes. Often happens close to the start of the new school year.'

'Surprised Mrs Milvern cares.' Ellie said this with her face to the letter but she caught her mum's foot tapping three times in quick succession and then stopping, as if in an attempt to control whatever emotion was rushing to the surface.

'She wants to see you succeed. We *all* want to see you succeed.'

Ellie nodded, and from somewhere she heard Amy's voice: *'The only thing you can control is yourself. Ignore those girls that are no good and do what is right for you. That's how you will succeed.'* A memory? Or is Amy nearby?

'Thanks, Mum,' Ellie said, breaking the silence. Her mum let out a sigh, as if she had been holding her breath, and beamed at Ellie. It had been a long time since Ellie had seen her smile at her like that. Her mum walked further into the house, leaving Ellie in the hallway kicking off her shoes. Out of habit, Ellie pulled her phone from her bag. There was a message from Mia. She didn't open it, just stared at Mia's name and then with a calm power, deleted the message without reading it.

'And Aria is in this class,' her mum called from the kitchen.

Ellie followed the voice into the kitchen and watched her mum pull out kale and chicken from the fridge. Stuffed chicken and creamed kale, mum's go-to weekday meal.

'Hey, Mum. Have you ever had kale soup?'

'Hmmm, no. I don't think so.'

'It's meant to be good.'

The cork of a wine bottle popped.

'I thought you didn't like soup.'

A wineglass clinked and the bottle gurgled.

'I don't. But someone said it was good ... Anyway, umm, do you have any pictures of Vicinity House?'

'Vicinity House?'

'Yeah, where nan's nana lived.'

Her mum took a sip of wine. 'Umm, possibly ... somewhere.'

Ellie hopped up onto the counter top and began chopping the onion.

'I want to see the colours it's painted. I reckon it is a brave person who paints their house pink and red.'

Ellie's mum put her wineglass down slowly.

'It's not pink and red. Your nan showed it to me last year, it's painted cream and green.'

Ellie paused. 'Oh.' *It was all a weird dream. I knew it.*

'Although, come to think of it, she did say her nana painted it pink and red. Apparently it worked, even though you wouldn't normally think of pairing those colours. Such a shame that the family lost the house because of a legal technicality. I've always wondered why Amy — your nan's nana —- didn't get advice on how best to organise the estate so it stayed in her family.'

'Not sure she liked people in authority,' Ellie said, and then bit her lip, hoping that her mum wouldn't notice.

'Yes, quite possibly,' her mum said.

The news from the radio buzzed in the background: 'train' ... 'Richmond' ... 'three people injured' ...

'What was that? About the train?' Ellie pointed her knife at the radio.

'Oh yes. I meant to say — there was an incident on a train this afternoon. Some man got on at Richmond and attacked some of the passengers. They don't know if the victims knew the man or if it was just a freak attack, but the trains have all been cancelled.'

'What ... what time was this?' Ellie's voice was no louder than a whisper.

Her mum started searching on her phone for articles, a murmur of news snippets escaping her like the buzz of sleepy bees.

'Here we are: the 3.10 from Richmond. That's the stopping service to Waterloo.'

The knife clattered to the floor.

'Darling, you okay?'

Ellie said nothing. Around her floated the smell of lilies and vanilla.

AUTHOR'S NOTE

The three ghosts in this story are all ancestors of mine. They were influential personalities within their family circles and all experienced love and loss, but their stories have rarely been shared and, in some cases, are barely known.

The life events that they share within this book are all based on actual experiences and their words, which I have taken from various sources, are frequently their own.

The idea for this book came during a visit from my parents-in-law. My mother-in-law told me about her nana (Amy Mello) and the blank spaces in her life story. I set about researching what I could of this remarkable woman and soon uncovered a trail of people and events that were revelations to the rest of the family. I realised that Amy was not the only woman in my family who had led an interesting life, mowing a path for themselves that went against the social conventions of the time.

This thought led me to research two other women: Charlotte Sophia Burne – my great-great-great aunt – and Winifred Margaret Davies – my granny. With the enthusiasm of family members who helped with the research, shared their memories and stories they had heard, as well as producing mountains of letters, diaries and photos, I managed to piece together these three fascinating lives. With that in mind, any errors are all my own.

The direct link to all three women is really my daughter rather than myself, so I decided to create an older version of her, a girl struggling with the transitions and challenges that I know I faced as a young teenager and which I am sure many others can relate to: moving to new places, trying to fit in, being bullied, and so on. I alighted on the concept of each ghost giving Ellie a message to live by, in order to express what I saw as their own approach to life.

In terms of the language of these three ancestors, wherever possible I have used their own words from letters and diaries or remembered conversations in order to let them speak and tell their story in their own style. Where this hasn't been possible, I resorted to other family members' words, where appropriate, and my own imagination.

The life events that I have covered are true; however, there are still gaps, so for the sake of posterity I would like to highlight where these gaps have been embellished or filled:

Charlotte Sophia Burne (2 May 1850 – 11 Jan 1923), otherwise known as Lotty, was born on 2nd May 1850 and much of her life is recorded due to her work with the Folklore Society and through her writings. My family has bundles of letters going back to the early 1800s, and diaries of family members spanning two decades, which helped to build up the picture of her life and her personality.

My grandfather, John Burne, dedicated his life to writing and researching hers. Growing up, I did not appreciate this interest, in fact I thought it all a bit boring! Now, though, I am eternally grateful for his work, which has saved me a lot of time and has meant that a lot of family history has been recorded and saved. His admiration for his aunt was well-placed. She was an incredibly intelligent woman who taught herself Latin and could debate with the best on almost any subject. Described by her aunt, Emily Burne, as being 'wise beyond her years', she was also fortunate to have had a mother who didn't care for social norms and encouraged all her children to be curious and to learn.

An element of Lotty's life that I did embellish was the involvement of Jim Vallings. He did exist and was a close friend of the family, having come into contact with the Burnes through his friendship with Lotty's brother, William. We know that Lotty and Jim wrote to each other regularly during the 1870s as well as visited each other's houses. In 1875, she visited her brothers at Oxford while they were at university and also saw Jim Vallings, who was a student with William. Lotty wrote to her mother: 'Jim is so nice, it does not seem nearly two years since we met – we were on our old terms from the first minute.'

We do not know for sure, though, if this was a courtship or if Lotty felt anything more than friendship. However, in 1883 Lotty wrote about an unnamed person: 'I still think of him but I don't love him anymore', and the poem she quoted in the story was one she had written while staying with the Vallings. So although the protagonist in both the quotation and the poem is unknown, my grandfather firmly believed it to be Jim Vallings, especially as 1883 would have been around the time he married.

What we cannot even speculate on is whether there was any time during the 1870s when the feelings were reciprocated by Jim Vallings. Either way, they kept in contact all their lives and the last record we have of them together is in a letter from Lotty in 1910 where she mentioned that Jim came for lunch.

I also embellished her questioning of Christianity, as I wanted to highlight the kind of conflict of choices that life can throw at you. The truth is that I simply don't know how religious she was; she attended church and her mother, Sambrooke, and both surviving sisters were all devout. Her involvement with the Girls Friendly Society (at the time a deeply Anglican charity) would also point to a person with religious inclinations. However, her surviving letters that mention family deaths all lack any reference to faith-based acceptance in stark contrast to other people's condolence letters, and the comments scattered through her writings (some of which I used in the book) have led me to interpret her as someone who was not particularly religious. This is all, of course, circumstantial evidence, and my own interpretation. Her work collecting folklore stories and her extensive knowledge and appreciation of history, suggested to me that she was a person who saw Christianity as an extension of other beliefs that came before it and that she did not have the unquestioning faith of her siblings. I would, however, hesitate to go as far as to declare her an atheist, considering the times and her upbringing.

Winifred Margaret Davies (9 Sept 1920 – 10 Jul 1999). Winifred died when I was a teenager having suffered from Alzheimer's. I have limited childhood memories of her but what is clear from everyone I spoke to is that Winifred rarely spoke about her own childhood. What I know and have retold here came from family recollections and research. It is true that my grandfather didn't know about Winifred's father's, Pryce Davies's, incarceration in a hospital until after Winifred's death. The family story was that he had spent the family savings on cows, speculating that the price would rise. When the price of cows fell, he was unable to cope with the guilt and worry.

In his medical records the doctors did not verify this story, but they did record his repeated worry that 'they would famish' and that he had 'ruined them' suggesting some truth in this family tale.

The family always felt that he was there longer than necessary; however, based on the doctors' reports over the thirteen years he was incarcerated, I can only surmise that he continued to struggle all his adulthood with guilt over this financial mistake and that while he could be calm and at peace in the security of the hospital, trial visits home were always unsuccessful, often ending with an early return to the institutionalised world. I cannot imagine what the harsh reality of Welsh tenant farming in the 1920s must have been like, but clearly this, combined with the constant reminders of his error that being home would probably have unearthed, was too much for him.

His wife, Maggie, was an incredible force. Said to have always been smiling and happy, she really must have been a wonder when you consider she was left with a farm and four children, one of whom was only a few months old, to run entirely by herself.

The story of the visit to the hospital is based on a family story; however, I haven't been able to confirm if, or when, the family did visit Pryce at the hospital. I feel it is more likely that the 'visit' that is often talked about is one that he paid to them at the farm, but I wanted to portray the place that Pryce was sent to. It was built at the turn of the 20th century but kept the sombre Victorian veneer that you often see in such buildings.

Irrespective of where or how the visit occurred, what is true is that my granny refused to take off her dress after a visit, and this must have been so out of character for Winifred that seventy years later her sister, Orian, still remembered it.

The other reason for taking the reader to Talgarth was because I saw a striking similarity in architecture to the hospital that Winifred was stationed at during the war. Both had that Victorian severity that makes you think of Gothic novels and tragedy. She once wrote to John: 'This will be the last letter I'll write you from Prewitt for some time, unless I get returned in disgrace', and it made me wonder whether, even if only subliminally, she didn't like it because it reminded her of Talgarth.

The story of Winifred volunteering to assist in what became known as 'Dunkirk' was a story that only my cousin had been told. I have assumed Granny was at Dover with the Red Cross, as she was working at a Red Cross hospital (Parkwood Convalescent Home) at the time and I believe the Red Cross were present at the docks to help those arriving off the boats. All my cousin was told by our grandad was that Granny 'went to the south coast with the medical team', so my assumptions could be incorrect. Granny did not share many wartime stories, happy to let my grandad recount his. Grandad was fond of saying that Granny was in more danger in London than he was in India, and judging from his letters at the time, I would say he was right.

Of the three women, we knew the least about **Amy Pacheco Mello** (31 Jan 1897 – 1 Jun 1968). We also have very little by way of her own voice as there are no letters or diaries to refer to. I have done my best to give her her own voice based on how her grandchildren and other family members and friends remember her. I have had to use a bit of artistic licence and some events or experiences have been embellished:

We don't know why Amy and her first husband chose to move to America but Joseph Simons' family ran a business in Massachusetts and, at the time, I found records that, at the very least, a brother was living out there. It is, therefore, likely they felt they could use these connections to find work.

We also have very little detail for the reason she later moved back to Bermuda. Although Ernest did request to be called Al after Al Capone, all the family knew was that they left Cambridge because Amy was concerned about him. There was no further detail than that so the bootlegging gin story is entirely my own fiction. We are also unsure of the exact date they returned to Bermuda. They were recorded in the 1930s census but no further record of them can be found. The family's view is that Amy had moved to Bermuda by the time Ruth was 5 years old, making 1930 a likely year for the move.

Although she didn't leave behind the written evidence of the other two women to use to establish her personality, I have tried to reflect it based on her life choices as well as traits seen in younger generations that are commented on as being similar to Amy's. The main frame of her life is entirely true, although much of it was news to the family. We knew she had a first husband but his name and place of death were uncertain. We did not know about the baby she lost or that she lived in different parts of Massachusetts.

The story I told of her leaving Bermuda in 1918 with her brother and his family, her first husband and their toddler, while seven months pregnant, is all true. As are the tragedies that then struck her within weeks of each other also happened as I described; but these events were also revelations to the family.

I do not know for sure when she moved to Cambridge after James and Joseph's deaths. I have assumed it wasn't immediate, especially as that would have meant they were travelling during the winter months. She is recorded as being in Cambridge in January 1920, so I assumed she moved at some point in 1919. An interesting small mystery is over who she stayed with when she first arrived in Cambridge. In the 1920 census she is recorded as living with a Joseph and Mary Beuvi, which may be a mis-spelling of Benevides, who were related to the Simons. I left this out as it wasn't clear and they are all quite common names, so could be coincidental. But the fact that it was the same address as the one they stayed at on their journey to New Bedford in June 1918 leads me to think it is quite likely.

The next mysteries I uncovered were about Amy's second husband, José Mello. The family story was that he died in a car accident, so I was surprised to learn that in fact he died of tuberculosis, until a historian told me that often people hushed up a death from TB because of the connotations of poverty.

We also did not know he had been married, was a widower at the time of his marriage to Amy, and had lost a child. I have been unable to find out when his first wife, Gloria, died and can only surmise that she died in the Azores or on the way there. She was alive in June 1922 when her son died, but José is declared a widower on his marriage certificate in April 1923.

José and Gloria's son died the day that his passport was issued. A tragic coincidence, but one of many coincidental timings that occur. For example, Lotty and her great nephew, Roger, share the same birthday, and John and Roger's grandfathers on both sides died on the same date although in different years.

This journey has given me a new appreciation of the little coincidences in life that attach us to our past and our ancestors. Whether through nature or nurture, I have been amazed at the number of similarities I have found in these women to those in future generations who are related to them. History is all around us and closer than we think. The most ordinary of families will have their secrets and surprises, and I hope this story and my adventure in writing it will inspire others to ask older generations about themselves and their memories.

I wanted to give these women a voice and have them tell their stories because they were too busy with other cares to talk about themselves when they were alive. I would like to finish with a quotation that, to me, sums up these remarkable women. In the words of Oprah Winfrey: "Step out of the history that is holding you back. Step into the new story you are willing to create."

APPENDIX

Menu Du Souper

I chose to base the menu for the protagonists' meal on the 1920s because 1920-1923 were the only years when the three women were alive at the same time (albeit at very different ages). Given how central food was in all of their lives, it seemed fitting to celebrate this coincidence through a menu of that era.

Caviar served with blinis
Sherry

Beetroot and Horseradish Soup
Sherry

Halibut à la Béchamel
Chablis

Lamb Noisettes with Mint Sauce
Beaujolais

Roast Duck with Plum Sauce
Buttered Green Beans
Stewed Red Cabbage
Baked Potatoes
Châteaux Margaux

Poires Condé

Sliced Pineapple

Coffee and Chocolate Truffles

SOME FAMILY RECIPES

I've included a small selection of the family recipes that I came across while writing this novel and mentioned in the story. I haven't modernised these recipes, so some measurements and ingredients may seem strange and you may also notice that there are no serving totals and some have very vague timing and heating instructions. I decided not to update them as I wanted to share the recipes just as one of my family would have used them.

———

Welsh Cakes

As far as I am concerned, Welsh cakes taste best in Wales. This recipe was my granny's and thus, I assume, her mum's before her. I remember my great-aunt Orian making these. She kept a tin that was constantly filled with these cakes and they were offered out with cups of tea.

6 oz flour

½ level tsp salt

¼ oz baking powder

2 oz margarine

2 oz sugar

2 oz fruit (currants or sultanas)

1 egg

½ gill milk

Sieve flour and salt

Rub in the fat

Add dry ingredients

Beat up egg and milk and mix to soft dough

Roll out to ¼ inch thickness

Cut out with 2-inch cutter

Cook on griddle

Allow 6-7 mins for each side.

Simnel Cakes

This recipe was copied from Charlotte Burne's grand-mother's (Mary Goodlad's) recipe book. Lotty believed it to be one that her grandmother had inherited from her mother and grandmother, both of whom were inhabitants of Bury:

To 3 lbs of flour, add 3 lbs of currants, ½ lb of butter rubbed into the flour, 2 oz of candied lemon, 1 oz and a half of bitter almonds, ½ oz of cinnamon, ¾ lb of loaf sugar, the rinds of 2 large lemons, ½ lb of yeast, 5 eggs, the whites and yolks beaten separately, and a pint of cream. Mix it together and make it up immediately into Simnel's [i.e. in the shape described below]. Let them stand to rise well on the tin and bake in a moderate oven.

Lotty wrote an article in the *Folklore Society Journal* 1919-20 titled 'Reminiscences of Lancashire and Cheshire When George IV was King' where she described them:

'My mother was one of five daughters of Mr William Good-lad, a surgeon of considerable local note, living at Bury, Lancashire, where she was born in 1820 and where her childish days were spent ... My mother had a vivid childish memory of "Fly" the greyhound ... walking over the "Simnel-cakes" which had been laid on the hearth to "rise" before baking, and leaving footmarks on every cake. "Bury Simnel's" are flat round plum-cakes, thicker in the centre than at the circumference, having the edges turned up and folded into a sort of scallop-pattern, and are made every year for "Mothering Sunday", the fourth Sunday in Lent.'

Fava Bean Stew

No one has the exact recipe that Amy used but this one is in the family and I have been assured is similar to what Amy's grandchildren remember simmering away on the kitchen stove.

My mother-in-law said: "there was for sure a very strong and delicious smell to the dish. This was a favourite with Mom and Uncle Arthur."

- Sauté 1 large finely chopped onion and one small clove of garlic finely chopped in a pot with a little olive oil.

- Season with salt and pepper.

- Once onions are soft add 1 tin (15 oz) of tomato sauce + 1/2 cup of ketchup and 3 tsp paprika and simmer on low.

- Add to the mix 4 tins (15 oz each) drained green fava beans.

- Bring to boil then turn down to a low simmer for 20-30 mins stirring lightly. Taste to see if any additional salt or pepper is required.

———